**A knock on the driver's window startled her, drawing a shriek as she whirled about in the cramped space.**

Ben was standing there, bent down from his substantial height of six feet four inches to gaze in at her. He wore a slicker, the hood pulled over his head, but his face was streaked with rain, and he looked grim.

"Oh, please, no." The groan was torn from Yashi at the sight of him. Ben was stoic. He had the best poker face she'd ever seen. He rarely let his emotions show, particularly on the job. He was quiet and calm and studied, and no one could ever guess what he was thinking, but now—

He pulled the door open a few inches and said in a flat voice, "Drive over to my house. I'll talk to you there."

\* \* \*

**If you're on Twitter, tell us what you think of Harlequin Romantic Suspense! #harlequinromsuspense**

D1041218

Dear Reader,

When it comes to books, I'll read pretty much anything—any genre, any subject, any trope. If asked, I would probably say I don't have a favorite. As long as it has well-ordered words and tells a story, I'm a happy camper. But after a lifetime of reading anything—everything—I realized I do have a favorite.

Women in jeopardy are intense, secret babies fun, cowboys heroes to die for. But what really makes my heart glad are reunion romances. Second chances. Once more finding that love you'd thought lost forever. Getting to right old wrongs and live happily-ever-after. I gravitate to those types of stories like my pupper is drawn to a tasty piece of broiled fish. (Yes, offer my dog a special doggy treat or fish and he'll go for the fish every time. And then come back for the treat.)

I love couples who have history and, boy, do Yashi and Ben have history. I knew in writing the other Cedar Creek books that Ben had a special heartache, but I didn't know much else until Yashi popped into my head and poured out their story. Their love. Her betrayal. Throw in a few kittens, a bloodhound named Booger and all the usual Cedar Creek characters and my heart was downright dancing with gladness. I hope this book makes you take a twirl or two, too.

Happy reading,

*Marilyn Pappano*

# DANGEROUS
# REUNION

———

**Marilyn Pappano**

HARLEQUIN

ROMANTIC
SUSPENSE

ISBN-13: 978-1-335-62658-5

Dangerous Reunion

Copyright © 2020 by Marilyn Pappano

This edition published by arrangement with Harlequin Books S.A.

For questions and comments about the quality of this book, please contact us at CustomerService@Harlequin.com.

Harlequin Enterprises ULC
22 Adelaide St. West, 40th Floor
Toronto, Ontario M5H 4E3, Canada
www.Harlequin.com

**Printed in U.S.A.**

Oklahoma, dogs, beaches, books, family and friends: these are a few of **Marilyn Pappano**'s favorite things. She lives in imaginary worlds where she reigns supreme—at least, she does when the characters cooperate—and no matter how wrong things go, she can always set them right. It's her husband's job to keep her grounded in the real world, which makes him her very favorite thing.

**Books by Marilyn Pappano**

**Harlequin Romantic Suspense**

*Copper Lake Secrets*
*In the Enemy's Arms*
*Christmas Confidential*
*"Holiday Protector"*
*Copper Lake Confidential*
*Copper Lake Encounter*
*Undercover in Copper Lake*
*Bayou Hero*
*Nights with a Thief*
*Detective Defender*
*Killer Secrets*
*Killer Smile*
*Detective on the Hunt*

Visit the Author Profile page at Harlequin.com for more titles.

As always, for Robert.

# Chapter 1

Though it was well after sunrise, the sky over Ben Little Bear's house was barely lighter than midnight, so black and rain-filled were the clouds that hung low. No glimmer to the east hinted that the sun had risen, and no glimmer to the west suggested the rain would move on any time soon.

Of course not. It was Saturday. His first day off in a week. Instead of mowing his yard, cutting firewood and going fishing with his cousins, he was going to stay home and...he didn't know what he would do, besides the start he'd already made: sleeping in late and having a cup of coffee that he'd made himself, exactly the way he liked it.

With a plate holding toast, ham and slices of tomato, he went onto the porch, to his favorite wicker chair that creaked when he sat in it, and found it already occupied. "I thought we talked about this."

The tiny gray cat looked up at him, his emerald eyes unblinking, before Ben shifted his gaze to the woman on whose lap Oliver sat. "I don't mind picking you up when you're drunk. I don't mind you sleeping in the guest room until you sober up. But I do mind you making yourself and that cat at home in my chair."

Morwenna Armstrong gestured to three matching wicker chairs. "They're all alike. How can this one be your favorite?"

"Because I said so."

Heaving a sigh, she picked up Oliver and transferred him and herself to the next chair. "I'd make a clever comparison here between you and Dr. Sheldon Cooper on TV, but since you don't even own a television, it wouldn't be worth my time."

"But it was worth your time to tell me that?"

She waved a hand dismissively.

"You're not hungry?"

"Not until my head stops throbbing and my stomach settles down."

"My mother knows a hundred hangover cures."

"Any of them work?"

"I don't know. I've never had a hangover." He put together a sandwich of toast and made a big show of taking a bite. Morwenna reacted by holding her hand to her face like a blinder and directing her attention very deliberately elsewhere.

"Do you know your neighbors?"

He didn't need to ask which ones. For this mile-long

stretch of winding road, there were only two houses. He gazed at the farmhouse set back a hundred feet across the road. "Yeah." Because she was never satisfied with a simple answer, he went on. "The Muellers. Mom, Dad, Brit, fifteen, and Theo, eight."

"Do you know them well?"

He drank some coffee before fashioning another sandwich. "We're…friendly." He helped out over there with cutting down trees, hauling building supplies and taking care of their yard when they were out of town. For a time when he was dating Will Mueller's cousin, they'd exchanged dinner invitations and gone out together. When he discovered that Yashi Baker was not only brilliant, beautiful and sexy, she was also sly, manipulative, wickedly ambitious and untrustworthy, all those invitations ended, and things had gone back to the way they'd been before. Neighborly, nothing more.

And one thought about Yashi was one more than he usually allowed himself in a day.

"Do they always leave their door open when it rains?" Even after fifteen years in the US, Morwenna had kept enough of her accent to let listeners know she was a proud Brit. He liked it. Liked that it was such a difference to the local drawl.

He shifted his attention across the road. The front door *was* open, and the lights in the living room and hallway shone in the dim morning like a weary beacon. The wind wasn't blowing, so rain finding its way inside wasn't a problem. But it was around eighty-five degrees with a hundred percent humidity, sticky at best. Inside, his air conditioner was humming along, keeping the rooms a cool seventy-two, but that would be a harder job if the door stood wide-open.

"You haven't seen anyone?"

"Nope. I've been out here since six thirty."

It wasn't a big deal, and it was his day off. It wasn't his business if the neighbors wanted to invite the dampness into their house. Both cars were home, so likely both Will and Lolly were, too.

But it was Ben's business if something was wrong. It might be his day off, but truly a cop was never off duty. He supposed the same could be said for a good neighbor.

He pulled out his cell and called Will's number. It rang a few times, then went to voice mail. He hung up and moved on to Lolly's. Her voice mail also picked up. After disconnecting one more time, he dialed Brit's number.

She answered on the second ring, sounding rushed and out of breath. Music played loudly in the background. "Hey, Officer Bear, what's up?"

Her nickname for him usually made him smile. Not this time. "Are you at home?"

"Oh God, Mom doesn't have you looking for me, does she? I left a note, I told her I was going to Jared's. I knew she'd freak out if I asked first, so I put the note on my pillow, but I thought I'd be home before she woke up and I could tear it up, and she'd never know, but—"

"So you're not at home."

"No," she said guiltily. "Is she really mad?"

"I haven't talked to her. Is she home?"

"If the cars are there, she's there. She doesn't walk, doesn't ride a bike, and the cute scooter Dad got her just sits in the shed because she says the helmet messes up her hair."

"What about your dad? Is he home, too?"

"Yeah. The only thing on the schedule this morning is soccer practice for Theo, and obviously that's canceled. Why all the questions?"

"Do me a favor, Brit. Don't come home until I call you back." Ben hung up and stood, gathering his plate and cup. "Brit sneaked out last night for a sleepover at Jared's—"

"Sweet," Morwenna said as she lifted Oliver to the floor, then also stood. At his scowl, she said, "But not really, her being only fifteen and all." She gave an emphatic nod that didn't make him forget for an instant that she'd been a wild child herself and still found those impulses difficult to resist on occasion, despite being twenty-nine years old.

She followed him into the house, closing the screen door behind her. "So Mum and Dad are supposed to be home, but they're not answering their phones, and their door is standing open. Do you think they realized she was gone and ran out in a panic to look for her?"

"Jared lives about as far from here as he can and still be in the city limits. They would have just called Brit, or maybe gone to pick her up. But the cars are both there." Ben went into his bedroom and took his gun from the nightstand. He grabbed an extra magazine and a radio, then dragged out a slicker labeled Police.

When he got back to the front door, Morwenna was ready to go, too, her Wellingtons in lime green a bright accompaniment to her red shorts, yellow shirt and purple slicker. Her psychiatrist mum had once asked her if she dressed the way she did to gain attention, and she'd honestly answered, *I like colors*. Sometimes her colors and patterns made his eyes hurt, but she was never dreary, and Ben appreciated that.

They jogged across his saturated yard, the narrow two-lane road and into the Muellers' equally wet yard. Their driveway, like his own, was dirt and gravel, so they stuck to the grass until they reached the sidewalk to the porch. At the top of the steps, he motioned to Morwenna to step aside, out of the rain and out of sight of the hallway.

He rapped on the open door, noting the film of moisture on the tiles just inside, and called, "Will? Lolly? It's Ben Little Bear." When there was no answer, he raised his voice and called again, this time adding Theo's name. Silence.

Drawing his gun, he glanced back at Morwenna. Her face was pale, her eyes wide, and her cell phone was clenched in one hand like a lifeline. She was a dispatcher for the Cedar Creek Police Department, where Ben was a detective, and he could trust her, if she had to make the call, to do it efficiently.

He stepped inside, gazing down the empty hallway, then up the stairs. Something caught his attention about six feet ahead, where the tile turned to hardwood. A smear, thin, watery, reddish in color. On the table to the right, beneath the stairs, a handbag sat next to a wooden bowl holding two sets of keys. A cell phone lay with them.

Every muscle in his body tightened as he walked,

sticking to one side of the hall until he reached the double-wide doorway into the living room. There he stilled instantly, everything but his gaze. He saw the rug, the couch, the armchair, the wood floor, the quilt on the ottoman, all splattered with red. Pillows had been knocked from the furniture. A wineglass was upended on the coffee table, along with a plastic cup and a puddle of white. Probably milk.

Oh God, this was not looking good.

Barely breathing, he stepped into the room, just enough to see that no one was there. No bodies—*thank you, Jesus.*

Backing up, he pivoted and went to the porch, where he handed his pistol to Morwenna. "Call Sam," he said grimly. He shucked his slicker and his shoes, pulled off his T-shirt, dried his feet the best he could with it, then tugged it back on.

"Are they...?"

He took back his gun as he pulled his cell phone out. "There's blood in the living room. Signs of a struggle." After fiddling with his phone a moment, he held it out. "Then call her and ask her to get here."

"Yashi Baker. Who's she?"

"Will Mueller's cousin. Brit will need somebody." He breathed deeply of rain, flowers, weeds, woods, then blew it out. "I'm going back in."

When the phone rang while she was in the middle of a jaw-popping yawn, Yashi considered not answering. It was all the way at the other end of the house, she reasoned, and she was so comfy on the window seat with her tablet, a glass of chocolate milk and half a honey bun.

But all the way at the other end of her tiny house was only twenty-six feet, and in her barely-a-business, she couldn't afford to ignore any calls. With a sigh, she nudged Bobcat off her legs, grinning when his gold eyes narrowed in response. "Sorry, Bobbo, some of us don't have the luxury of lazing twenty-four hours a day."

With just a few strides, she snatched up the phone on the kitchen counter, giving the screen a cursory glance even as she answered. The name there stopped her, though. Everything inside her went hot, then icy, and trembling started at the top of her head and swept all the way to her bare feet. She sank onto the dining seat behind her, heart thudding, and wondered if she could choke out any recognizable words around the lump in her throat when she realized the voice coming from the phone wasn't male. Wasn't Ben.

Still shaking, she lifted it to her ear in time to hear the woman say "—you there, Ms. Baker? Hello?"

"Y-yes. Sorry. Th-this is Yashi Baker."

"This is Morwenna Armstrong. I'm a dispatcher with the Cedar Creek Police Department, and our officers are requesting that you meet them at Will and Lolly Mueller's house as soon as possible."

Virtually all thought of Ben—how much she'd loved him, how badly she'd betrayed him—disappeared, replaced by instant concern for her cousin's family. "What's wrong? Is it one of the kids? Are they all right?"

"I'm sorry. I don't have information to give. Can you go to the Mueller house?"

Jumping from the chair, Yashi dashed up the stairs to the loft, grabbing running shoes and socks. "Yes, of course. I'll be there in ten—" Rain pounded on the roof inches above her head. "Fifteen minutes. Do you at least know if they're okay?"

The dispatcher hesitated. "I know Brit is."

Meaning Will or Lolly or Theo might not be. *Dear God.*

Yashi dropped the phone on the bed, shoved her feet into the shoes and socks, then ran back down the L-shaped stairs. Immediately, she rushed back for her phone, hit the bottom step and started out the door before turning back for her purse and keys. At the last instant, she remembered her rain jacket, yanked it on and ran out.

What could have happened to warrant the police wanting her presence? Had one of her cousins been assaulted? Arrested? Had someone broken into their house? Had Will done something to protect his family?

His family. Her family. The only family she had in the whole world. If anything had happened to one of them, any of them, she would… God, she didn't know what she would do.

Her lemon-yellow Volkswagen Bug was the only bright spot in the sodden morning. It was small and dinged and scratched, but it was paid for, and that counted for a lot in her world.

Her office, with the house on wheels parked behind, was located on Highway 66 halfway between Cedar Creek and Tulsa. Weather wasn't keeping anyone from running their Saturday morning errands, so she forced her attention narrowly on traffic to keep it off the fear in her gut. Her hands gripped the steering wheel until her fingers hurt, and bands were tightening around her chest. Periodically, she glanced at her phone in the passenger seat, but she resisted dialing Will's or Lolly's number. Whatever was wrong, she didn't want to find out while driving in torrential rain.

She turned west on First Street, which became Highway 66 again in a few miles, and she followed the road out of town. When her cousins had bought their house out here after Theo was born, they'd been in the county, but the city had incorporated section after section until they'd wound up within city limits. They hadn't liked that, but they'd been philosophical about it. They loved the house, loved the fifteen acres that kept anyone from building too close, so they'd accepted it.

By the time Yashi reached the short road where the long-extinct Dixieland Amusement Park had grown up nearly a hundred years earlier, she was having trouble breathing, and her knees were quivering. She was a lawyer. She'd been an assistant district attorney. She'd had dealings with law enforcement most of her adult life. Where was her professionalism? Her much-touted ability to stay calm in any crisis?

After she turned left onto Ozark Trail Road, the old original Route 66, the road wound through a shadowy curve, trees canopying overhead, underneath an old railroad bridge and around another curve cut through rocky hillsides. She slowed, always her habit, as the left-hand turn into Will's driveway came when the road began to straighten, but this time her speed dropped to practically nothing.

Police vehicles filled the driveway and the short stretch of grass along the road. There was barely room for her little Bug between a big white pickup and a black SUV, both bearing police markings. She eased the car into the space, cut the engine and sat there trying to breathe.

*Oh God, oh God, oh God.*

The rain hadn't let up. Four figures huddled together on the porch, talking: Sam Douglas, the chief; Daniel Harper, a detective she'd dealt with only a few times before leaving the DA's office; Lois Gideon, a uniformed officer who knew more about the department and the town than the rest of them combined; and a young woman in shorts and a T-shirt, dark haired and pale skinned and, considering that she'd made the official call requesting Yashi's presence from Ben's personal cell phone, probably Morwenna the dispatcher.

She'd probably been at Ben's house when whatever had happened, happened.

He liked to sleep in late on his days off. She'd probably been sleeping in late, too.

With him.

*Not important*, Yashi's brain reminded her. Her family was the important thing here, and there was no sign of them.

At least there were no ambulances or fire trucks among the vehicles. That was good. That meant no one was hurt.

Or they were beyond the help of paramedics.

Sweat broke out across her forehead, the trembling of her hands increased and anxiety fluttered in her chest. If she didn't calm down, she was going to go into full panic mode, and that—

A knock on the driver's window startled her, drawing a shriek as she whirled about in the cramped space. Ben was standing there, bent down from his substantial height of six feet four inches to gaze in at her. He wore a slicker, the hood pulled over his head, but his face was streaked with rain, and he looked grim.

"Oh please, no." The groan was torn from her at the sight of him. Ben was stoic. He had the best poker face she'd ever seen. He rarely let his emotions show, particularly on the job. He was quiet and calm and studied, and no one could ever guess what he was thinking, but now—

He pulled the door open a few inches and said in a flat voice, "Drive over to my house. I'll talk to you there."

A moment later, he passed in a blur behind her car. She grabbed her cell, praying for a call from Will, saying, *it's all right, just a misunderstanding.* After pulling her keys from the ignition, she jumped out, slammed the door and ran after Ben. The air was muggy, too thick to breathe, a combination of August heat and a deluge of biblical proportions.

In seconds, everything from her hips down was soaked. When he stepped across the ditch, then climbed up the path there to his yard, she did the same, missing the flat wide stepping-stones, setting her feet into the cool water rushing down the slope. Her shoes squished and slid as she started up the path, nothing but a stretch of grass kept mown to provide easy access between neighbors.

Ben never once looked back at her. He climbed the steps to the porch, paused at the door and then finally faced her. The grimness was still there, but it was better concealed. This was more in line with what people jokingly called his detective face. The joke: it was also his normal-conversation face, his reading-a-good-book face and so on.

"Do you want to go inside? It'll be cold."

She shook her head so strenuously that water streamed from her hair. Even while getting drenched, she hadn't thought to pull her hood over her head. Ben used to tell her that she resembled Bobcat when he got a much-hated bath.

"Sit. I'll be back in a minute."

When the door closed behind him, she walked to the end of the porch, turned back and went to stand at the railing directly across from her cousins' house. Now there was a crime scene vehicle, and pulling in behind the others was a pickup truck. Quint Foster—former assistant chief, demoted to just officer—climbed out of the driver's side, and a shorter form, definitely a woman, got down from the other side. They joined the people on the porch, took off their jackets, their shoes, put on booties and went inside.

Yashi's hands gripped the railing while she bounced on the balls of her feet. She wanted to go inside, too. She wanted to see Will and Lolly, wanted to find out what was going on and how to fix it. She wanted assurance, comfort, a fear-soothing hug, an absolute promise that whatever was wrong would soon be okay.

The door closed behind her, and she felt rather than heard Ben's approach. No comforting or hugging would be coming from him. She'd destroyed all his softer feelings for her. The first year without him had been impossible, the second merely miserable. She'd cried a million tears over him, had flung two million curses at him and a billion more at herself. She'd missed him more than she'd ever missed anyone.

For a kid who'd lost both parents at age six, that was saying a lot.

Ben brought a notepad and an ink pen with him. He left his jacket on a chair to drip, wiped the sweat from his neck and sat in his favorite chair to begin the interview. Daniel and Sam had both offered to do it. It was common knowledge Ben was more comfortable interrogating than interviewing. Or, Sam had suggested, they could wait for their newest hire and first female detective, JJ Logan, to arrive. But he'd said a stiff no, thanks. They didn't know he had reason to avoid all contact whatsoever with Yashi Baker, and he didn't intend to tell them. No one outside the Muellers had known about their yearlong relationship, and he meant to keep it that way.

"When was the last time you saw the Muellers?"

Yashi was still, her head erect, her spine straight. Though she looked tall and elegantly lined, tension radiated from her. She stared at the house a long time, seeing nothing, before turning to face him. "Last Sunday. We had dinner after church at Pablo's." Her voice quavered, but a breath steadied it. "I talked to Will on Wednesday about Theo's next soccer game, and Lolly emailed me some recipes Thursday. I had a text from Brit yesterday. She wanted to know if I'd teach her to drive the Bug. She's got high hopes of getting a car for her sixteenth birthday, and she thinks a Bug might suit her."

"Did they mention any plans for today?"

Yashi slipped out of her jacket and, as he'd done, draped it over a chair back to drip. She was dressed for a morning at home: gray cotton shorts and a T-shirt that had seen better days. It was a leftover from her days at the University of Texas, and she usually wore it to sleep in.

Gathering her blond hair in her hands, she wrung water from it, then shook it back. "Theo always has practice of some sort on Saturdays. Lolly picks up groceries during practice, Will works in the kitchen and Brit tries to put as much distance between herself and them as she can. Not," she hastily added, "that there's a problem. It's just… She's fifteen."

Ben hadn't asked for or needed an explanation. He knew the Muellers were close, probably unusually so these days. Besides, he had three younger sisters and two brothers. One of them, George, had put so much distance between him and the family that none of them had seen him for coming on twelve years.

Whatever had happened with the Muellers had nothing to do with their teenage daughter longing to be grown up.

Yashi was silent until he finished making his notes, then she met his gaze. "What happened?"

Part of him wanted to refuse to answer her questions. That wasn't the way a police interview worked. He asked the questions. She answered them. Simple. But the part of him that might be a better cop than he was a man wasn't juvenile enough to resort to that. They were her family. She had a right to know at least the basics. Trouble was, the basics were all he had to offer and raised nothing but questions.

"Morwenna and I were having breakfast when she noticed the front door was open there." He didn't look at her, didn't care if she wondered whether he and Morwenna were involved, didn't care if she did or didn't give a damn who he slept with.

"I called Will and Lolly and got no answer," he went on. "I called Brit, and she'd sneaked out in the night to go to her boyfriend's house. She thought she'd be back before anyone woke up. They're supposed to be home. Their cars are there. Lolly's purse and keys are on the hall table, and so are Will's keys and phone. And…" His mouth thinned as he recalled the scene in the living room. The amount of blood wasn't an incompatible-with-life scenario, unless it all came from one person. It was the lab's job to figure that out.

Yashi's face had gone pale, making her eyes seem ridiculously blue in contrast. She pressed her lips together, and muscles clenched in her jaw, her neck, her hands. "And?"

He didn't want to go on. Delivering bad news to a family about their loved ones was always hard, and the fact that he knew both the family and the loved one made it even harder. Especially since the family in this case was pitifully small. Yashi was an only child; so was Will. Their parents had died when they were kids, and their grandparents before that. Both sets of great-grandparents had immigrated, one from Canada and one from Russia. Other than distant relatives back in their homelands, the family line was down to Yashi, Will and his kids.

Maybe just Yashi and Brit.

She waited, motionless. Her eyes were fixed on his face, steady and unyielding, and her breaths were measured. To anyone watching her, she appeared calm and patient. To the person unlucky enough to be the focus of that stare, she appeared slightly less lethal than a nuclear warhead.

He took a deep breath, wished he'd let Sam or Daniel or JJ have this job, then quietly answered. "There was a struggle in the living room. Things knocked about, spilled milk and wine, table upturned. It doesn't look as if any of the beds were slept in, but the kitchen is clean and there are leftovers in the refrigerator, so we're guessing it happened last night, between dinner and bedtime. Do they still stay up late on Fridays and watch movies?"

Yashi's nod was vague, not as to the answer, but lacking the strength to be emphatic. No wonder. While she'd been cozied up doing whatever occupied her Friday nights these days, three of the four members of her family had been fighting for their lives.

And it was absolutely not the right time to remember that *he* used to occupy her Friday nights.

He closed his eyes briefly, let himself see the scene again in his head, then looked at her. "There was blood in the living room. A lot of it."

She'd been pale earlier. Now she turned white, and her body began sliding to the porch floor. If not for the balusters behind her, she would have pitched back into the yard. As it was, she slid down until her butt hit the floor, knees drawn up, and she hugged herself tightly, hiding her face in her arms.

Ben listened for tears, watched for the shuddering of her shoulders. This was one of the things he hated about interviews. It wasn't in him to offer emotional or physical support to someone whom he'd just given bad news. JJ could do it if she had to. Sam was really good at it. Lois excelled at it. Even Daniel, who was a little on the stiff side, could unbend much better than Ben could.

But no tears came from Yashi. No shudders. No sobs. No great sorrow unleashed. Dragging a wheezy breath into her lungs, she lifted her head. The sorrow was there on her face, shifting her appearance from pretty blonde to tragic beauty, but her eyes were dry. "So my family's been attacked, injured, kidnapped and possibly—" her voice caught, a hiccup, then turned steely "—possibly murdered. Do you have any clues yet? Any ideas why this happened to them?"

He was shaking his head when his cell beeped with a text. Seeing it was from Sam, he automatically glanced across the road and saw that everyone over there had gone inside the house except Morwenna. Morwenna knew her limits when it came to the job, and she observed them strictly.

The text was short and terse. You need to see this. Putting down his pen and notebook, Ben shrugged into his slicker and set off. Even as he said, "I'll be back," Yashi scrambled to her feet. He didn't tell her to stay put. He wouldn't in her situation. She wasn't just any citizen or worried family member. She'd been an assistant district attorney for six years. She was more familiar than most with the damage people could inflict on others. If Sam didn't want to let her in the house, she could wait on the Mueller porch.

The rain was showing signs of easing up finally. It still fell with a steady patter, but the rivers running down the road were narrowing, and the ditches were slowly draining. Ben and Yashi climbed into the shelter of the porch, took off their jackets, kicked off their shoes and put on booties before Ben gave the partly opened door a push.

Sam pulled it open, gestured for Ben to come inside, hesitated with Yashi, then gave her a nod. When they'd joined the small group of grim people in the foyer, Sam closed the door.

There was a message written in red on the inside of the white door. Clunky letters, paint running in drips from the overspray, looking all too much like drops of blood, and the text—the promise—was chilling.

I'll trade them for her.

Yashi walked outside, barely glancing at Morwenna. Some small part of her brain that was still functioning in Normal Land noted that Ben's friend was younger, prettier and possibly color blind. That part of her hoped that if he wanted her, he got her, complete with happily-ever-after.

She took the steps one at a time, grasping the railing, unable to see through the rain and the dampness in her eyes, unable to make out anything without that gruesome bloodred message superimposed over it. She walked to the driveway, past Lolly's minivan and Will's SUV, and stopped where the ground dropped steeply into a small valley. The creek that cut through it rushed with surplus water. It was the kids' favorite playground: wading, climbing the boulders that edged it on both sides, sailing makeshift boats. Brit liked to stretch out on the flat rock in her bikini, invisible from any vantage point except where Yashi was standing now. It was the only time she welcomed Theo's splashes because they cooled her baking skin.

Every time Yashi saw her in a bikini, she was struck anew by how young she seemed to Yashi and how attractive she was to the males out there. Though Brit was restricted from the more revealing clothes her friends wore, she could be covered head to toe and guys would still notice her.

One pervert in particular wanted her badly enough to come take her from her house in the night. Badly enough to kidnap her family when he found she wasn't there. Irrationally enough to think he could trade them for her. *Oh dear God.* Where had Brit met him? She was too savvy to fall for someone online. She knew the hooks, the lures, had been taught internet safety along with *use your napkin* and *brush your teeth* and *reuse, reduce, recycle.*

Was it a teacher at her school? The coach of her soccer team? Someone sitting in the pew behind her at church, benignly singing hymns? The parent of a friend? A neighbor? Her doctor, her dentist, someone she trusted as a friend?

The possibilities were endless. Yashi knew too well that more often than not, criminals didn't look like criminals. Sure, there was the guy with *Kill all cops* tattooed on his forehead who'd, surprise, shot a cop. The unshaven, unbathed, wild-eyed terrors who made protective instincts scream from a hundred yards away.

But so many looked normal. Behaved normally. Did everything but think normally. The ones whose friends and neighbors said, *But he seemed like such a nice guy. He coached my kids. He treated his grandmother like a queen.* The ones no one would ever look at and think, *He could be an embezzler, a rapist, a predator, a kidnapper, a murderer.*

Everything inside Yashi shuddered with despair. She hugged herself tightly, willing the sickness back into her stomach, calling on years of coping to gain some semblance of emotional control. She was bending forward at the waist, eyes closed, taking short, steady breaths through her nose, when a light touch on her arm startled her upright again.

"Sorry. I didn't mean to surprise you." Morwenna stood there, concern lining her face. Like Yashi, she'd left her slicker on the porch. It was too hot a day to swelter inside rainproof fabric. "I'm Morwenna. I'm the one who called you."

Yashi sniffed and dashed her hand across her face, wiping away raindrops—teardrops—only to have more appear in their place. "Yashi."

"Would you like to go back to Ben's to wait?" Morwenna's sympathy was sincere, but different from what she'd seen on the faces of the officers and crime scene investigators when she'd walked inside Will's house. There was an innocence to it that offered both acknowledgment and hope. She knew this was a bad situation, but she expected only the best outcome. Her faith touched that cold, hollow spot in Yashi's gut.

"Yes. P-please."

Morwenna took hold of her arm and guided her around the vehicles in the driveway to the road. She wasn't chatty—Yashi had expected chattiness—but got her across the yard, onto the porch and seated before she disappeared inside the house. The moments until her return passed unmarked, no thoughts, no words, only images of Will and Lolly, Brit and Theo, the way Yashi had always known them. Laughing, happy, teasing.

Morwenna came back, arms full. First, she set two bottles of water on the round table between the chairs, then she shook out a thick fluffy bath towel and handed it to Yashi. "I'd offer something stronger than water, but the only other thing Ben has in the house is coffee, and trust me, his coffee isn't drinkable."

Yashi knew that. He drank the other stuff at work and in restaurants because no one made it his way, but he insisted the only good coffee in the world was his.

In the time they were together, she'd come up with a dozen good uses for his brew—cleaning sludge from car engines had topped the list—but drinking wasn't among them.

And Morwenna knew. How long had they been together? Was it dating, a relationship, all good fun, friends with benefits or more? Did he love her? Did she love him? Did she deserve him?

Yashi hoped so, because *she* certainly hadn't.

Morwenna gave her dark hair a quick rub with the second towel, then wrapped it around her before she sat down. No sooner had she settled in, when a tiny gray kitten appeared from nowhere, leaped into her lap, rested its paws on the chair arm and lifted a disdainful nose in Yashi's direction before curling into a ball.

"Ben's got a cat," Yashi said blankly. He'd registered official complaints against Bobcat practically every time he'd come to her apartment. The cat was possessive and always lying where Ben wanted to sit. He sharpened his claws on Ben's holster, shed an immense amount of yellow hair on Ben's uniform and preferred to sleep in the center of the bed—claws on Ben's side, of course.

"This is Oliver. He had to find a new home after his human went to jail for making meth."

"And Ben volunteered?"

"Oh no. He lost to Sam and Daniel in Rock, Paper, Scissors." Morwenna gave a boys-will-be-boys shrug before uncapping her water and taking a drink. She waited while Yashi did the same, then cautiously said, "So you know Ben."

Knew him. Had loved him. Tennyson, in her never-humble opinion, had been so off the mark when he'd written, "'Tis better to have loved and lost than never to have loved at all." She'd loved deeply, lost deeply and could live without the pain again.

Not that falling in love with Ben had been a choice.

Aware that Morwenna was waiting, Yashi gave the easiest answer. "I used to work in the DA's office. I prosecuted some of his cases."

Let her think that was all there was between them. Nothing but business. Not that it mattered. Ben wasn't the type a woman got insecure about. He was solid and steady and loyal. He was an emotional rock, and it had nothing to do with his height or the broad shoulders and granite muscles that went with it. He was a man who never strayed from his beliefs, who did the right thing not because he should but because it was who he was.

"He's a very good detective. They're all very good."

A ghost of a smile quivered on Yashi's lips. "I know."

"They're the people I'd want looking if it was my family missing."

Eyes misting, she whispered, "I know." They were dedicated. They did their best on every case. Will, Lolly and Theo deserved the very best.

She was taking a drink when her cell phone rang. Cold water spilled over her chin and dripped onto her shirt. More splashed her legs as she dropped the bottle to dig the phone from her pocket. The screen identified Brit, and when she lifted the phone to her ear, she was greeted by her cousin's hyped-up, high-pitched and breathless voice.

"Yashi? What's going on? Officer Bear called and

told me don't come home, and Mom and Dad aren't answering their phones, and he said they're not home. Where are they? Where are you? I'm at your house, but you're not here. What's happening?" The last words came out a wail, accompanied by the soothing sound of a male voice in the background. Her boyfriend, Jared.

"Honey, I'm at Ben's house." Yashi needed less than a breath to choose a lie to tell—a partial one, at least—because no way was she breaking the news over the phone. "Sweetie, your house was broken into and—"

"Oh God, are they all right? Mom? Dad? Are they hurt? What—who—" The shriek dropped to a frantic, fearful whisper. "Is Theo okay?"

*Dear God, I pray so.*

Without stopping for air, Brit went on. "I'm coming out there right now. I want to see—I want to talk to Officer Bear. I want— Jared, come on! We have to go! We have to—I have to—"

"Brit, listen to me." Yashi's words were sharp, the only way to cut through the girl's emotions to reach the rational part of her brain. "You still have the key to my house, right? Go on in and wait for me. I'll be there as soon as I can. Brit?"

The only answer was a thud. A moment later, Jared got on the phone. He identified himself, his sixteen-year-old voice quavering with fear and the effects of Brit's drama and trauma. "Should I bring Brit home now? Officer—Detective Little Bear told her to wait until he called, and she's called him, but he's not answering."

Yashi got to her feet, repeating the instructions, feeling the brush as the towel fell to the floor. "I'll be there as quick as I can. Just get her inside and—and let her cuddle with Bobcat for a while." The cat usually managed to bring Brit back from the edge of hysteria to the-world-hasn't-ended balance.

The world hasn't ended *yet*.

Or maybe it had.

She was halfway down the steps when she turned to Morwenna. "I don't know if Ben has more questions, but—"

"You have to go. Of course. I'll tell him. He knows how to reach you."

The rain had become little more than a mist that dampened their faces as they hurried across the road. Yashi began patting her pockets for her keys, then remembered they were in her jacket. With a quiet word, Morwenna jogged ahead to the porch and brought the slicker back to her. Apparently stricken by impulse, she gave Yashi a quick, tight hug.

"Have faith," she said when she let go.

Faith. Hope. Trust.

Yashi was feeling pretty low on all three at the moment.

# Chapter 2

Ben stood in the doorway of Brit's bedroom. It was on the second floor, at the back of the house and had a view of a lot of wet, densely grown trees. There was no sign of another house even though he knew Kenneth Brown's house was a short distance to the southeast and Marlon Pickering's was about the same distance to the southwest.

Could either of them be involved with this?

Kenneth Brown was a mean SOB who was quick to anger and married to a woman just as mean. Except for regular smackdowns with her family—every reunion and holiday turned into a disturbance call—they kept to themselves.

Marlon Pickering was Native American, belonging, like Ben, to the Muscogee Creek Nation. He was a successful artist, doing watercolors that depicted their ancestors' lives after their forced removal from the southern states to Indian Territory nearly two hundred years ago. He and his wife, recognized for her pottery and basket weaving, were active in tribal affairs, the art world, their family and community. Last Ben had heard, they were raising two grandchildren along with the youngest of their four kids.

Morwenna came around the corner, laying her hand on his shoulder. "I said I'd tell you— Ooh, pretty room."

He glanced at the sage-green walls, the pale gray trim, the thin white curtains, then looked at her, one brow lifted. "Your room is painted in primary colors."

"Doesn't mean I can't appreciate something different. Yashi got a call from Brit. She's going to her house to talk to her. You should answer your phone when a distraught family member calls."

Yeah, he should have, but Brit was melodramatic by nature. He'd watched her do a complete meltdown over the most insignificant things. Who knew what her response would be to hearing her family had been attacked and kidnapped?

And now, he admitted with both satisfaction and chagrin, he didn't have to tell her because Yashi would do it for him. It wasn't fair, but life so often wasn't.

Seeing Yashi this morning, beautiful and golden and vulnerable, had reminded him of that.

"I told her you would find her when you were ready to interview Brit. I assume you're going to?"

Could he put it off on someone else without feeling like an ass? Like he'd somehow let down the Muel-

lers, the department, even himself? The other officers wouldn't hold it against him. They all had their
strengths and weaknesses; one picked up the slack for
the others.

But the Muellers were his friends. He'd known Brit
since she was five. He'd held Theo when he was a baby,
had given him a finger to hold on to when he was learning to walk, perched Brit on his shoulders so she didn't
miss a thing at the Christmas parades. They were in
danger, and he needed to help them.

Even Yashi.

He sighed heavily. "Yes, I'm going to. I'm going
now."

He was down the stairs and halfway to the door when
Sam stepped out of the living room. "Did I hear you say
you're going to interview Brit?"

Ben glanced up the stairs, judging the distance from
where Sam stood to where he'd been talking to Morwenna, and gave a shake of his head. "Fatherhood has
sharpened your hearing."

Sam's look was wry. "Who knew a baby not much
bigger than a football could bellow like a herd of cows
at feeding time? As long as Sameen's making noise,
it's okay. It's when she gets quiet that I start to worry."

"She's three months old. You think she's gonna crawl
out of her crib and make a run for it?"

"Nah. That's what the little Harper's going to do."

Daniel turned away from his conversation with a
crime scene guy long enough to scowl. His wife, Natasha, had been engaged four times, earning the nickname Runaway Bride, before she'd finally married him

last fall. Now, two weeks past her due date, running anywhere other than the hospital was the last thing on her mind.

Sam returned to the subject. "Stay with Brit until we figure out what to do with her. Don't forget to collect her cell. Oh, and we need her prints."

Ben didn't resent the reminders, though he didn't need them, either. He had a list of things to do running in his head: interview Brit; get the names and contact info of every friend and enemy she had; find out everything about her current boyfriend, her ex-boyfriends, any wannabe boyfriends. Track her movements for the past days or weeks or months; listen to her voice mails; read her texts, emails, instant messages; scour her social media; study every single photograph on her cell.

Basically, he intended to go through her life with a fine-toothed comb, and then through the lives of her family and friends. He intended to keep her safe, to get her parents and brother back, to make their lives right again.

And he intended to do it all without putting himself in danger with Yashi again. Daniel had forgiven his commitment-shy wife for breaking his heart and started over new, but Ben didn't have that in him. Given the nature of his job, there were a lot of people he couldn't trust in his life, but damned if he would invite one who'd proven herself so right back in.

After a stop at home to change into dry clothes and pick up his badge and weapon, Ben drove into town, automatically heading for the older neighborhood where Yashi rented a high-ceilinged apartment in a 1940s-era house. Her bedroom windows overlooked a detached garage so overgrown with wisteria and honeysuckle that the doors no longer opened, and she'd sworn the place was worth every penny just for the view and the fragrance.

He pulled to the curb in front of the house and gazed at the empty spot where her yellow car had always sat. She wouldn't have taken Brit anywhere. She'd understood the message spray-painted on the door as well as he had. Her cousin was in danger, and Yashi would protect her like a mama bear.

Annoyed he hadn't considered the possibility of her moving to a new place sometime in the last five years, he called the station and asked one of the dispatchers on duty to run her driver's license.

"Don't need to. Her office is on the new highway, a couple miles past the fire station, and she lives behind it. Cute place. My brother bartered some work on it in exchange for her help when him and his wife adopted their little girl."

Ben thanked him and headed that way. Not many lawyers in Cedar Creek got rich. At least in the DA's office, Yashi's office space and staff had been supplied by the county. Now that she had to cover those expenses, it made sense to combine the work space with the living space if she could.

He found the office easily enough, a nondescript building with large plate-glass windows that were tinted against the afternoon sun. The parking lot was wide enough for four spaces, none of them occupied this morning. But a narrow lane led around the south end of the building, reminding him the dispatcher had said she lived behind the office, not in the back of it as Ben had assumed.

He didn't know what to expect, but it wasn't what he got. Instead of a paved lot, there was a large square of lush grass, and in the center was a Victorian-style playhouse. It was white with trim and curls in very pale shades of blue and green, and a matching set of wood lawn furniture sat beneath a canvas sail in the same shades. The Bug occupied one-half of a concrete parking pad, and shrubs, flowers and a white picket fence edged the three sides of the yard.

Ben didn't often find himself taken by surprise, but now he was. He climbed out of the truck that dwarfed Yashi's car and followed a path of stepping-stones to the tiny front porch. He was lifting his hand to knock on the pale blue door when it swung open and Brit flung herself into his arms.

"Officer Bear, have you found them yet? Are they okay?" Her voice came muffled from somewhere below, but the misery and fear relayed clearly.

He patted her back. "Not yet, Brit. Do you feel okay to talk to me?"

"Yes." But her muscles tightened and she burrowed a little harder against him.

He walked inside without releasing her, then closed the door behind them. His head was literally a few hairsbreadth from touching the ceiling, and he could easily reach both outside walls if he tried.

Yashi stood a few feet away, arms hugging her middle. She'd changed into dry clothes, too, another pair of shorts and a T-shirt. Her feet were bare. Their position, one foot resting on top of the other, brought back the earlier image of vulnerability. She looked in need of comforting, too, and left out. She'd told him once that she'd spent most of her life being left out. No big deal. She could handle it.

It had broken his heart.

For just a moment, he let himself wish things had turned out differently between them, the way they were supposed to have been. He'd wanted what Sam and Mila had, what Daniel and Natasha and Quint and JJ had. He'd never meant to be thirty-six and single, with the only women in his life family, coworkers and occasional relationships that were doomed to end before they started.

Sometimes life sucked.

"Sweetie, why don't you go wash your face and maybe change into some of my clothes?" Yashi waited until Brit let go of Ben and ran up the stairs to the loft before finally releasing her hold on herself and gesturing toward the living room chairs. She didn't have a couch—the window seat served that purpose—but there were two large comfy chairs that each unfolded into a twin-size bed. They were quite possibly the only furniture in the house that would fit Ben comfortably.

Along with her bed.

He walked to the nearest chair, where Bobcat stretched then gave Ben a bored look that ended in a yawn and an indelicate display of licking.

"He still holds me in high regard," Ben said as he moved to the other chair.

Yashi tried to smile but couldn't. She lifted the cat and sat in his spot. As soon as she settled him beside her, he jumped up and gracefully leaped from one perch on the wall to the next until he reached the loft. "He's a cat," she said, as if that explained everything.

She wished it was that easy in human life.

"While we waited, I asked Brit to write down a timeline for last night," she said, nodding to a notebook on the coffee table. "She also made a list of her friends and their phone numbers, and the usernames and passwords for her social media accounts."

He picked up the notebook, glanced at each page. Brit's handwriting was like her, spirited and energetic. Yashi tried to remember if she'd scrolled so many loops and frills with a pen, but her teen years seemed so very long ago.

Ben's dark gaze lifted from the timeline. "She climbed out the second-floor window?"

Yashi parroted the response her cousin had given her. "She couldn't very well sneak down the stairs and out the door with her family right there in the living room."

"She's so girly. I didn't know she had it in her."

"Young love." This time she managed a tiny smile. "Jared's parents were out of town. It was their first chance to do it somewhere other than the back seat of his car." As a responsible adult, she should be worried and cautioning, but she'd been fifteen when she'd lost her virginity. She remembered what it was like to be young, discovering the world as well as herself, and the earnestness of the boy named Caleb who swore he would love her forever.

That time, forever had lasted seven months and two weeks. He'd dumped her when he'd gotten the chance to take a cheerleader to the prom.

Yashi didn't have a very good track record with *forever.*

Ben flipped back to the first page in the notebook. "She told me she left a note on her pillow."

"I did. It's in there." Brit came down the stairs, wearing a pair of black spandex shorts and a T-shirt that swallowed her. It was faded brown, hung from her shoulder and draped so that it was difficult to see the logo: an outline of a buffalo with Oklahoma written across it. It was an ancient shirt, one that had already outlived its useful years before Yashi had worn it home from Ben's house one early dawn long ago.

Brit passed on to the bathroom in the back corner of the house, and a moment later, the faint sound of water drifted out.

"I didn't see the note."

The air-conditioning kicked on, and Yashi automatically reached for the lap quilt folded over the back of her chair. It had been a gift from Lolly, a Victorian crazy quilt pieced in velvet and brocade, and it warmed her soul as well as her body. "Maybe the crime scene unit had already collected it."

He shook his head, his black hair gleaming in the light from the nearest overhead. "I was the first one in the house. The first one in her room. There wasn't any note."

"Maybe Lolly found it." Right away, though, she

shook her head. "No, she would have called Brit immediately with steam coming out her ears. Will, too. I saw the phone. She didn't have any calls last night after Jared texted to say he was waiting down the road."

Brit returned from the bathroom, her hair held away from her face with a band. Her skin was sallow, and she wore a cloak of fear and uncertainty that left her grimly subdued. "I left a note. I put it on my pillow." Instead of settling on the window seat, she nudged and slid her way into the armchair with Yashi. "Then I climbed out the window and down to the back porch roof and onto the railing and then the porch. I had a flashlight, and I cut through the woods and met Jared up the hill at the driveway where the old house burned down."

Stroking Brit's blond hair, Yashi privately agreed with Ben. She hadn't known Brit had it in her—sneaking out, walking through the woods alone at night. Forget young love; this must have been raging hormones.

What did it mean that the note was missing? It could have blown off the bed and onto the floor. The techs could have bagged it without mentioning it to Ben.

Or the kidnapper could have taken it. Wanting something she had touched, handled, put on the pillow where she laid her head.

A shudder rocketed through Yashi, then passed into Brit. The girl drew her feet onto the cushion, huddling as small as she could, and tugged the quilt over to cover her, too. Her expression was resolute, but it was all bravado. Bless her heart, she wanted to be brave and strong and help find her parents, but she was a scared little girl. "I'm ready, Officer. You can ask." Beneath the quilt, she clasped Yashi's hand tightly.

Regret tightened Ben's mouth, but it passed quickly, his face moving into impassivity. He was strong and steady. He would get Brit through this, because that was what he did. He fixed things for other people. He made things all right again.

Yashi wished she knew how to make things right. The only time she'd ever had that kind of confidence had been in the DA's office. She'd been a warrior in the fight for justice…until she'd learned she was as fallible there as every other part of her life.

"Have you noticed anything unusual lately?"

Brit chewed the tip of one nail while thinking. "Marliss Matlock complimented me the other day. She's super smart. She doesn't do compliments." Then her forehead wrinkled. "I know that's not the kind of thing you mean, but it's summer. I don't see that many people. Theo and I have been going to soccer, and we go to church, and we help Mom with the garden and the yard and stuff. No one's doing anything weird. The only people I talk to online are people I know, and I haven't argued with anyone in ages, not even Theo. The most exciting thing happening is school starting in a couple weeks."

Her voice broke with the last words, and she swiped her free hand across her face. "I haven't seen any strange guys, either. I've never seen anyone watching me like they shouldn't. Grown-ups don't pay any more attention to me than my friends, and guys my age… This can't be a guy my age, can it? What kid could make my mom and dad do anything? My dad would pound 'em. My *mom* would pound 'em. They would never let anyone near Theo or me."

Ben didn't explain what Yashi already knew: the kidnapper had to get physical control of only one family member. Yes, Lolly and Will would both go crazy-vicious on anyone who threatened their son…but not if the man already had a knife at Theo's throat. Ditto, if he grabbed Lolly first, Will and Theo would cooperate to stop him from hurting her.

Had he expected to take Brit without any interference from her family? Had he sneaked in the way she'd left, only to find her bed empty and the note saying she'd gone off with her boyfriend? Had the man's anger, jealousy and frustration been so strong that instead of leaving to try another time, he'd taken it out on the others?

Ben's steady voice broke through her thoughts. "What about your neighbors?"

"Neighbors?" Brit hiccuped the word. "You're our only neighbor."

"The people who live down the road," Yashi explained. "The ones on the other side of the railroad tracks. Anyone out there. Do you see them out walking or working in their yards? Ever played with their kids or gone to their houses for dinner or seen them in town?"

Brit shook her head helplessly. "I don't *know* them. I could see them right here and not know who they are. Except for that one Dad calls the crazy old coot. Mom says he's a bad son. They told me and Theo to stay out of his way because he's always ticked off about something."

Yashi's heart pounded a little harder, making even breaths tougher to come by. Crazy old coot didn't necessarily equal stalker/sex offender/kidnapper, but it could. She looked at Ben, and when he finished with his notes, he met her gaze briefly before looking away.

"Is that enough?" Brit asked, her voice small and drawn. "I don't want to talk anymore."

Ben's voice softened. "Yeah, Brit, that's good for now."

She gave Yashi a hug, pulled the quilt away from her and wrapped it around her shoulders before hugging Ben, then climbing the stairs to the loft. A moment later, a soft whoosh came from the mattress, followed by a whimper. "Oh Bobcat, what if they don't come back?"

Yashi felt the cry, and its accompanying tears, deep in her heart. What if they *didn't* come back? What if she and Brit had lost them forever?

Judging by the snores Ben heard from overhead, Brit was asleep by the time Yashi came downstairs from comforting her. She looked as drained as Brit and even more apprehensive. Of course, it was an entirely new situation to Brit, while Yashi had experienced loss up close before. Mother, father, aunt and uncle, all because some idiot had tried to drive and make a phone call at the same time.

"Who is the crazy old coot?"

"Kenneth Brown. A few alcohol-related arrests, a lot of domestics that don't result in anything."

Her nod indicated she remembered the man. "The family that brawls together..." She'd pulled on a sweatshirt while she was upstairs, and now she fiddled with the too-long cuffs. "If you want to come back in a few hours, give her some time to rest—"

"I'm staying until Sam gets a place for her."

"Oh." She didn't protest that Brit should stay with her. He didn't have to argue the idea with her. Yashi the cousin didn't want to let Brit get farther away than the bed upstairs, but Yashi the lawyer knew protection was the uppermost concern.

Finished with folding the cuffs, she smoothed the sweatshirt over her hips, and he saw the faint lump of a weapon on the right side of her waistband. As an assistant DA, she'd been the object of some threats, mostly flashes of temper when guilty verdicts were read, so Ben had taught her to shoot, and she'd gotten a concealed-carry permit. She was in the job to help victims. Not become one.

She looked around the room, at a loss for anything to say or do. "I, uh... You want something to drink? I have water, milk, lemonade and a coffeepot you can throw some mud in."

"No Coke?"

"I gave it up. Too many calories and no room to expand."

He looked her over, his gaze going all the way down to those bare feet, then up again. With her long legs and lush curves, she couldn't live comfortably at her "ideal" weight, but he was willing to bet she'd never met a man who cared. She looked as good in her clothes as out of them. *Almost*, old memories whispered.

She went to the kitchen, a distance of maybe ten feet,

and opened the refrigerator. Besides the armchairs, it was the only full-size thing he'd seen in the house. Hidden behind its open door, she said, "How about lunch? I've got sandwiches, leftover pizza and a bowl of pasta salad."

"Pizza." She liked it the way he did: thin crust, extra cheese and vegetables, and served cold. The meat was insignificant.

He stood up, noticing again the proximity of the walls. Confined areas didn't bother him, but he couldn't imagine living in this tiny space. From what little he'd seen of the loft, he wouldn't even be able to stand up in there. Not that he would ever be there. His time in her bedroom, though always amazing, was long past.

"Bring back old memories?" she asked as she handed him a plate, then set the pizza box on the counter.

He stilled in the act of removing a slice. How could she possibly know he'd been thinking about them, together, sex? He had the best blank face in the business. Even when he was a kid, no one had ever been able to guess what he was thinking, and it had only gotten better with age.

"Your great-grandfather's travel trailer? In Great-Aunt Weezer's backyard?"

Heat warmed his face, and he took another slice of pizza to hide it. Of course she was referring to the first place he'd called his own. It had been even smaller than her dollhouse, though when he'd done away with the living/dining room and kitchen, he'd been left with a reasonably sized bedroom and bathroom. Provided he didn't mind barely fitting into the shower.

Best of all, it hadn't been his mom's house, shared with her, three sisters, two brothers, various dogs, hamsters and friends.

"Yeah," he mumbled in agreement, tearing a couple of paper towels from the roll and balancing his plate with the glass of lemonade she offered. One look at the dining table—barely big enough for two and currently collapsed against the wall to provide some space for moving about—and he returned to the chair in the living room. "Why didn't you just fix up the back of your office?"

She padded in, carrying a bowl filled with pasta salad and a glass of water. "A lawyer starting out solo doesn't pay a lot of bills. If things get bad, I could lose the property but not the house. I'd just hitch it up to a truck and go someplace else."

His brain had noted the skirt around the house without really registering it. Of course it hid wheels. She wouldn't even have to pack. Just batten everything down and go. If her practice improved to the point where she wanted and could afford a regular house, she could sell this one or buy an acre of land near one of the nearby lakes and have a weekend getaway.

"Will and the kids and I did what we could, with lots of help from the internet," she said as she reclaimed her seat. "I traded services for everything else. It's not for everyone, but it suits Bobcat and me."

It did, Ben had to agree. Soft colors, clean lines, no fussiness. It was definitely much nicer, inside and out, than his old travel trailer. Sturdier, too. Walking through his trailer had been like crossing the deck of a pitching boat, and when the high winds came—as much a part of Oklahoma as the blue sky—he'd half expected to be rudely awakened while tumbling through the air.

Silence stretched out while they both got down to the business of eating. Not companionable—there was too much awareness between them for that—but tolerable. Like eating next to a stranger in a restaurant.

If he'd slept with the stranger. Gotten his heart broken by her. Hoped to never see her again.

Her spoon clinked against the bowl when she set them aside. She huddled in the chair, arms around her legs. Her shirtsleeves had come unrolled and fell down to hide her hands where they were clasped. "Is it true…" Her gaze shifted to the loft, then back to him. "Is it true that the chances of survival drop with each passing day?"

He swallowed the last bite of pizza and wiped his hands before setting his plate on the window seat. "I've never worked a kidnapping, so I don't know the latest statistics, but…yeah, that seems to be the case. But this isn't a typical kidnapping. You don't kidnap an entire family for access to one of their kids. If he went there to take Brit, why didn't he just leave and try again?" Presumably, he would have been equipped for one victim, not four. One against one was relatively simple. One against four, not so much.

"Maybe they caught him. Maybe he made a noise or Lolly went upstairs to change for bed or he knocked something over."

"Maybe. Maybe he was angry that Brit was with another guy and took it out on them. Maybe he really thinks he can trade them for her. Or maybe he's just freaking crazy and there's no logic to his actions."

Ben and Yashi had agreed on most things back in the day, among them that last line. There was no logic to be found in illogic, no sanity in insanity. This person, this secretive friend or relative stranger admiring Brit from afar, was clearly operating in a different reality from the rest of them.

As a rule of thumb, Ben hated different realities. Most of his cases were pretty straightforward; the *why* of a crime was usually revealed early on. Anger, greed, jealousy, revenge, love, power—those were the big motives. But throw mental illness into the mix, and up became down, rationale became fantasy. Sadly, he'd dealt with enough psychopaths in one year to last his whole life.

Yashi was about to speak when his cell signaled a call. Instead, she gathered their dishes and took them to the kitchen. A gesture that hinted at privacy, but not given the distance here. It didn't matter. He kept his responses to Sam's conversation brief before hanging up less than two minutes later.

She watched him from the kitchen, eyes wide. It would be like that in the upcoming days, he knew: every phone call a jump start to the fear and panic and dread. A knock on the door a reason for the heart to beat double time. Even the sound of a car door outside would startle her and make her hands shake.

"JJ and Quint are on their way to pick up Brit. For her own safety, you can't know where she's staying." Her head bobbed automatically, but he doubted she was processing his words that quickly. "Sam asked if you know the house well enough to tell if anything's missing. If you could walk through it with us."

She began another automatic nod but stopped, and the color drained from her face. She'd looked that pale on his porch, when he'd told her about the blood in the living room, just before her legs had given out and she'd plopped onto her butt. A part of him wanted to tell her they would skip the living room; she didn't have to look at her family's blood.

A part of him always wanted to make things easier on the victims' family, but nothing about victimization and violence was ever easy.

She gulped, straightened her shoulders and lifted her chin. "Of course," she said in a calm, steady voice. She sounded like the cool, never-fazed prosecutor she'd been for so long, but all the professionalism in the world couldn't hide the panic in her blue eyes.

And all the self-righteous resentment in the world couldn't stop him feeling bad for her, way deep inside.

Detective JJ Logan was originally from South Carolina and radiated confidence and assurance that wrapped around Yashi and made her feel safer just being in the room with her. Quint Foster, formerly the assistant chief of police before grieving his fiancée's death had sent him plummeting to rock bottom, seemed to feel better with JJ around, too. It was nothing overt; they didn't touch, didn't stand too close, but even the slightest glance her way softened his face and warmed his eyes.

It sharpened Yashi's awareness of how alone she was. How wistful.

Brit came down the stairs, sniffling and holding Bobcat tightly to her chest. Judging by his face, the cat was longing to be out of reach of every human in the place, but he let Brit hang on. His one compassionate-cat act of the week.

"I want to stay with you, Yashi," Brit whimpered for the fifth time. "You're all I've got left. Please don't let them take me away!"

Yashi wrapped her arms around her, and Bobcat wisely seized his moment to leap away, landing on a ledge on the nearest wall. She held Brit tightly, repeating reassurances. "It's for your own safety, sweetie. We don't know what this person will try next, but we have to make sure he can't get to you. It'll be all right. I'll call you. I'll visit you." She'd gotten that confirmed by JJ while Brit was still upstairs.

"But I want to stay here! You have a gun. You can protect me."

She smoothed Brit's hair from her face and looked intently into her eyes. "But I'm not going to be here all the time. I'm going to help find your mom and dad and Theo." She caught a flinch shuddering through Ben in her peripheral vision, but she brushed it off. He knew her too well to expect her to stand back and do nothing.

"I'll be all alone." Brit's words came out weak, half sob, half plea.

"Only for a little while. And only for your own safety." She hugged her tightly again, whispering, "I love you, sweet pea. Do this for us. All of us. Please."

Shudders rocketed through Brit's body, but after a moment, her grip on Yashi loosened. She swiped her hand across her face, stood taller, accepted the tissues Ben offered with a polite thank-you and nodded. "You don't have to worry about me, too. Just find my mama and daddy."

Yashi forced a smile. "And Theo."

"Um…well, if you have to." Brit's one moment of lightness disappeared. She wriggled free of Yashi, pushed past Ben with a squeeze of his arm, then walked out the door without a look back. Somberly, JJ and Quint followed. A moment later, three car doors sounded, quiet thuds in the muggy afternoon, and Yashi felt her own shudders.

This day had started out with such promise: rain, a contented Bobcat, nothing more pressing than eating on their schedule. Then it had become one ugly thing after another, and the next one was up on her list.

She offered to take her car. Ben said he would drive.

The silence was excruciating. All she could see was Brit's stricken face. All she could hear was her heart-breaking plea. *I'll be all alone.* As they turned onto First Street, she drew a breath, willing to talk about anything to get that memory out of her mind. "How is your family?"

Ben didn't look surprised that she wanted conversation. He rarely looked surprised at anything, and he well understood the value of taking one's mind off one's troubles. "Good. Mom's thinking about expanding the restaurant again."

"Not into the family room." The large private din-

ing room was the only space in the building to expand
into. She'd eaten a few meals there with Ben and various
relatives—not as a couple, just grabbing a meal while
they worked on a case together. She'd loved the idea of
family gathered around a table full of good food, talking
and joking and teasing, loud and boisterous and always
affectionate—had thought that someday she would have
a right to be there. That someday she would be part of
that lively, loving bunch.

That was before the Lloyd Wind case had come
along.

"She says we can eat in the kitchen." Ben's voice was
implacable, as if thought of the restaurant or the family
held no connection whatsoever to her. She always felt a
pang of loss when she passed the Creek Café. Probably
the only pangs he felt were hunger.

"She says better yet, we can eat at home. Save the
café the cost of feeding us all on a regular basis."

"Your mother lives to feed her family."

"That's what we tell her. She says she lives to feed
families who pay. A nice tip afterward is exceedingly
appreciated."

The SUV bounced over the railroad tracks. "I always tip nicely," she remarked. That earned a glance
from him.

"You still eat there?"

"The best place in town?" she asked with a lightness she definitely didn't feel. "Having to live without
your mother's food would have been cruel and unusual
punishment."

And living without him? No less than she deserved.

The silence came again, and this time she let it linger. They followed the western leg of the same highway she lived on to the municipal golf course, where Ben slowed to make a right exit onto an older, narrower road. Long-time residents of Cedar Creek called her road New 66, though it was closing in on seventy years old. Not a youngster, but still nearly three decades newer than the section of Old 66 they now traveled.

They rattled across Rock Creek Bridge, its steel trusses the color of rust. It was as old as the road, making her wonder about the structural integrity of every one of its 120 feet. Brit and Theo had loved it when they were kids, and Ben still did. He appreciated things that lasted. He'd told her once, the most serious he'd ever been, that he intended for them to be a thing that lasted.

They hadn't, of course. Good things didn't last—not for her, at least.

When he slowed for the final curve before the house, Yashi's breath caught in her chest. She didn't want to do this, but she would. She could face anything that might help get Lolly and Will and Theo back.

The number of police vehicles there had diminished, but there were three vans from Tulsa news stations parked alongside the road. The reporters perked up when Ben parked in the driveway, heading their way with their photographers before he even turned off the engine. Yashi appreciated that he didn't tell her to say nothing. She hadn't faced a journalist in a long time, but in her last go-rounds with the media, after Lloyd Wind's conviction had been overturned, she'd perfected the stoic face and stony silence.

"Detective Little Bear, can you tell us—"

Yashi shut out the question, the voices, and fixed her gaze on the house. She'd come here a thousand times, and nothing had changed. The trees had grown taller, the roses wilder, a little more lawn carved out of the surrounding woods. The five of them had built a gazebo in the side yard; she'd helped Lolly plant her full-acre garden. They'd had dinners and cookouts and parties; she'd babysat so Will and Lolly could have alone time; they'd just hung out, doing nothing special but doing it with the people they loved best.

Nothing had changed, except that the happy family that lived here had been shattered. *Please, God, let it be temporary.*

"Hey, you're Yashi Baker, aren't you?"

The sound of her name jerked her attention back to the media, to a tall, lanky photographer with red hair in a ponytail longer than her own.

"The assistant DA who wrongly convicted Lloyd Wind in that homicide case."

In her head, she politely pointed out that the jury convicted Wind, not her. In reality, she kept her mouth shut, careful not to clench her jaw, and her face blank.

Recognition lit a female reporter's eyes. "Last week he received a $7 million settlement from the state because of you. You want to comment on that?"

She continued walking, passing Lolly's minivan, and Ben stepped in behind to block her from their view. "Seven million," she muttered. She'd seen the headlines, of course, about the settlement, but she hadn't yet made herself read the stories. The biggest case of her career. The one that ended it.

"Considering he was in prison four years, it's not so much," Ben muttered back.

"He wouldn't have made a fraction of that working for four years."

"But he would have been free, not locked up for a crime he didn't commit."

"That's a matter for debate." Yashi said it quietly, unsure whether he heard, grateful he didn't respond. Thinking about that case made her head hurt, and she already had enough going on today. The sun was bright enough to scorch the dandelions, but it couldn't dissipate the moisture in the air. The humidity was heavy, a wet blanket that hugged everything and made breathing an effort. It was too hot and miserable for anything besides lazing with a cold drink.

She stopped at the bottom of the porch steps, Ben still right behind her. It would be cool inside the house. Cool and empty and ugly and threatening.

*Don't worry about me*, Brit had said.

"Don't worry about me," Yashi repeated, the words nothing more than a few puffs of air.

Theo, Will and Lolly. Those were her only worries.

# Chapter 3

Yashi's back was rigid, the muscles in her neck bunched, when she walked inside the house. She moved far enough to allow Ben to close the door, shutting out the smallest glimpse a telephoto lens might capture from the road, then stopped. She took short, shallow breaths, then her jaw clenched a couple times and she began breathing through her mouth. Had she caught the faint tang of blood on the air?

Crime scene techs still worked while Sam, just visible through the kitchen door, thumbed through the calendar hanging on the wall there. He let the pages drop and joined them, bringing booties and gloves. "I'm really sorry, Yashi, but I appreciate you doing this. We'll start in Brit's room."

She nodded stiffly before fixing her focus on the

protective coverings. She made a point, Ben noticed, of not looking toward the living room, of not letting the painted message on the front door edge into her vision. When Sam nodded toward the stairs, she led the way to the second floor, walked straight to Brit's room and went to stand in the center, beneath a glass light fixture painted with clouds on a clear blue day. "Did the lab guys find the note?"

"We assume he took it. Probably because it was something personal, something she'd touched." Sam let that sink in before he went on. "JJ—Detective Logan— packed a bag for Brit—clothes, makeup, that sort of stuff, and the lab bagged her electronics. Do you see anything else that's missing?"

Moving carefully, Yashi walked around the room, opened drawers, looked in the closet, scanned the bulletin board above the desk. After a while, she gave a terse shake of her head and moved on to the next room.

By the time they went downstairs, Ben was feeling the stress of the day all over, every nerve and blood vessel and muscle throbbing. All he'd wanted was one day to relax. Not a kidnapping. Not a potential triple homicide. And damn well not Yashi back in his life.

And damn it, that last part made his head hurt worse. He should be worried about the victims. His focus should be one hundred percent on Will and Lolly. His heart should be hurting for Theo, who was likely terrified, probably injured or possibly dead, and for Brit, who was definitely terrified because her entire world had just been upended. Not because his ex was standing three feet away, looking lost and vulnerable and grief stricken.

He did hurt for Theo and Brit. But he could hurt for Yashi at the same time. Hurt because of her.

In the kitchen, full of cream-colored cabinets and honeyed walls, Yashi studied the refrigerator a moment. "There's a picture missing." She stabbed her gloved finger at a spot on the right side. "It was from a vacation we took a few years ago in Arkansas. We were hiking across a creek, and I fell in. Lolly took the shot after Brit and Theo helped me out. I was soaked, and they were hysterical. She stuck it on the fridge in a plastic sleeve with a magnet."

They spent an extraordinary amount of time in the kitchen, given that she'd seen everything within a few minutes, but still she lingered, and they let her. After it would come the dining room, and then the living room. Nobody wanted to go into the living room.

Yashi stood at the kitchen table, staring out the window at the garden. Lolly spent a lot of time in the garden, and her crops showed it. At least once a week, she gave Ben baskets of tomatoes, corn, cucumbers and squash, radishes and okra and whatever else was flourishing. She shared with others, too. Right now an old table on the porch held filled baskets with ribbons tied to the handles, tagged *JL*, *KA* and *SB*. Before he could ask, Yashi said, "I don't know who they are. She loves giving stuff away as much as she does growing it. Where is Detective Harper?"

The sudden change of subject made Ben blink, but Sam didn't. "He's interviewing the neighbors. When we're done here, Ben, give him a call. He's saving Kenneth Brown for when you're with him."

Ben nodded. Every jurisdiction had its quirky people, and after a while, an officer learned the precautions for each one. Kenneth Brown was angry, argumentative, uncooperative, as quick to throw a punch as he was to run his mouth and threatened lawsuits over every run-in. In dealing with him, backup was advised.

After another moment or two, Yashi turned and walked back down the hall to the dining room. Brightly lit, small, sparsely decorated, the room couldn't sustain more than two minutes of scrutiny.

Mouth set, hands fisted at her sides, she paused just out of sight of the living room. Sam touched her arm, murmuring, "Are you sure?" She nodded grimly and took a step, then another.

After seeing her own little house, Ben could recognize similar touches to this room: the soothing blue-green walls, the golden oak flooring, the light, fluttery curtains at the windows. Instead of shelves for an entitled cat, this room held a fireplace tiled in opaque glass. Instead of double duty for every space, this room was large, the furniture oversize, the soft, plush area rug wider than Yashi's whole house. There were plenty of shelves and tables to display art made by the kids, photos, plants, fresh flowers. There was no paring down here. Lolly and Will had a lot of space to fill with everything that meant anything to them.

Yashi stared at the bloodstains for a long, painful moment, then picked her way toward the couch. Wine had dripped a deep purplish-red stain onto the cream rug, and the milk on the coffee table was thick. She bent as if to pick up a pillow on the floor, remembered where she was and straightened again before detouring to the fireplace.

"There's a picture missing here, too," Sam said quietly. He pulled a bagged item from an evidence bin and held it for her to see. A picture frame, glass shattered, the frame itself twisted and warped. "Do you know what?"

Her mouth barely moved. "It was a family picture. All five of us. Brit thought we needed a formal portrait for our family history so her great-grandkids would have something to look back on. We had it taken last—last month." After a moment to control the wobble that had entered her voice, she asked, "Can I go out back? I need some air."

Sam nodded, and she walked with deliberate calm out of the room and down the hall. Ben was pretty sure her speed picked up dramatically as she neared the back door off the kitchen.

Ben scowled. "So the guy took a note Brit wrote and two pictures that included her but left a lot of pictures of just her."

After returning the evidence bag to the bin, Sam shrugged. "Something about those two spoke to him. He probably has tons of pictures of her already. He's probably been at this awhile."

*At this.* Obsessing over a fifteen-year-old girl. Did he actually know her? Did he understand the true nature of the relationship, if any, between them? That he was one of Dad's business associates, the husband of one of

Mom's friends, the father of one of her own friends. A guy not important enough to register amid the everyday drama of a fifteen-year-old's life.

A guy who meant nothing to her while she apparently meant so much to him that he would do anything to claim her.

Sounded like a mental health issue, but Ben knew better than to assume that. In her dealings with the Cedar Creek PD, Morwenna's psychiatrist mother frequently reminded them of two facts: people with mental health issues had a history of mental illness, while criminals had a history of criminal behavior. The two groups did overlap, but not nearly as much as people wanted to believe. Truth was, people with mental illnesses were far more likely to become the victims of crime rather than the perpetrators.

But that overlap was there. The serial killer who'd tried to add both Sam and Mila to her trophies had had a list of psychiatric diagnoses as long as her criminal offenses. The stalker who had brought Daniel back together with his ex-fiancée, now-wife Natasha, had been a true-blue psychopath.

But they were exceptions. The rest were just bad people who did bad things. Like the woman who killed JJ's friend, not because she couldn't control herself. She was competent as all hell. There'd been no mental demons driving her. Just good old jealousy and greed. And the boyfriend who'd helped…too lazy to hold a job and clinging to an unshakable conviction that he deserved an easy and luxurious life.

"You gonna stand here awhile or check on Yashi?"

Ben blinked before focusing on Sam. "Today's my day off."

Sam snorted. "You know days off are exceptions, not rules. Besides, if I told you to go home, you wouldn't do it. You and she used to be friends, didn't you? Before she left the DA's office. So go check on her. I'll let Daniel know you're available."

An innocent word, *available*. Perfectly good in the context Sam used it. But add *Yashi* and *friends* to it, and all the innocence leaped off the nearest roof. This was a difficult time for both him and Yashi. She couldn't help being vulnerable, but he could stop himself from being affected by it. He could summon up his famous control, could handle this like the capable detective he was. Professionally. Rationally. Unemotionally.

Sure, he could.

Yashi was sitting on the steps that led into the backyard, chin resting on her knees, hands loosely clasped over her ankles. Water dripped from the roof, the giant oak, the black locust tree. It ran in tiny streams down the pillars that supported the porch roof and made quiet little plops on the mulch when it fell from the plants. With that much rain in this kind of heat, Lolly insisted she could actually hear the cornstalks growing. Yashi had been listening, but all she heard were Brit's tears, and all she felt was the ice inside herself that wasn't going away soon.

When the back door opened, she knew it was Ben. Not that it would be unusual for Sam to come and talk to her, but her body had never reacted to Sam's proximity. He was a gorgeous guy, compassionate and honest and just really super all-around good, but her hormones preferred a different all-around good guy.

Ben towered over her for a moment before taking a seat as far to the left as he could. She'd known people made uncomfortable by his sheer size, but it had never bothered her. It took more than size to make her cower. She wasn't sure how much more, because she'd never let herself do it since she went out on her own at eighteen. She'd come closest this morning.

"Will's an accountant," she said after a moment. "His clients are mostly businesses, though of course he does a lot of taxes when the season comes around. He's been an assistant coach for both Theo's and Brit's soccer teams the last few years. He's been doing some running with Theo to help improve his speed on the field. He's on the building committee at church and also handles their books. He belongs to one civic group and was on the planning committee for the new soccer complex."

She was rambling about things Ben probably already knew, but saying them out loud helped organize her thoughts. "Lolly's been taking classes at OSU-Tulsa, one or two a semester. She's planning to go back to work when Theo starts junior high. She wants to teach elementary school. She's active with the kids' school and sports. She's taking classes to become a master gardener, and she belongs to a knitting group that meets at the park on pretty days and at the coffee shop on bad days. She volunteers with the election board, she loves antique shopping and she's trying to find time to take a basket-weaving class with Louise Pickering."

When she paused for breath, Ben took the chance to speak. "We aren't going to fixate on the idea that this is tied to Brit. We'll look at everyone, everything. We know the message on the door and the photos could be misdirection. Do they have any enemies?"

She had asked that question of people before, about their loved ones. She'd never imagined it being asked of her. "Maybe a few soccer parents who want their kids to have more time on the field. A client or two wanting to fudge their taxes." Finally she turned her head to gaze at Ben. His black hair gleamed in the sun, and a thin sheen of perspiration dotted his forehead. She was as wrung out as the kids after a hard-fought soccer game. He looked as if, yeah, it was a little warm today, but nothing he couldn't handle.

"You know Will, Ben. He—" She broke off, realizing that was the first time she'd used his name to his face. First names with strangers could be fine. Same with friends. First names with a man she'd once been intimate with… It wove a disquieting feeling.

"He's a nice guy. Everyone likes him. He likes everyone. He has a talent for dealing with people," Ben finished for her. "And Lolly is the same. Kids love her, their parents adore her, everyone wants to be her friend. Theo's a typical kid. The only time he gets aggressive is on the soccer field, and even then he'll stop to help up the kid who falls." He paused and his voice softened. "You know we need to consider everything."

She nodded.

"What about financial issues? Do they owe money? Are they living above their means?"

Money was about as close a sacred subject to Yashi as anything got. She'd never had an abundance of financial security. Her foster parents had covered everyday expenses, she'd gotten loans and jobs for college and law school, and then she'd gone to work in the district attorney's office. There'd been no big paychecks coming out of that office, not even for the DA himself. Livable wages that covered an occasional splurge. That was her life.

Of course Will had more money than she did. The house, the vehicles, the kids' activities, not needing a second income, Lolly's college classes and frequent passions. How much he made, how much they spent, how much they owed—none of her business. She edited all that down to a simple, "I don't know."

"What about other family?"

The steady question startled her into a blink. *She* was their family. The one who knew them best, saw them most, loved them dearest. But of course, they had other family. When their parents died, Yashi had had no one, but Will's mother's family had taken him in. He'd begged them to let her come, too, and his aunt had cried when she said she couldn't. So had Will. So had Yashi.

Lolly had parents living in Maine, a brother in the army in Korea and another brother at sea on a Military Sealift Command ship. The soldier was married with a wife and daughters; the sailor was divorced but brought his two kids to visit every couple years. There was the full complement of aunts and uncles and cousins and in-laws, a good-size bunch that gathered every five years in Maine.

Enough to make Yashi's world look empty.

"The ones she's closest to are in her cell phone," she responded, sitting straight and trying to unobtrusively press her shirt against her breasts to dry the trickles of sweat there. "Probably the biggest disagreement in their lives is whether lobsters are better boiled or steamed. It's hard to imagine anyone traveling all the way to Oklahoma to duke it out over that."

The sigh that escaped her was miserable. She was steaming, energy draining from her cells. She wanted to go inside—but not inside Will and Lolly's house. She wanted to jump in her car and drive wildly around the county, searching for the specific one of the fifty million possibilities where someone was holding her family prisoner. She wanted to line up every person who had ever gotten cross with them, ever scowled or honked their horn or made a snide remark, and inter- rogate them relentlessly. To polygraph everyone who'd ever met them, every soul in Cedar County, and ex- pand as necessary.

She wanted Will back. And Lolly and Theo and Brit, home where they belonged.

Ben's cell signaled, and after a glance, he moved to stand up. He didn't get far, though, before settling onto the step again. "Daniel's waiting for me over at Kenneth Brown's. Do you want to wait at my house or take the truck home or have Sam find a ride for you?"

The decision required no thought.

"I'll wait at your house."

With a grim nod, he stood and led the way back through the Mueller house and out to his vehicle. It seemed an extravagance to drive a few hundred yards, but with two of the media vans remaining on the shoulder of the road, she was grateful for it. Though cameras turned her way as they climbed out a moment later, she focused on Ben's broad shoulders, following him onto the porch, blocking her from their view while he unlocked the door, then stepped back to allow her to enter.

He looked for a moment as if he was about to say something. *Bathroom's down the hall. Help yourself to whatever you need. Lock the door behind me.* A shiver washed over her. Simple words, a threat or a promise depending on the circumstances. God, she wished these circumstances were better.

"Be careful," she whispered, but the door was already closing behind him.

Though Kenneth Brown's house sat no farther from the road than the Mueller house, his driveway was easily five times as long, snaking up the incline, following the path of the creek. Shrubs slapped against the sides of Ben's truck while tall, thick stalks of johnsongrass brushed featherlight over the cab windows.

Halfway up, hidden from both road and house, Daniel was leaning against his car. He was in uniform—black tactical pants and polo shirt—with his badge and holster on his belt. For every notch that marriage had loosened him, impending fatherhood, wifely hormonal swings and one hot summer had ratcheted him back up. Though he should have looked casual, leaning there with his ankles crossed, he was visibly tense.

Granted, it could just be the prospect of another run-in with Brown.

Ben rolled down the window as he stopped and Daniel approached. Before the other detective could speak, he asked, "You want to get behind me when we go in? I only ask because the last time you went in first, you landed kind of hard when he threw you back out."

Daniel's responding look was flat. "I wouldn't have landed so hard if you hadn't stepped aside."

"The guy heaved you like a javelin, and you wanted me to just stand there and wait for you to crash into me?" Ben snorted, swatted a fly that came too close and gestured toward the thick growth. "What do you think?"

Though his tone didn't change, Daniel knew from years of working together what he meant. He scratched his jaw, then waved away a cloud of gnats that had found him. For a Los Angeles–born and-raised kid, he did okay in the country. Mostly.

"He's an ill-tempered pain in the ass, but I don't buy him for this. Kidnapping three people, stashing them somewhere... Brown's too lazy. And the last time his wife saw his attention wandering to another female, she took a baseball bat to his head."

Ben agreed. Plus, by the time the sun went down on any given night, Brown was settled in for a long evening of drinking, arguing—even if it was only with the TV—and more drinking. Chances of him having seen or heard anything of value were slimmer than slim.

Daniel stiffened his spine. "Let's get on with it. I've got reports to write."

Daniel went back to his car, and they continued the

drive to the clearing at the top of the hill, parking behind Brown's vehicle. The house was older than dirt,
a simple square with no porch, no identifiable color. A
chicken coop off to one side had collapsed in on itself,
and a workshop of corrugated tin leaned precariously
on the other side. There was hard-packed dirt instead
of grass, and the woods surrounded it all with a claus-
trophobic margin of about ten feet.

A person might think the people who lived there
were poverty stricken, but Ben knew that wasn't quite
the case. He had no clue about their debts, but Brown's
current vehicle was a luxury SUV still bearing the
showroom shine, and Pamela Brown drove a Mercedes.
A satellite for television and another for internet sat side
by side on the roof, and stacked outside the workshop
were empty boxes that hadn't been out long enough
for the weather to disguise their contents: a sixty-inch
television, two laptop computers, an espresso machine.

When Ben joined him, Daniel murmured, "Deputy
was telling me about a house out in the county that looks
about like this from the outside. Inside there's a $5 mil-
lion art collection. Me, I'd rather find a nice balance."

"Bet the art collector doesn't have a fallen-down
chicken coop. But then, maybe he could call it modern
art and slap a price tag on it." Ben drew a breath and
started toward the front door. The stoop consisted of
fiberglass steps that had been hauled to within a foot
of the house and called good. When he set his foot on
the bottom step, the door above opened.

"Ain't nobody called you."

Brown stood in the doorway, arms crossed, fingers

of one hand clasped around the neck of a beer bottle. Drink of choice, weapon of choice, all in one. He'd never grown taller than five-seven and had spent most of his sixty years trying to convince everybody he was a six-four badass son of a bitch. He was wiry, tough, his blue eyes faded and squinty, and his hairline had receded to the back of his head.

He reminded Ben of his grandmother's old bantam rooster.

Brown's second weapon of choice—an old-fashioned .38 caliber revolver—was holstered on his belt.

"We'd like to ask you a few questions, Mr. Brown." Ben called a lot of people by their first names. As long as Little Bears had been in Cedar County, he knew a *lot* of people. "Put the gun down and step outside, please."

Ben could see the thoughts running through the man's mind. He had a right to be armed on his own property, but he'd learned to be cautious of law enforcement officers whom he'd thrown ten feet through the air. Daniel hadn't been the first.

With a scowl, Brown set the pistol down nearby, stepped out and closed the door behind him. "'Bout what?"

"Were you home last night?"

"Yep."

"Was Mrs. Brown here?"

He took a long drink from the bottle, draining it, then tossed it to the ground. It bounced on the hard dirt before settling. "She went out to dinner with her sisters. Come in about eleven and went to bed. Why? Who's saying it and what are they saying?"

"Did you see or hear anything unusual last night? Any time from sunset on?"

Brown's jaw jutted forward. "Look around. We don't see nothing, and the only thing we hear is the train going past. We don't even hear traffic most the time."

"You know Will and Lolly Mueller?" Daniel asked from a spot a few feet to Ben's left.

"Know who they are. Don't really know them." Brown smirked. "We don't sit down to dinner with them. They're not really our kind."

Lolly would have tried to befriend them, Ben knew, because that was the kind of person she was. She'd probably shown up one day with a basket of vegetables or fresh-baked bread to say hello and been turned away rudely. It had probably happened several times, because Lolly was a big believer in second chances.

"Do you know their kids?" Daniel asked.

"I know they got some. Can't say as we ever met. Why? Did something happen to them?"

Ben shifted to gaze in the direction of the Mueller house. Back in the day, the trains, with their cast-iron brake shoes striking sparks on the steel rails, had been a regular source of wildfires, clearing the deadfall and keeping the woods fairly neat. Then they'd gone to composite brake blocks, which minimized the sparks, and left years of dead leaves, debris and new sprouts to form a virtual jungle. He doubted even blazing lights at the Mueller house could penetrate the growth.

He tuned back in to hear Daniel speaking again. "So you didn't hear any noises at all last night? No shouts? No screams? You know how sound carries at night."

There had been nothing to alert Ben to trouble, neither before he left to pick up Morwenna nor after they'd returned, and his house was much closer.

Brown's eyes lit up, and his posture straightened. "Screams? Something did happen, didn't it? What was it? Did he go crazy and kill them all? Or was it the kids? Did they stab their parents in the night and take off? Was there a home invasion?"

Ben's nerves clenched. How had everyday people developed such a taste for violence? He hated what people did to their children, their families and total strangers, and detested how so many otherwise normal people salivated over every grisly, gory detail. Just the possibility of something bad nearby had brightened Kenneth Brown's day.

"Come on," he cajoled. "If it was anything serious, it'll be on the internet. If someone's running around here killing people, I've got a right to know. I have to protect me and my wife."

"So you didn't hear anything unusual," Ben said. "Thank you for your time, Mr. Brown." He turned his back on the man and headed back toward the truck.

Daniel fell in step beside him. "You feeling a little twitch between the shoulder blades right now?"

"Nah," Ben lied. He was never eager to turn his back on trouble. "He wouldn't want to risk damaging his new truck. I assume you got the same thing from the other neighbors."

"Without the beer, the gun and the sick excitement." Daniel stopped next to his car. "Sometimes I hate people."

"Sometimes they deserve to be hated."

Including the one waiting back at his house?

No. There was a saying: the opposite of love wasn't hate; it was indifference. He'd loved Yashi more than he'd known he was capable of. She'd hurt and betrayed him. He'd stopped loving her and now felt pretty much nothing for her. He'd gone months, maybe even years, without ever thinking about her. She was nothing to him.

Until this day from hell had brought her back front and center.

Ben's house was the only Craftsman bungalow Yashi had ever set foot in. Despite the coziness of the word *bungalow*, it was easily four times the size of her house, with oak flooring, airy spaces and exposed beams. The outside was deep gray with white trim and a burgundy door. Inside were creamy tones, white walls with a touch of peach above mahogany cabinets and book-cases, solid furniture and rugs woven in rich earthen tones. It had belonged to a great-aunt of his, and when she'd died, he'd been fortunate enough to work a deal with the family.

Yashi had paced from living room to kitchen and back again so many times, she thought she could see a trail emerging on the carpets and flooring. She'd gotten water from the refrigerator and gone to the bathroom to wash the sticky remains of sweat from her face and arms, and she'd resisted peeking into the master bed-room. She'd helped Ben paint that room, a lovely barely green hue, and had picked out the shades for the broad windows and the linens for the bed. She didn't want to see that Morwenna's influence had replaced her own. Lime green? Neon orange?

After Yashi banished herself back to the public spaces, a knock had sounded at the door, and she'd rushed to it, only to catch a glimpse of the red-haired photographer standing on the porch with his reporter. Quietly, as if they didn't know she was there, she had scuttled to Great-Aunt's library, a tiny nook off the living room, with built-in shelves all around, shared between books, baskets, beadwork and pottery. It held one cushy chair, one table, one good lamp and no window to allow the outside world—or reporters—to intrude.

Now, long after the knock, she stopped handling the art, quit trying to pretend interest in reading and returned to the living room. She was cold, so she wrapped herself in a quilt from the sofa. It was Lolly's work, a geometric pattern in rust and brown, mossy green and dusky blue, and it brought tears to Yashi's eyes. She was counseling herself to be strong—there would be plenty of time to cry when everyone was back where they belonged—when she heard footsteps on the porch.

Another knock came, followed almost immediately by a deep, quiet voice. "Son, trust me, you don't want to be trespassing on a police officer's property."

She sidled closer to the window and saw the photographer again, with Ben behind him on the steps, looking unimpressed by the guy's status as media. He made a shooing gesture, and the redhead shooed. It was so easy to be intimidating when you had presence, Yashi reflected with a sigh, and Ben had it in spades.

He had everything she'd ever wanted. But she'd been

stupid enough to think she could have both her ambition and his trust, and she'd ended up losing everything.

She sank into the nearest chair as he turned the key in the lock. By the time he opened the door, she probably looked as if she'd been huddled there the whole time.

"I didn't hear your truck."

"It's across the road."

Of course. He'd had to check in with Sam after talking to the cranky neighbor. He looked hot, and sweat dampened his black hair, but he didn't bear any bruises or scraped knuckles. "I take it Mr. Brown was in a good mood."

Something dark and fierce passed through Ben's eyes, but it disappeared immediately. "He was."

Finally he moved from his spot in front of the door, passing her with long strides, trailing a scent of sun and perspiration. She was focusing on shallow breaths and restraining old memories when he came back with a bottle of water and a plastic container of cookies. He pried off the lid and offered her a choice of chocolate chip and oatmeal. She chose a chocolate chip cookie, as he'd known she would, and he took an oatmeal, as she'd known he would. She'd just bitten into hers when he spoke again.

"Where were you last night?"

Her breathing stopped, her chewing, the beating of her heart. In her whole life, no one had ever asked her that question with anything more than minor curiosity. Her foster parents, a friend who'd had a last-minute change of plans and no one to hang with, a vaguely jealous boyfriend.

She tried to swallow, realized she'd forgotten the cookie and choked it down with a swig of water. "I was in the office until six, then I went home. I finished my work there, ate dinner, watched TV with Bobcat and went to bed about eleven. I didn't have any visitors or any phone calls, but my cell was on, so you can verify that it was there."

Which didn't mean anything. If she was going to commit a crime, she would leave her phone at home. There would be no pinging signals off cell towers to track her movements.

Ben looked a little more implacable than usual. "I have to ask."

"Of course you do. I understand." That first bite of cookie had tasted incredible. Now it was just filler for an unsettled stomach. "Will and I have had our share of disagreements, but we haven't come to blows since I was five and I gave him his first black eye. Lolly and I don't even have disagreements. She says as long as she's happy, she'll keep the rest of us happy, and she does."

A single tear slid down Yashi's cheek, and she brushed it away. She absolutely believed in the catharsis of tears, but now wasn't the time, and in front of Ben wasn't the place. Even in his warmest, most touchy-feely moments, he wasn't a *there, there* sort of person.

But he'd always given her a *there, there* sort of feeling. Quiet, stoic, confident in his ability to take care of his world. She thought her father had been like that, though she didn't have a lot of memories to support that conclusion. Just two constants, really: she'd always been happy to see him, and she'd always been aware of the change in her mother when he came home every night: her voice a little lighter, her touch a little gentler, her face a little prettier. Everything was better when Daddy was home.

And it had been. Until the night neither Daddy nor Mama had come home, nor Uncle Joey nor Aunt Shannon. For the next twenty years, until she'd moved to Cedar Creek, Yashi hadn't even had a place to call home.

And then she'd met Ben, and everything had been all right again.

Ben chose another cookie, breaking it neatly in half and taking a bite before setting the piece down again. When he raised his gaze, it landed somewhere over Yashi's right shoulder. "I also have to ask… What about Brit?"

Righteous disbelief flared inside her, sputtering out almost as quickly. How many times had she asked witnesses similar questions and provoked similar responses? *I'm just covering the bases*, she'd assured them. *I have to consider all possibilities.*

She unclenched her hands, rested them on the arms of the chair and drew a deep breath. "Absolutely not. She's moody sometimes, and self-absorbed sometimes, but she's also got the kindest heart a person could want. Lolly is good at picking her battles with Brit. She always says, 'Is this the hill I want to—'"

The rest of the adage caught in Yashi's lungs, turning her breath into a wheeze, but she forged on. "—'to die on?' Is proving her authority worth the fallout over something simple like green hair, or is it better to save the big guns for the big battles? That sort of thing." She swiped one hand across her nose. "They get along great. Lolly sets the rules, and Brit mostly follows them. When it calls for compromise, Lolly does. When she doesn't, Brit always knows why. And she knows Lolly's always, always got her back."

"And Will?" Ben asked.

A moment from last Sunday flashed through Yashi's mind: Brit pulling her dad to the restaurant steps, climbing onto his back, and Will giving her a piggyback ride the twenty feet to their car. "He still looks at her and sees the eight-year-old pigtailed tomboy who will always be Daddy's princess. In his head, he knows she's growing up and away, but in his heart, he pretends it's not happening."

"Were they aware that she and Jared are having sex?"

Suddenly weary all the way to her toes, Yashi tugged the quilt closer. "Lolly has had the abstinence-is-good talk with both kids since before they even understood it, and she's given Brit the if-you-can't-wait-be-prepared speech a dozen times. She'd scheduled Brit's first appointment with a gynecologist for next month, and she was more or less resigned to the fact that birth control was going to be the topic of the day."

Because Lolly also remembered what it was like to be fifteen, with a sweet boy swearing he would love her forever.

In the silence that followed, Yashi thought wistfully of a dark room, a bed, cold air, warm covers and a solid breathing being beside her to remind her she wasn't alone. To let her ease her muscles, relax her nerves, to take deep breaths and stop thinking, stop worrying and sleep, please God, without dreams. Being awake was enough of a nightmare.

There was a bed down the hall, and Ben was more than enough to make her feel safe, but that wasn't going to happen. Her own bed would have to do, and whatever comfort she found would come from Bobcat. If she woke up, alone in the dark and afraid… She'd been there before. Would be there again. She always found her way back into the light.

"One more question, and I'll take you home."

Her eyes had drifted shut while she longed for peace. She opened them to see Ben's gaze steady on her. No, she felt it first. Had always felt it. From the very first time they'd met.

He looked tired, too. Nothing obvious like bleary eyes or drooping features. It was just an indefinable something about him that only those who knew him well would recognize. Feeling bad that fate had forced him back into her presence, she sat straighter and pretended she'd found a new source of energy.

"What do you know about Jared?"

She blew out a breath. "He seems like a nice kid. Never been in any trouble. Honors student. Polite within limits."

Ben's snort was so faint she barely heard it. It had been an ongoing joke in the DA's office that the more times a suspect said *please* and *thank you* and *sir* and *ma'am*, the guiltier he was.

"I can't imagine Jared ever plotting anything more devious than—than—" She couldn't even think of a way to finish the statement. He was a nice kid. She liked him.

"Than inviting his girlfriend over for the night when his parents are out of town?" Ben stood, towering over her, prompting her to stand as well. "The problem is, individuals do all sorts of things we don't imagine them capable of. That's why trust is an issue."

He said it blandly, as if it applied to this conversation and nothing else, but it sent a flush of heat through her. She'd broken his trust, and she doubted that was something he would ever forgive.

Sliding the quilt off her shoulders, she folded it, then laid it across the back of the chair, one hand smoothing the fabric before she forced herself to speak calmly, unaffectedly. "You got two questions for the price of one. Can I go home now?"

## Chapter 4

Ben drove around the back of Yashi's office and parked beside the Bug. Neither of them had spoken after their last remarks at the house, making the drive one of the more uncomfortable ones in his recent experience. She hadn't acted stiff and insulted. She'd just sat in the passenger seat, turned slightly to the right, and stared at her cousins' house until it was out of sight, then continued to stare that way. Her shoulders were rounded, her breathing quiet except for an occasional huff.

At their destination, it took her a moment to realize the reason they'd stopped, to click back into the present and recognize where they were. Clenching her keys and cell—all she'd brought with her—she slid to the ground, started to shove the door shut, but stopped. "If you hear anything…"

"We'll let you know." Not him. Not if it was bad news. That would be Sam and Lois's job. If worse came to worst, Yashi deserved someone who could hold her, console her and be her shoulder to cry on. Ben couldn't be that for her, not anymore.

She murmured thanks, closed the door and walked through the opening in the white picket fence. She looked bereft as she followed the stepping-stones to the house. There was no backward glance when she climbed the steps, no wave from the door when she let herself inside.

The door closed. He knew she locked it behind her, because that was what she did. Next, she would turn on a light, but it didn't happen right away. He could too easily imagine her leaning against the door or sliding to the floor, letting loose the tears that had been close all day, crying the way she always had: alone.

Sometimes Ben's family and friends drove him crazy, but at least he'd never known all the different ways of being alone that Yashi knew.

He lifted one hand from the steering wheel to rub the middle of his chest.

Finally, he backed around the Bug and left. Halfway through town, he slowed and pulled into the Creek Café parking lot. His plan to get dinner to go and head back home to write his reports took a hit when he saw the greeter seated just inside the door, but he hesitated an instant too long to successfully retreat.

Great-Aunt Weezer crooked her finger at him through the glass. Ben sighed. He was a cop, carried a gun and a Taser, and still, ignoring a summons from his great-aunt was more than his life was worth. Swallowing a sigh, he pushed the door open and walked inside.

"I figured you'd get hungry sooner or later and stop in. I didn't think you'd leave it so late," she announced from her perch on a bar stool at the hostess station.

"It's only—" His gaze flicked to the wall clock above her. "Five forty-five." It seemed weeks since he'd woken up this morning with nothing more than coffee, breakfast and rain on his mind. Not even ten hours.

"I seen you drive by. Several times."

"I'm working, Great-Aunt."

"You think your face is so pretty, I'd be wanting to see it if you wasn't?"

Yep, that was Great-Aunt Weezer. Not a sentimental bone in her body. According to his other great-aunts, she'd been born cranky, and time hadn't improved her one bit. She was blunt and bossy and could sour fresh cream with a look. She didn't trust anyone but family, and she didn't like them most of the time. Along with his mother, she was one of the constants in his life, and he loved her.

"I didn't think you worked on Saturday nights."

"I'm not working. I'm meeting someone."

Meeting someone? People didn't arrange to meet Weezer. She just sort of happened to them when they weren't looking.

She slid to the floor, a solid clunk drawing his gaze as she held out her arms wide. "How do I look?"

*What?* She never cared about her appearance. Or her behavior, her attitude, her reputation, her temper or anything else. She gave people two choices: take her or leave her. It didn't matter to her.

What was the best way to compliment a crotchety ninety-some-year-old woman with a penchant for pinching and scowling, who opted for comfortable and cheap in her clothing and bought most things a size too big?

This evening, the long skirt was pink cotton, a step up from the usual faded denim skirts or floral housedresses. Her white T-shirt didn't have a picture or a logo on the front—another indication that she was fancying up—and holy cow, those were real shoes that had made the clunk when she stood up. No broken-down suede moccasins or fuzzy house slippers. And one of those real shoes, brown leather with a low heel, began to tap impatiently. "You've got words, nephew. Use them."

"You clean up real good."

Her faded gaze narrowed, then she let out a bark of laughter. "You know, you're not my least favorite relative. Now, I don't have much time. What happened out there?"

Ben didn't want to discuss the Muellers' disappearance. Gossip spread effectively in Cedar Creek; Weezer probably knew almost as much as he did. It wasn't his policy to talk about cases with family anyway, so he deflected his great-aunt with a question of his own. "Who are you meeting?"

Weezer did something he'd never seen her do before—never thought her capable of doing. She…fluttered. Patted her iron-gray hair. Tugged at her shirt. Adjusted her mussel shell necklace. Flushed as pink as the shell. "Aw, it's just that Fred Allbright. Met him over at the community center. Plays a mean hand of Texas Hold'em. Not anything special. Just dinner."

Ben drew a startled breath. Good God, Great-Aunt Weezer had a date. His weary brain was trying to process that when the door opened and her fluttering vanished. Her gaze swept to the newcomer, and she actually smiled. Well, as close as she ever came.

His senses returning, Ben grabbed the opportunity to escape. "I've got to see Mom," he said quickly, gave a nod to the wizened, gnomish little man and beat it into the kitchen. When he walked through the door, he collided with his mother, two sisters and an aunt. He expected, oh, maybe a greeting of some sort. What he got was shoved to the side by youngest sister Mercy, who would have made a great linebacker, especially with Aunt Denise at her back.

"He looks harmless enough," Mom whispered, peering out the narrow space between door and jamb.

"He looks sane, too, but he's going out with Great-Aunt, so what does that prove?" middle sister Toni shot back.

"He's just as cute as a little bug," Aunt Denise said.

Ben straightened to his full height, laid one hand on the door high above their heads and closed it. "Spying on guests in the restaurant?"

All four women raised their gazes to his. His mom stood as tall as she could, too, though she fell about fifteen inches short of him, and bristled. "It's not spying when it's my restaurant. I own every single thing in here—including you. Besides, just like you, I have a duty to serve and protect, and I'm looking out for Great-

Aunt's best interests. At least, I was. If you want food here tonight, let go."

He did, and she cracked the door open, then sighed. "They're gone. I hope you're happy."

"About as much as usual," he lied as the other women scattered.

His mother stepped back and folded her arms over her middle to study him. She was sturdy and tireless. Life had given her no choice once her husband ran away with her last paycheck, their only car and his girlfriend. He'd left Mary Grace with six kids, no money and the quickest recovery from heartbreak humankind had ever seen.

*I loved your father dearly, right up until I realized how desperate our circumstances were, and that was it. I fell out of love with him—* She'd snapped her fingers. *Like that.*

He wished he'd been that lucky with Yashi. But he would have to have been a different person. He hadn't just loved her; he'd let her inside, let her become a part of him.

*Let her?* He hadn't had a say in the matter. It had just happened. He'd discovered one day that he wasn't just dating her, wasn't just having sex with her. He was savoring her when she was with him and missing her when she was gone. He was changing from a man alone, responsible only to himself, to a couple, from Ben to Ben-and-Yashi. Decisions he'd once made alone suddenly merited her input; his focus shifted from enjoying the present to looking to the future. He'd changed, and he was happy with it.

Then she'd ripped his entire life apart.

His mother's look turned sympathetic. "Bad case?"

"Triple kidnapping. Will and Lolly Mueller and their boy."

"Oh Lord. He comes in more often than she does— during the workday, you know. The whole family's here probably once a week. They seem like very nice people. They're never difficult—kids shut off their electronics, they tip well. I can't imagine who could possibly want to hurt them."

"I'm hearing a lot of that, but apparently someone's got a reason." He breathed deeply of the rich, gorgeous aromas: frying peppers, onions and garlic; rolls and biscuits and corn bread; beef stew and goulash and fried pork chops; sugar and butter and vanilla. Home, for him, had never been a specific place but rather smells. These smells were the backdrop for his entire life.

His stomach growled, and his mother patted his arm. "Go sit down somewhere, and I'll fix you a little something to take with you."

Knowing her *little something* would feed him for at least three meals, he did as she suggested, taking a seat out of the way in the back of the kitchen, where he tilted his head back, closed his eyes and pondered the two most important questions of his day.

Who had taken the Muellers?

Would they get out of this alive?

And less important but still in his mind: Would he come away from this new contact with Yashi intact, or was he about to find himself in deep trouble again?

* * *

When Yashi woke Sunday morning, for one lovely moment, it was an ordinary day. The sun was sending rays through the small, high windows just below the roof, casting bands of light across the interior. Bobcat was snuggled beside her, one ear propped on the edge of her pillow, and the only sound out of the ordinary was the low whistle of a train passing two miles to the west. Was that what had awakened her from a lovely, delicious dream that had left her warm and tingly and feeling oh, so relaxed, limp and happy in Ben's—

All the good feelings inside her deflated as quickly as if popped by a pin, and yesterday's memories rushed in to fill the void. Will and Lolly and Theo… Oh God, how could she have forgotten them even in her sleep?

Because she wasn't Superwoman. She'd been exhausted when she'd crawled into bed last night. She'd barely remembered her own name.

Were they all right? Injured? Dear God, were they still alive? Was the kidnapper keeping them together, or had he separated them? Poor Theo must have been so scared. He was only eight, a brave kid but a little unsure about the comfort of any bed besides his own. He felt best in his ninja pajamas, with his matching comforter and his snuggle buffalo named Bernie.

And his mom and dad: Lolly, always so content with life, now terrified by the threat against them, praying frantically for their rescue, and Will, feeling he'd failed in protecting his precious family. The blood in the living room was probably his; he would have put up a hell of a fight. Yashi prayed most of it belonged to the kidnapper. She hoped he'd suffered severely—*but, please, Lord, don't let him die while he's got my family hidden somewhere.*

Her thoughts were switching to Brit, physically safe but probably an emotional wreck after last night, when Bobcat roused. With easy grace, he stretched, his back forming a fine arch, then he gave her a chastising look and, with a few leaps, traded the bed for a sun-bathed windowsill. His morning routine: a stretch, grooming in the warm sun, another stretch, then a graceful descent to the kitchen, where he naturally expected breakfast to be waiting. He could turn to grumpy cat very quickly if he was disappointed.

Not nearly as ready to start her day as he was, Yashi pushed herself from the bed, shoved her feet into her oldest, most worn-down and comfiest slippers, and started down the stairs. She'd gone only partway when a solid *rap-rap-rap* rattled the door and shook her whole world. Her feet in the battered house shoes slid out from under her, and she landed hard on her butt on the landing. Above her, Bobcat arched again, fur standing on end in a perfect illustration of a scary Halloween cat, and his hiss warned her exactly who was at the door.

Heart pounding, she jumped to her feet, rubbed her hip ruefully, kicked off the shoes and hustled to open the door. Ben's broad-shouldered frame filled the porch. Filled her entire existence in that moment. The thud of her heart stopped abruptly, and her chest tightened so she couldn't breathe as she studied his face for a hint. No relief lightened his dark chocolate eyes or softened the thin line of his mouth. Not good news, damn it.

But whether it was bad or indifferent, he gave no clue. If she were uncharitable, she might say he was playing the stoic warrior stereotype to the hilt, but it wasn't play. Quiet, unfazed, controlled—that was just his way. He felt things deeply. He just didn't wear his emotions on his face or anywhere else.

Before she could ask any questions, could even think of anything to say, he spoke.

"Did you see the text?"

"What text?" She whipped her head around so quickly that the ends of her hair slapped her in the face. The chair where she'd curled last night to stare at the television was empty save for the quilt. The tray that served as an end table held the TV remote and a box of tissues but nothing else. What had she done with her phone? Plugged it into the charger in the kitchen? Of course not, not with Will and Lolly and Theo missing.

Spinning around, she dashed across the living room and up the stairs. She'd made a mess of the bed, tossing and turning all night, and she had to yank off most of the covers to find the cell phone. The screen showed a message received nearly ten minutes ago, probably the reason for her sudden awakening. The note was simple and to the point.

Let's trade.

Accompanied by a poorly lit photo of Will.

Her legs gave way, and she sank onto the bed. Though the trembling in her hands and the stinging of her eyes made seeing difficult, the man in the picture was definitely her cousin. He wore a T-shirt for Theo's soccer team, his jaw was in need of a shave, his brown hair was rumpled and his face lined with stress. What appeared to be a bruise darkened his left cheek, another on his jaw, and a smear across his upper lip and on the shoulder of his shirt looked like blood, possibly from the punch that had made his nose so puffy. The shot had been taken so close that his head and shoulders filled the frame, allowing no hint of a background. It could have been taken anywhere.

And there was no sign of Lolly or Theo.

She should have been startled when Ben appeared on the stairs a few feet in front of her, but she wasn't. She'd always marveled at how quickly and quietly he could move. It came in handy in his job, he'd said, and it had been invaluable in helping his mother raise his brothers and sisters. The kids might have sneaked something past Mary Grace, but never past Mary Grace and Ben.

He didn't come into the bedroom proper. At its peak, the ceiling nearly brushed the top of her hair. As it was, three steps down, it did brush the top of his. "He sent it to me, too. I texted back, asked when and where but haven't gotten a response. It's probably a prepaid phone. Next contact will probably be from a different number."

Yashi squeezed her eyes shut as the screen blurred even more and tried to think with her brain and not her heart. "Why didn't he send a picture of Theo? People are naturally more willing to negotiate when it involves a child. Or Lolly. Women are still seen as more vulnerable than men."

"Rational people." He glanced around the loft, his

gaze taking note of the railing that encircled the area and the narrow strip that stretched along the south side all the way to the front of the house. The space gave the house a defined entry with the lower ceiling below, the builder had explained. All Yashi cared about was the built-in storage it held.

"Do you think they're together? That he's keeping them in one place?"

Ben eased down to sit on the top step. "Look at Will's eyes. He's not looking at the camera. He's focused on something off to his right. I bet that's Lolly and Theo."

She looked at the photo again. Ben was right. Will wasn't gazing listlessly into the distance. He was looking *at* something. Someone. And those lines on his face weren't just stress. There was ferocity. Anger. Fear. Hope.

As long as they breathed, they had hope.

"Should I text him, too?" She didn't want to—didn't want to even pretend for one second that she would give Brit to some pervert nutjob—but if Ben thought she should, she would compose a response and send it onto the airwaves with wings.

"Not yet. We'll talk about it with the rest of the team. Can you come in to the station?"

"Of course." She jumped to her feet, grabbed a dress, shoes and underwear from their various storage cubbies, then stopped short. Usually, she would strip where she stood or dress in the bathroom after a shower. Usually, she didn't have Ben Little Bear in her house. "I, uh…"

He stood, bumped his head and retreated a step. "Did

you never consider you might bring someone of normal height up here sometimes?"

His voice, dark and warm with just the slightest hint of humor, sent shivers through her that made the pink panties she held slide loose and flutter to the floor between them. His gaze skimmed over them before she ducked and scooped them up.

"Six foot four isn't normal height around here for anyone except you." *And you would never come up here of your own free will.* A pang of regret twinged in her chest.

He headed down the stairs. "Has the demon off-spring been fed yet?"

"No. I'll get it—"

He made a dismissive gesture before disappearing from sight. Bobcat watched him walk into the kitchen, then leaped to the floor and stalked after him. Ben had never made his favorites list—except possibly under the heading of Humans Most Entertaining to Annoy—but he clearly understood the connection between people and their ability to provide the food he loved.

She undressed quickly, put on the clothes she'd chosen and went downstairs to the bathroom. When she passed through the kitchen, Ben was leaning against the counter, arms crossed, and Bobcat was sitting next to his food and water dishes against the wall, their gazes locked. She passed between them, not slowing when she said, "You know he won't eat while you watch him."

Ben snorted. The cat sniffed.

Like old times. She closed the bathroom door behind her, letting herself slip into the memories she rarely visited. It was a cold, wet day when she'd come home from work and found a tiny, bedraggled lump of something curled next to her door. Her first thought had been a dead bird or rodent, but when he heard her approach, Bobcat had lifted his head and issued the most pitiful meow in feline history. She hadn't wanted a cat—in fact, her plans had included a dog, the bigger and doggier, the better—but no one with a functioning heart could have turned away that kitten.

Ben had snickered when he'd seen them a few hours later. He didn't dislike cats in general, just Bobcat, but to be fair, Bobcat had started it by hissing every time Ben came into his line of sight. The cat had escalated to "accidental" bites, swipes across bare skin, sharpening his claws on Ben's clothes and calves alike and generally doing everything to alienate the other male except piss on him.

Yashi's sigh was wistful as she met her own gaze in the mirror. She had a lot of sad memories, a lot of bad ones, but she'd had her share of good times, too. It was okay to remember them, as long as she didn't lull herself into thinking that she could have those times with Ben back again. His presence in her life this time was dictated by one thing—this crime—and when it was resolved, he would disappear again. She had to be ready for that. No relying on him. No mistaking his professional interest for personal. No thinking that this time might be different.

Sunday mornings were usually quiet at the police department. When Ben parked in the lot, Sam's and

JJ's cars were already there, along with Morwenna's. She wasn't on the schedule for the day, which meant another dispatcher must have called in.

He got out of his truck and waited on the sidewalk for Yashi. She'd insisted on driving her own car so no one would be bothered later by giving her a ride. It had been a good idea. The less time he spent with her, the more he could pretend that nothing had changed. That this was just another case. That she was just another victim's family member. Not an old friend. Not someone he'd once slept with. Not someone he'd once loved.

She hadn't often worn dresses when they were together, which had made the times she did more special. Seeing her long, muscled legs had always been cause for celebration, and when the dress also bared her arms, that was a double pleasure. This morning's red dress did both, clinging to her breasts, flaring out at her hips—which, memory wouldn't let him ignore, were covered by a delicate scrap of pink. A tiny, fragile scrap not meant to conceal but to tease and tempt and titillate.

Despite his efforts, a small sigh escaped. He'd seen her in every piece of clothing she'd owned, and out of them, too. Dressed, naked and everywhere in between, she was an inspiring sight.

And he didn't need any inspiration of that kind this morning.

Her shoes, sandals that revealed hot-pink toenails, made little clacky noises on the sidewalk alongside his running shoes, and her hair fluttered in the breeze while her gaze seemed distant. Was she remembering all the times her job had brought her to the police station? Or maybe the times when the job had just been an excuse to see him there? Her office had been only two minutes away, in the courthouse behind them, but as far as he knew, she'd gone back only when cases required it, and none of the work she did now required dealing with the police.

He held open the heavy door, and she stepped past him, leaving some sweetly floral note tickling his nose. The fragrance was light and teasing, a scent to lift the spirits with each breath.

Just like the inspiration, he didn't need that today, either.

A walking psychedelic display was coming down the hall from the direction of Sam's office toward them. Morwenna's smile bloomed when she saw Yashi. "Did you get any sleep last night? Have you had breakfast? Need coffee? I'm about to make a run to Mama Little Bear's. Anything you want?"

Ben watched peripherally as Yashi's gaze moved over Morwenna. She took in the leggings, the layered shirts, the mismatched jewelry, the plaid headband paired with a polka-dotted one, and she smiled as fully as she seemed capable of. Good. Morwenna wasn't delusional—she knew her fashion style didn't appeal to most people—but no one got to hurt her feelings over it.

"Coffee would be lovely," Yashi said. "And one of those cinnamon rolls?"

"And maybe a little protein to give you energy? You can't run on sugar all day. Believe me, I've tried." Morwenna made a face before moving to pass them.

"Hey." Ben stopped her, one arm out. "Aren't you going to ask what I want?"

She rolled her eyes. "Coffee, scorched. Eggs, rubbery. Toast, burned. Sausage, just disgusting." Feigning a shudder, she walked on.

Ben watched her, a fluidly shifting mass of color and light that made the rest of the space look drabber than ever. He hadn't been too happy when Sam hired her four years ago. She'd seemed flighty and forgetful and totally lacking in competency—he'd later learned she always got that way when nervous—but she'd turned out to be smart and capable and exactly what the department needed to lighten and brighten up.

"How long have you been together?"

Yashi's question was so far off the mark that for a moment, Ben debated whether he'd heard her properly. When he turned to look at her, he saw by the look on her face that he had. He liked Morwenna—loved her, even—but in such a nonromantic way that, despite the guys joking about it yesterday, they were in a different universe. But he could see why Yashi might think differently. He'd told her himself that he and Morwenna had been having breakfast when they realized something was wrong at the Muellers' house, and she knew he didn't indulge in hookups at his house.

Her expression was such a failure at casual interest that he was tempted to let her believe the ridiculous. But getting intimate with Morwenna—ugh—wasn't something he could even pretend in. "She went out with her girlfriends Friday night, had too much to drink and called me for a ride. She didn't want her mum getting upset with her."

Yep, there was relief in Yashi's blue eyes. As if she still cared.

Caring had never been the problem, he sternly reminded himself. It had been the things she did in spite of the caring that came between them. Betraying his trust. Using his words against him. Violating the intimacy of their relationship. Those had killed the relationship, not lack of love.

She drew a breath, blinked, and the relief was gone, her expression neutral. "She's a grown woman. Unless she has a drinking problem, why would her mom be upset?"

"You haven't met Dr. Armstrong, have you? She's an extreme marathoner—she's done some hundred-kilometer runs—and she's religious about staying in shape. Nutrition, exercise, meditation, focus, yoga, sleep—it's all a huge deal to her. And Morwenna…" He gestured. She was softer, rounder, carrying a few pounds more than her mother would ever dream of. She loved good food and junk food and lived on caffeine. Meditation was an alien concept—energy hummed through her even when she slept—and she tended to like a little more of everything than was good for her. Mum's passion was fitness. Morwenna's was life.

"Isn't one of the inspired. Okay. Got it."

Yashi shifted her attention to the lobby where they stood and the desks behind the counter. Ben looked, too. Nothing had changed in the years since she'd been there: same desks, same floors, mostly the same people. For those people, though, everything had changed. Sam had gotten married and become a father. Daniel's ex-fiancée had walked in that big door one day last year and turned his world upside down. Quint had practically grieved himself right into the grave alongside his own fiancée, but with a lot of struggle, he'd found his way back to where he belonged, and he'd brought JJ with him.

And then there was Ben. Still single. Still alone. Still regretting what might have been. Rather than reflect any more than that on the past five years of his life, he started toward the conference room.

Sam and JJ were there, as he'd expected. So was Daniel, who lived only a couple blocks away, and another surprise: Sam's three-month-old daughter, looking bright-eyed over her daddy's shoulder and happily babbling. She had her mother's dark hair and eyes and her father's outgoing nature, evidenced as she reached for Yashi the moment she saw her.

"Oh Sam." Yashi took the baby and held her out for inspection. "She's gorgeous. She must take after her mother." She smiled brightly at his smirk. "Did you stick with the family tradition in naming her?"

Family traditions were important to her, enough to make Ben feel a tiny pinch deep inside.

"We did."

"Okay, let me guess." Yashi's words were mumbled around the chubby fingers with which the baby was exploring her mouth. She removed the tiny hand, cradled her on her hip and pursed her lips. "The obvious would be Samantha, but you've got one already. And a Sam-

son and several Samuels and a Sammy. If I recall, your
wife's name is Mila, so Samila would be my choice."

"That was his choice, too," Daniel murmured from
his seat at the table, "but he didn't get it."

"You gonna get your choice on naming your kid?"
Sam asked.

Daniel grinned. "He's gonna be a Harper. That's all
I care about."

"Being named after one parent is enough. I didn't
think she needed both our names." That was Mila, coming through the doorway, dabbing at the shoulder of
her dress with a damp cloth. She was accompanied by
a faint hint of sourness, courtesy of the baby and her
morning milk.

Yashi shifted Sameen and extended her right hand.
"Yashi Baker."

A few years ago, Ben reflected, the gesture would
have bewildered Mila. Thanks to a horrific upbringing,
she'd had no one in her life but her grandmother, her
dog and the coworkers she didn't interact with. It had
taken several murders—and Sam—to bring her out of
her solitary existence.

Now she shook hands as if she'd been doing it all her
life. She even touched Ben's arm as she passed. "Mila
Douglas, and this is Sameen. I'll warn you, she has
no sense of propriety. She'll stick her fingers in your
mouth, chew on anything she can put in her mouth, even
if it happens to be attached to you, and she overflows
her diaper without warning."

Yashi grinned at Sam. "Mama's looks. Daddy's manners. She's perfect." Her gaze shifted back to the baby, and the lightheartedness slowly faded.

Was she thinking about the babies she'd expected to have by now? Envying Mila and feeling the sense of loss before she even handed Sameen to her? The sweet smells, the soft skin, the bright eyes, the warmth and movement and sheer contentment that made up Sameen's existence?

That longing sometimes sneaked into Ben's consciousness—when Sam announced Mila's pregnancy, when Natasha announced her own, especially when he saw the little fair-haired babies snoozing in car seats or screaming their lungs out in shopping carts. Biology stacked the odds against it, with his black hair, brown eyes and Creek heritage, but for years, he'd had a yearning for a pretty little girl with her mother's blond hair and blue eyes.

"We've got to get to church," Mila said, and Yashi handed Sameen over after one last snuggle. Yashi quickly turned away, going to the end of the conference table and looking out the window before finally taking a seat.

There was a moment's bustle while Mila and Sameen left and everyone else got settled, then Sam grimly said, "Let's look at what we've got."

What they had was essentially nothing. The blood in Will's living room was of three different types. The paint on the door was spray paint, sold at a half dozen places in Cedar Creek. They'd lifted dozens of fingerprints, belonging mostly to the family and to Yashi.

They'd interviewed the neighbors and were expanding to everyone else in the family's lives.

They had no clues. No leads. No answers.

As Yashi walked out of the police station after two depressing hours, her head throbbed in time with her steps. The breakfast from Creek Café had gone down easy but now sat like a rock in her stomach, and excessive caffeine jittered through her body with every heartbeat. She went to her car, stood there awhile, trying not to think about the long empty day ahead of her—a day she would normally be spending with her family—then turned and crossed the grass to First Street.

It was hot. Humid. Piercingly bright sun, achingly blue sky and not a breath of a breeze. A typical August day. The heat seeped into her skin, slowly chasing away the chill, forming tiny drops of sweat, pleasantly comfortable for the moment.

That moment wouldn't last.

Cedar Creek's downtown consisted of two- to five-story buildings, mostly brick or sandstone. Businesses occupied the ground floors, with an emphasis on antique shops, and most of the upper floors held offices, apartments or were waiting renovations to bring them new life. She turned west, alone on the sidewalk for as far as she could see, and walked mindlessly, her reflection in the windows distorting as she passed from one building to the next.

She loved this town. Had been charmed by it the very first time she'd visited. Hadn't hesitated for one second when Will suggested she move here. It was funny that two Texans, born and bred and happy with their state, had ended up in a little Oklahoma city neither of them had ever heard of until college. His best friend had been from Cedar Creek, and when Will and Lolly had been looking for a small-town environment to raise the kids they intended to have, one trip to Cedar Creek had decided them. His friend had moved to Chicago a year after they settled there, three years before Yashi joined them. None of them had ever regretted their choices.

At the moment, though, Yashi felt as if the town had betrayed them. It was silly. The town hadn't abducted her family. It hadn't forced the kidnapper to do it. Every place had good people and bad. It wasn't Cedar Creek's fault this particular bad guy lived here, or that he'd chosen her family. The key word was *chosen*. All the guilt, all the blame, lay squarely with him.

The ring of her cell phone startled her into the moment. She'd walked to Main Street, the end of the downtown district, crossed to the other side of First and was halfway back to her starting point, and she couldn't name a single thing she'd seen besides her wavering image.

Heart pounding, she pulled the phone from deep pocket of her dress, squeezed her eyes shut for a brief, fervent prayer, then looked at it. The number was blocked.

Though her hands trembled and her knees were suddenly unsteady, she answered the call, unable to make her voice as strong and sure as she wanted it to be. "This is Yashi."

"Yashi!"

Brit's voice broke halfway through the name, and

Yashi's heart broke, too. Glancing around, she spotted a couple of '50s-era metal lawn chairs in front of a shop and sank gratefully into one. The green metal was shaded by the overhead awning but still made her grateful her legs weren't bare.

"Brit, sweetie, how are you holding up?"

The question unleashed a flood of unhappy words. "I don't like this, Yashi. I want to go home, and I want Mama and Daddy and Theo to be there, too, and I want this to have never happened! I want to water the garden and help Mom deliver her vegetables to Mrs. Lewis and Mr. Adams. They'll go bad if they just sit there on the porch, and you know how she is about letting things go to waste. I want to practice soccer with Dad, and I want to lie by the creek and yell at Theo for splashing water on me and getting my hair wet, and I want to have goulash for dinner!"

Yashi's throat tightened, as did her grip on the phone. The Douglas family had their naming tradition; through the Muellers, Yashi had a few traditions, too. More Sundays than not, she was at that dinner table eating goulash with them. She helped in the garden, too, and knew Lolly's opinions on every aspect of recycling and re-using, and how many times had she listened to Brit yell at Theo? Too many to count.

"Honey, I'm so sorry. I should have come to see you. I should have asked Ben where you are and gotten permission." Should have put Brit first, before absolutely anything, most certainly herself. She was an adult. She could handle trauma. But Brit was new to this kind of upset and fear, thank God. Of course she would have trouble coping.

A hiccup, then a loud sniff came from the phone, followed by a softer, calmer voice. "It's okay, Yashi. Officer Lois said I could see you maybe tomorrow."

The mix of formal title and informal first name tempted a small smile. Brit had been little when she met Ben and, through him, Lois Gideon. Lolly's disapproval of children calling adults by their first names had led to a compromise that Brit had never outgrown. It had always tickled Ben when she tilted her head way back, gave him her best princess/tomboy smile and called him Officer Bear. Sentimental guy that he was—a label no one would slap on him at first or even twenty-first meeting—it still pleased him to know he had a special place in her heart.

"Do you have everything you need, honey? Clothes, books, makeup? A banana split from Braum's? Some frozen pickle pops?"

"I just need my mama and daddy and brother." Brit's whisper was tiny and forlorn. "I can't have my computer or phone, and the only real book I'm reading is the sixth *Harry Potter*. I can't do that without Mom and Theo."

Another Mueller tradition: group-reading *Harry Potter* in the summer. Even Will, who loathed it all, found the eye rolls and heavy sighs a fair trade for the sweet picture of the three people he loved best snuggled together with the books.

"We'll get to finish it, won't we, Yashi?"

Yashi's heart hurt. Could she promise Brit that of course her family would return to her? It was the natural thing to say, but a lifetime ago, Yashi's mother had promised she would be home in time to tuck her into bed, and she'd never come. Yashi had never seen her or her father again. There'd been no viewings before the funeral, no final kisses or hugs. Just a promise Mama hadn't kept. It had taught her that promises were iffy things. You could do your best, but a pickup slamming into your vehicle at seventy miles an hour needed only an instant to obliterate your best.

"Who do you trust most in the world outside our family?"

"Officer Bear."

"Well, he's spending every bit of his time looking for them." She didn't go so far as to make promises on his behalf, but she didn't need to. Brit's faith in him was complete.

"Okay. And when we're all home again, I'm never sneaking out of the house again as long as I live."

"You bet you aren't, because I'm going to help your dad put iron bars on your windows, and I was thinking of getting an ankle bracelet for your birthday, the kind that sets off an alarm if you go more than twenty feet from your room. You know, they're a little bulky, and they only come in black, but I figure you can glam it up a bit."

Her cousin almost giggled. "I have to go to school, Yashi."

"One word—homeschooling. Better yet, you could be the first and only student at the Baker Law Firm and Online School. We'll put your desk in my office.

Six hours a day, five days a week. No holidays, breaks or vacations."

This time the giggle fully formed but faded too soon. "I love you."

Yashi swiped her hand across her eyes. "I love you, too, sweetie."

"Pray for us. Daddy and Mom and Theo and me and you."

"I am." As the call ended, she sighed heavily. Too often it seemed that praying was the only promise she could keep.

# Chapter 5

On the walk back to her car, Yashi sweated out the jitters from too much caffeine. Unable to face the emptiness of home, she checked the police department parking lot for Sam's vehicle, didn't see it—or Ben's, though she wasn't looking—and sent Sam a text instead, asking permission to pick up the vegetables. Delivering them would ease Brit's mind a degree or so and give Yashi something to fill an hour or two.

She was turning onto the two-lane that led to the house when his affirmative text came back. Don't go in the house, he instructed, but he gave her free range over the outside. That was okay. She wasn't sure she could bear going in that house ever again until her family was back where they belonged. A flash came from her childhood: Will's aunt, taking responsibility for gathering funeral clothes, leading her inside their snug little house. Yashi had been too confused to understand, too scared to ask why this woman was taking her mama's best clothes and too worn out to cry anymore. Instead, she'd plopped herself on Daddy's chair, snuggled in the jacket he'd left lying there and pretended herself right out of the moment.

She'd pretended herself out of a lot of moments over the next few years.

Though the pavement had dried from yesterday's rain, the leaves and bushes still glistened. The branches that met over the road were heavier, sagging lower, and the very air seemed too thick to breathe. She gripped the steering wheel tighter, concentrated on keeping to her side of the narrow road. A couple of big water drops plopped onto her windshield when she drove through the tunnel beneath the railroad tracks, but everything else was still.

The Mueller driveway was a muddy mess. She parked as far to the left as she could, where rocks showing through dirt offered a more solid trail, and climbed out. Sourness churned in her stomach, and even as her hair turned lank from the humidity, the fine hairs on her neck stood on end. Other than Ben's house across the road and the highway sounds from the turnpike, there was no other sign of life. No dogs barking, birds flying, trains chugging past.

Damn it, she was scared. She was alone in a place where something awful and violent had happened, a place where no one could hear her scream if it happened again. But she had her phone and—reaching under the driver's seat, she drew out a black nylon holster—her gun, and she'd never been one to give in without a fight.

Wishing for a waistband to clip the holster onto, she gripped the gun in one hand, the cell in the other, and walked to the house. Up the steps, also covered with mud, and around the porch to the back side. Nothing had changed in twenty-four hours. Everything was still saturated with water. The grass had grown another inch, the corn probably two inches. Tiny footprints tracked along the porch railing—from Ben's Oliver?—and droplets of water remained on the garden baskets. They held heirloom tomatoes, sweet yellow onions, herbs and lettuce, cucumbers and eggplant and summer squash.

Sliding her pistol into her dress pocket, she picked up both baskets, walked back to the front of the house, then stopped. There had been three baskets yesterday morning, the third one tagged with more initials. *SB*. It had stuck in her mind because they were her mother Sonia's initials.

She carried the baskets to her car, leaving them on the hood, then returned to the porch. The steps where she and Ben had sat yesterday afternoon appeared the same, lacking the mud of the front steps. She climbed to the bottom one, narrowed her gaze and tried to find a sign that someone had crossed the grass. As if she had any talent for finding such signs. The woods a few yards away were thick and wet. No one would come to the house that way when there was a perfectly good road out front, with plenty of muck on the ground to hide their movements.

It was probably no big deal. SB, whoever that was,

had probably expected Lolly's delivery and come to pick it up herself. Or maybe another neighbor—someone nosy like the old coot next door—had come over to get a glimpse of the crime scene and decided to help himself to the food.

But wouldn't someone other than SB taking the food have taken all of it? People around there had a fine appreciation of homegrown tomatoes, onions and cucumbers. Why leave two baskets to spoil when he was already stealing one?

Wishing she'd worn sturdier shoes, she stepped into the grass. Within a few feet, her sandals were wet and moisture was seeping between her toes. She walked alongside the garden plot, wondering why no bees were buzzing in the nearby crape myrtles, why the occasional red wasp didn't circle her, where the flies were. She didn't like unnatural things, and unnatural stillness topped the list. It lent an ominous air to the scene and roused her fear once again.

The cornstalks rustled when she passed them, and her gaze darted that way, her mouth going dry. She stopped, her feet planted, not wanting to go forward or back. The woods began just ahead, a heavy growth of oaks, mimosas, maples and a profusion of red cedars, ranging in height from two feet to forty. The red cedars were pretty, always green and Christmassy, and they invaded everywhere they could get a tiny root. Over there was one that had completely surrounded a black-jack oak, leaving gnarly dead branches poking through. On the other side, eight or ten small red cedars were growing together, blocking light from the other plants around them.

Standing there, she could count at least a dozen of them big enough for a kidnapper or two to hide behind.

Nothing around her indicated that anyone had come this way, but her gaze settled on something discarded in the grass ahead: small, red, ragged edges. Before she recognized it, a voice from behind startled her out of her skin.

"What are you doing?"

In her panic, all she heard was a deep, male voice; all she realized was that she was utterly alone; all she felt was the pounding of her heart. It took only an instant to recognize the intruder as Ben, though, quickly enough that she hadn't had time to yelp or spin around or maybe throw herself into his arms. She drew a breath before slowly turning.

He looked so good that, oh yeah, she would have loved to throw herself into his arms. Once she got there, she would never want to leave again, while he would be counting the seconds until he could push her away.

"Sam said I could come."

"I know. But the baskets were on the porch, and you're standing out here staring into the woods like you've seen a spirit."

"Not a spirit. A tomato."

His brows arched, giving her the impetus to walk forward to the red object resting in the grass. "There were three baskets on the porch yesterday, weren't there?"

He nodded.

"When I got here, there were only two, and that to-

mato appears to have been eaten recently." She pointed
to the chunk, mostly stem and skin.

Ben came to stand beside her and crouched. The
position allowed her to look down on his glossy black
hair for one of the few times in their lives. The others
had usually occurred in the bedroom, and he'd been
kneeling, not crouching, and she hadn't had the least
interest in his hair or much of anything else besides
pure pleasure.

Looking at him in any position was incredibly plea-
surable.

After a moment, he stood again. "Could have been a
deer, a squirrel or raccoon. Could have taken a tomato
off the vine." They both looked that way, at the less-
than-vigorous vines that bore only green fruit at the moment—then his broad shoulders shrugged. "Could have
helped itself to one from the baskets before SB came."

She knew he was right. It wasn't likely someone had
come out of the woods, stolen the basket, then disappeared back into the overgrowth. She'd come to that
conclusion before he arrived. Still…

"Do you know who SB is?"

"No idea."

He walked to the edge of the grass, then pushed past
tree branches to the faded path there. It led to another
creek that ran through a narrow valley. It wasn't deep
enough to swim or fish in, and the hillside was steep
and rocky. Too little reward for too much effort. Lolly
and Will used the path only to get to the clearing a few
yards ahead where she kept her compost pile. He studied the ground, parallel lines of dirt packed by the gar-

den cart wheels, needles from the red cedars and weeds that Theo mowed when necessary. Standing next to him, Yashi didn't see any signs of passage in the last day and a half.

"Will and I need to come out here with the chain saws and take out these cedars."

Yashi's nerves sharpened. Her family was missing, and he was talking about trash trees? Then she got the message: he was talking about the future. When Will was back. When things were normal. He was giving her reassurance.

*Who do you trust most in the world outside of our family?* she'd asked Brit. She didn't need to ask herself the question. Her answer was the same as Brit's—had been for years, would be for years.

Ben *would* find Will and Lolly and Theo. He hadn't promised it. Didn't need to.

She believed it anyway.

Ben stared at the ground long enough to recognize individual blades of grass before he finally looked up and ahead. There was no neighbor between where they stood and the Pickerings' house, over on the new highway. Nothing but acres more of exactly what was in front of them: trees, rocks, shrubs, piles of dead leaves, with the added feature of narrow valleys that more closely resembled canyons. Lose your footing at the top of the hill above the creek, and you were likely to be in the water before you could catch yourself, with a fair share of aches and bruises.

The only thing out there besides the creek and the

woods was a pair of tunnels where the train tracks crossed the water, wide, shady and muddy. According to his great-aunts, in their youth, hoboes used them as resting spots while waiting for the next train. Anyone wanting to pass through that area would do so on the railroad tracks, where ties and gravel provided a reasonably level surface.

Anyone passing through who wasn't worried about being seen.

Someone just wanting to steal a basket of vegetables? Not likely.

He pulled out his phone and opened a satellite map feature. As he zoomed in, blobs formed into shapes: lines cutting through woods, clearings growing larger, houses becoming visible. The final image confirmed his assumption: in the rough triangle formed by the Mueller, Brown and Pickering houses was nothing but trees. No driveway snaking through, not even a hint of a trail. The only passable way through was the train tracks.

Still, it wouldn't hurt to bring a dog out here. CCPD didn't have a canine of their own, but there were several trackers they'd worked with before who volunteered their dogs' services. The heavy rains likely would have destroyed any scent of the Muellers or their kidnapper, but that bit of tomato had been tossed there after the rain, and anyone who'd taken this route to the house so soon after the owners' disappearance was definitely someone Ben wanted to talk to.

He texted Morwenna, asking her to contact their first-choice volunteer, and got back a quick On it. As he slid the phone back into its case, behind him, Yashi slapped at an insect, drawing his attention back to her. To quote Great-Aunt Weezer, she looked like a horse rode hard and put away wet. Everything about her was limp and damp, from her hair to her dress to her very self, and lines etched the corners of her eyes and her mouth.

And yet she was still double-take triple-take stop-a-man-dead-in-his-tracks beautiful. He'd never been particularly drawn to blondes, had never cared about the color of a woman's eyes, but one night he'd awakened in the middle of the night beside her, the lamp on the bedside table still lit, and realized that somehow, at some time, his definition of a beautiful woman had narrowed drastically to this woman. Not her hair, her eyes, her golden skin, not her breasts or the curve of her hips or her amazing legs, but everything that was *her*.

After they'd broken up, he'd figured he would eventually get past that, but he hadn't. Sure, he could look at other women and agree that, yes, they were beautiful, but it didn't mean the same thing. They didn't have the sucker-punch-to-the-gut effect on him that she did.

A mosquito buzzed his ear a half second before she swatted another one. "I was wondering where the bugs were," she said ruefully. "Now I just wish they'd go back."

"August is meant to make us appreciate September." Or so his mother had claimed. Of course, she'd had six kids at home who went back to school the third week of August, so she had likely referred to that rather than cooler days.

"I can appreciate September just fine without being

steamed and eaten alive by skeeters in August." She climbed the steps ahead of him, her dress too damp to swish but still allowing a pretty picture of her legs. "Lolly would have a fit if she saw all this mud."

"Lolly will be thrilled to see every clump and clod of it. Besides, Will, Brit and Theo all have experience at scrubbing."

Ben gazed across the road at his house with momentary longing. It was cool inside and there were leftovers from last night's dinner in the refrigerator and two dozen things he'd rather be doing, even if one of them was just lying on the couch and staring at the ceiling. But after stopping by to check on Yashi as Sam had asked, he still had a list of people he needed to talk to before calling it a day.

When they reached the driveway, he watched her pick up the baskets and put them in the passenger seat. Her skirt pulled snugly when she bent at the waist and her top half disappeared inside the car, revealing a lump in her pocket. He'd taught her to shoot a long time ago and picked out the weapon for her. It had surprised him, having spent his entire adult life as a cop, that seeing her with the compact pistol at her waist had given his usual arousal a little kick.

She straightened, caught him looking and raised one brow. "I could have put it in my purse, and then where would I be when I needed it?"

How had she known—? Because she knew him. Because she'd listened when he'd told her, *If you're going to carry it, wear it. Don't stick it in your pocket, don't tuck it in your waistband, don't drop it into that bottom-less pit you call a purse. Holster. Clip-on or shoulder.*

She'd listened to everything he said, even throwaway remarks that had been all joke and no truth, that she had *known* to be all joke and no truth. Things he'd said in private. In bed. Naked. Just him and her and Bobcat, giving Ben baleful looks between catnaps.

And then she'd gotten him on the witness stand at Lloyd Wind's trial and taken those remarks out of context to use against him. To bring his character into question and to convict an innocent man.

He waited for the clenching of his jaw, the tightening of his nerves, the sense of betrayal and loss—those things that always accompanied memories of the end of their relationship. The anger that she'd sacrificed him for her career. The hurt.

A muscle in his jaw twitched, but that was about it. There was too damn much other stuff going on to focus on old regrets.

A car came around the curve to the west, slowed to a crawl at the clearing where the Mueller house sat, and the passengers, both front and back, began snapping pictures with their cell phones. Ben might have ignored them if they'd been kids, finding some stupid thrill in taking photos of a house where a crime had occurred, but these were women at least in their fifties. He shifted, blocking Yashi from their view, and gave them a hard look as they passed.

Neither of them had stopped with the picture taking.

"Bet they're already sharing them on social media," Yashi said, her voice as hard as his expression. "Got to be first on their friends list to stir up the ghouls. Whatever happened to empathy, respect and decency?"

"The internet. World's best invention."

They finished the statement together: "World's worst invention."

He swiped away the sweat trickling toward the corners of his eyes, then pushed shut the Bug's door. "Don't come out here alone again."

He didn't know what response to expect from her. Assistant DA Baker had always—almost—respected Detective Little Bear's advice. Away from work, Yashi Baker had sometimes found Ben Little Bear hardheaded and old-fashioned. So far, as family member of kidnap victims, she'd been amenable and helpful.

She looked around them, her gaze sliding over thick stands of trees, boulders bigger than her car, leaf canopies and tangled bushes, briars and weeds gone wild, and a shudder trembled through her. Was she thinking how isolated the place seemed, given that it was within city limits? Considering how many hundreds of hiding places were out there? How many countless secrets the woods could hold?

He loved the isolation. With his job, he needed the lack of other neighbors, the hundreds of trees per person, the quiet and peace. Yashi had loved it back then, too. Right now, though, he imagined it was hard for her to find peace in the place where Will and Lolly and Theo had been violently taken from their home. Hence, the pistol in her pocket.

After a bleak moment, she gave a shake of her head. "No. I won't."

She walked around the little yellow car and opened the door, but before she could climb inside, he spoke again. "Yashi…do you need anything?"

It was a question they had asked each other a thousand times: on the way to each other's house, on a trip to the kitchen for a drink, when heading out of the office for anything. The answer had been no, as often as not, but the offer had always mattered. Now her expression turned bittersweet. "Just my family."

"Will seeing Brit tomorrow help?"

She nodded.

"Lois will make arrangements."

After another nod, she slid into the car, finally releasing her grip on her phone, flexed her fingers, then backed around his truck and headed toward town. Ben called Morwenna as he walked to the truck.

"I was just getting ready to text you," she said in her bright way. It wasn't that Morwenna didn't feel complete sympathy for the victims the police department dealt with. Bright was just the way she was. "Did you know they have competitions for search and rescue dogs? They get to practice tracking and get prizes, and it makes the babies happy. Anyway, Booger and Zeus are both on their way home from Kansas City from just such an event. Booger's mom said she would call you in the morning. Will that be too late?"

"He's a bloodhound. I'm not sure there's such a thing as 'too late' for him." Zeus, despite the more noble name, was a beagle and a very good scent tracker, just not as good as Booger. Besides, with a good twelve inches or more of dead leaves piled on the ground under the trees, little Zeus might get buried, while nothing stopped the bigger, brawnier Booger from pushing on through.

After getting off the phone with Morwenna and climbing into the truck, Ben hoped that he was big and brawny enough to share that trait with the dog. That nothing would stop him from pushing on through.

Monday morning Yashi left her office less than an hour after she got there. She had paperwork to deal with, a couple of clients to call, but she was too frazzled to sit at her desk in an empty building. Regular everyday noises made her jump, reminding her of the prickling of her nerves at Will's house yesterday, and when she tried to concentrate, her mind diverted back to the only thing that truly mattered right now: her family.

She'd delivered Lolly's baskets yesterday before heading home. Juanita Lewis might have been the secretary in an office of youngish accountants, but she was also the mother hen who'd watched over them and made sure the older people—or the clients—didn't eat them alive. Tears had come to her eyes when Yashi handed her the vegetables. If she'd known anything at all about the kidnappings, she'd hidden it well.

Kirby Adams had been concerned, too, he and his wife sitting beside each other on their sofa and holding hands. He told her he'd given a list of Brit's teammates and the names of other teams and coaches in their league to the detective who'd interviewed him, and he'd asked her to please let him know when she had news. He was young enough and handsome enough, she'd thought, to catch the eye of most teenage girls, but maybe instead it was Brit who'd caught his eye. Maybe this happily-married-guy thing was camouflage. Maybe his wife, at twenty-six or twenty-eight, was too old for his tastes…or, more likely, Yashi was seeing things that weren't there.

It had been her job once to make judgments about people, to study evidence, to decide whether the police had built a sufficient case to convict a person of a crime, then to persuade a jury of that. It hadn't given her any kind of know-all magic, hadn't enabled her to look into a person's eyes and detect his guilt or innocence. She had no evidence that Juanita Lewis or Kirby Adams was even remotely involved in the kidnapping, and looking at them through the lens of suspicion wasn't fair to them nor healthy for her.

The call from Lois Gideon telling her she could see Brit at ten was what propelled her out of the office. It was another mucky, yucky day, the heat and the humidity both hovering in the high nineties. She broke a sweat as soon as she stepped out of the building, and the interior of her car was as stifling as an oven. As soon as the engine was running, she rolled down the windows, turned the air-conditioning to high and peeled out of the lot and onto the highway to get some wind blowing through the Bug.

Because she hadn't had any appointments on her calendar, she'd dressed in capris and a sleeveless top, and she'd braided her hair before securing it into a knot at her nape. As she sped toward town, she fumbled on a pair of dark glasses, then punched a button on the dash to start her favorite CD. Wayman Tisdale had been a gift to Oklahoma basketball, Ben used to say. Yashi thought his better talent had been his music. His jazz CDs never failed to make her feel—well, if not happy, at least better.

There was plenty of time for happy when her cousins were home.

She had put together a small bag for Brit the night before: a box of pickle pops to go in the freezer, a few magazines, an assortment of nail polishes and gems, her own iPod with a wide assortment of music and a small journal with pens filled with pink, lime and purple ink. After one more stop, she drove to the address Lois had given her, recognizing the house as Quint Foster's. Cedar Creek didn't have a lot of options to protect a minor that didn't involve juvenile facilities. The only place safer than this, in Yashi's opinion, would be Sam's or Ben's house, but they couldn't put little Sameen in possible danger, and they needed Ben out working on the case.

After parking next to Quint's old truck, she gathered her bags and walked to the door. He must have been watching from the window, because he opened the door before she'd had a chance to juggle the bags so she could knock. He ushered her in, closed the door and locked up behind her.

Yashi gave him a steady look up and down. He wore jeans and a T-shirt, along with a weapon and his badge on his belt. He'd aged a few extra years since she'd last spent any time with him—losing his fiancée would do that to a man—but he was as handsome as ever, and a hard-earned contentment had settled over him, softening his features. "You look good, Quint."

"So do you."

He hugged her, and the years slipped away, taking with them her regret for not attending Belinda's funeral, for not reaching out to him when she died, but she hadn't known if she would be welcome. After her stunt in the courtroom with Ben, for the short time she'd remained on the job, she'd become the ADA that no cop wanted to deal with. A few, Ben included, had been openly hostile. Lois had chided her. Sam and Quint, then assistant chief, had been polite but disappointed in her.

She'd never had anyone in her life to disappoint before, and it had been much worse than she expected.

When he stepped back, his nose wrinkled. "Do I smell pickles?"

She smiled. "Some people bring flowers or candy. I bring pickle juice."

"Huh. Brit is in the kitchen." He gestured toward the open door between the dining room and kitchen.

"Have you put her to work washing dishes?" Yashi teased as they headed that way.

"That's JJ's job, and she protects it fiercely. She's afraid if someone else does dishes, then she'll be expected to actually cook something."

Brit didn't jump up to greet Yashi the way she expected, in part, probably, because of the sizable bundle of tan fur curled in her lap. Its nose was hidden behind folded paws, but it lifted its brown eyes to inspect Yashi. The eyes narrowed at the pickle juice smell but widened when catching the scents from the other bag. "This is Chica," Brit said, giving the dog a hug that lingered. "Isn't she gorgeous?"

"Gorgeous," Yashi agreed. Even if it wasn't true, who insulted a pit bull who was at the perfect level to eat your face? She set the bags on the island, sliding the smaller one to Brit, then gave her a cautious hug, making sure Chica didn't mind. "How are you, sweetie?"

Brit leaned her head against Yashi's shoulder. "I'm okay. I mean, I'm not, like, in a jail cell somewhere with other kids who are in trouble, right? And Chica sleeps with me and growls if she hears anything, and Officer Lois or Officer Quint or Detective Logan is always here. She's nice. She's from South Carolina, and she beat up that girl that killed the rich girl and assumed her identity a while back, and the girl was, like, half her age."

Yashi smiled, too. She'd read about the case earlier that year—had even gotten a call from Hank Benton asking if she would represent his son, the boyfriend, Zander. She'd told him no. Everyone was entitled to the best defense possible, but that didn't mean it had to come from her. Getting involved with that case, when the killers had also tried to kill Quint and JJ, would have been impossible for her.

"JJ's half again her age," Quint said from the other side of the island, where he was chopping ingredients on a board. "She was twenty-five. JJ's thirty-seven."

Brows furrowed, Brit did the math. Yashi could actually see the moment "half her age" and "half again her age" revealed their separate meanings to her brain.

"Oh. Big difference. Good thing she's not here to kick *my* butt."

Drying his hands on a towel, Quint tossed it on the island, then headed toward the back door, where he lifted a leash from a hook. "Chica, wanna go out?"

The dog shifted from lazy and too comfortable to a tan blur streaking across the tile to the door. Yashi caught Quint's gaze and gave an appreciative nod, then slid onto the stool next to Brit, nudging her with one shoulder. "Want me to put your treat in the freezer?"

Brit started to push the bag toward her, then stopped and unfolded the top. Her mouth tilted in the faintest of smiles when she lifted out the carton and saw the choc-olate chip ice cream floating in a sea of warm caramel sauce. "I'd probably better eat it now. I wouldn't want any of the caramel to go to waste. You want a bite?"

"No, thanks, sweetie." If Wayman Tisdale made her happy, Wayman and ice cream made her deliriously so. She'd devoured her own rocky road cone sitting in the Braum's parking lot. "I delivered the baskets to Mrs. Lewis and Coach Adams yesterday."

Plastic spoon still depositing food into her mouth, Brit hugged her again. "Thank 'ou. Mom'll be—" She removed the spoon. "Mom will be glad."

"That other basket, the one for SB…do you know who that is?"

Brit's gaze went distant as she continued to eat the sundae. "Mom gives away a lot of vegetables, but the baskets only go to the regulars. The people who will bring them back. Everyone else gets theirs in plastic sacks. Mrs. Lewis always gives hers to Dad at work, and Coach Adams brings his to practice."

"And SB?"

"Theo and me have never met her. He thinks she's not real. He says it's like when Mom moved that silly Christmas elf every night after we went to bed, or when she put that rabbit in the yard on Easter morning and said he'd filled our baskets and left them on the porch."

The rabbit, paused in his hop across the Mueller yard, had been pure coincidence, but that hadn't stopped Lolly from taking advantage. Yashi had seen firsthand the awe and astonishment on little Theo's face. Brit had been delighted, too, but had known that even her mom couldn't make a rabbit hop by on cue.

"Where does your mom say SB lives?"

Her enthusiasm for sugar waning, Brit took a smaller bite of the sundae. "I don't think she really knows. She says she's an old woman who lives in the woods. People don't just live in the woods. That's so…" Her vocabulary didn't seem to have a word to describe what it was. "But wherever she lives, Mom puts little treats out by the Christmas tree for her, like a bouquet of flowers or some applesauce or cookies, and they disappear. And that's where the basket comes back."

Her nerves knotted, Yashi stood and scooted the stool back to the counter. She wanted to run out of the house, race out to Will's house and search every acre of the property for this woman, but she forced herself to remain calm. "Did your mom ever call her by name?"

Brit pushed the dish away, the spoon balanced on top, and restlessly turned to face Yashi. "Yeah, a few times she did, but—" Like any teenage girl, she hadn't been overly interested in a strange old woman who claimed to live in the woods. "It was something silly. I don't know. Sugar? Sweetheart?"

"Hey, I have a silly name all my very own." Besides, she and Lolly had had more than a few laughs over some kids' names in use. With parents' imaginations running wild, it seemed there was no such thing as a silly name these days.

A troubled expression came over Brit's face. "I should have told Officer Bear about this Saturday, shouldn't I? I just didn't think… I mean, sometimes I think maybe Theo's right that she's not real. Maybe she's someone Mom made up to, I don't know, try to keep us believing. You know, in magic. Mom loves magic."

Yashi's hand trembled as she brushed blond hair from Brit's face. "You know what she says the three most magical days of her life were?"

"When she married Daddy, when I was born and when we moved into the house." After a moment for impact, Brit relented. "Okay, yeah, maybe when Theo was born. It certainly changed *my* life." Then the bleakness returned. "Did I screw up? Officer Bear asked me about neighbors, and I didn't tell him."

"How could you tell him when you don't know her name or where she lives or even for sure that she's real?" Yashi herself wondered if the gifts went to a neighbor who lived west of the Muellers, and the rest of the tale was made up for the kids' entertainment. It *was* on the fantastical side.

Besides, if it was true, could an old woman who lived alone in the woods have kidnapped an entire family all on her own?

Not unless she was all sorts of crazy.

And violent.

Brit gripped both of Yashi's hands. "Will you tell Officer Bear? And tell him I'm sorry I didn't think of it Saturday?"

Yashi pulled her in close for a hug. "I will, sweetie. I'll do it right now."

## Chapter 6

When Ben glanced over his right shoulder to make sure the lane was clear so he could change for the up-coming turn, he got a full-face blast of doggy breath, something worse and two large brown eyes as innocent as a babe's. He grimaced, made the lane change, then rolled his window down a few inches. Beside him, Daniel's nose twitched, then his entire face screwed up. "Did your dog just fart?"

In the rear seat behind Ben, Dusty Smith snorted. "Oh, like you haven't done it yourself before." Then she tried to surreptitiously lower her own window a few inches. "Don't listen to the mean man, Booger. It's okay."

The rearview mirror reflected the hound's impassive face. With his long ears, saggy jowls and sad-looking eyes, he wasn't a classically pretty dog, but there were a lot of pretty dogs out there who couldn't begin to measure up to Booger when he was working.

"If he's got such a great sense of smell, how can he stand that?" Daniel asked as his window lowered all the way down. Hot air rushed through, replacing the gassy smell with exhaust, pollen and dust.

"If you keep insulting my dog, he's going to show you why people call bloodhounds slobber hounds. Nobody can scent like Booger, and nobody can drool like him, either." Under her breath, Dusty muttered, "City boy."

"I heard that," Daniel muttered back.

Ben shook his head. The plan had been for Dusty to meet them at the Mueller house, but the air-conditioning had gone out in her truck, so she'd hitched a ride with them. He didn't mind. He'd had bigger and stinkier dogs than Booger in his truck before. Just not with Daniel, who still retained come of his big-city ways despite living in Cedar Creek.

And not one whose noxious smells were quite so noxious.

He made two quick turns onto his road and, within a couple of minutes, was pulling into the Mueller driveway. His jaw tightened when he saw Yashi's car was already there. He'd figured she would spend as much time with Brit as possible this morning, but apparently he'd been wrong. She got out of the car as he shut off the engine and waited impatiently.

After his passengers unloaded, he rolled up the windows, though he hated to capture any remaining essence of Booger inside, and locked the truck. As he walked around to join them on the other side, Daniel's phone rang, and he answered on speakerphone.

It was Sam. "Did Yashi get hold of Ben? I told her you were heading out to the house."

"She beat us here," Daniel replied. "We just got here ourselves."

"Good. I told her I'd ask Lois about the old woman in the woods, and she just came in, too."

Ben suppressed a snort. He'd heard tales of the woman from his great-aunts, some of whom claimed to have met her, some who insisted they'd been having a little tipple when they saw her. That had been years before he bought his house, probably twenty. He'd figured the odds of it being true back then were slim, and after twenty years, it seemed even less likely.

"Sweetness Brown." Lois's voice came from the phone. "She's Kenneth Brown's mother, so she's not really old—probably eighty, maybe eighty-five. Wipe that skeptical look off your face, Ben. I know what you're thinking. I'm in my sixties myself, but I can still keep you under control. I've known Sweetness for years, long before she moved into the woods. If I had that ungrateful pig for a son, I would have put myself in long-term time-out, too."

"Sweetness?" Booger's handler echoed. "What kind of name is that?"

"Says the woman named Dusty who's standing with the woman named Yashi and the dog named Booger." Lois humphed. "I don't know exactly where her cabin is, but it's on Brown property, so the other side of the tracks from the Muellers'. I doubt Kenneth would be able to give you any better directions, lousy bastard son that he is."

Her last remark made him recall something Brit had told him Saturday when talking about Kenneth Brown: *Mom says he's a bad son.* In all his dealings with Kenneth, Ben had never considered that the man had a family of his own. It was his wife's family he was always getting into trouble with, and Ben had assumed his family was dead or wanted nothing to do with him.

But obviously, Lolly had known his mother was alive and that he treated her badly. And, of course, being Lolly, she'd included Mrs. Brown in her world, at least as far as the old lady had welcomed inclusion.

"What's the story on Mrs. Brown?" Daniel asked. "Is she likely to give us trouble when we find her?"

"Oh no, she lives up to her name. She's…" It wasn't often Lois had to search for a word, Ben thought. Like Morwenna, she usually had more than enough to fill any silence. "I guess the correct term today would be intellectually challenged. She has a rather simple outlook. She likes routine—change scares her, and chaos freaks her out. As long as her husband was alive, she was fine. She stayed home, raised Kenneth, took care of the house and the garden and the chickens, and Frank did everything else. I bet she hasn't set foot off the property for thirty years or more, except for Frank's funeral."

Ben gazed at the tree where Yashi had found the tomato. The old trail he'd remembered that led to the creek down there also led straight to the tunnels where the train tracks crossed. Someone as hermit-like as

Sweetness Brown might feel more comfortable passing through tunnels—narrow, contained, hidden from casual gazes—even though there were easier routes climbing fences and crossing the open hundred feet of tracks and railroad right-of-way.

He felt someone watching him and shifted his gaze to meet Yashi's. She'd known to ask Sam about Mrs. Brown, which meant Brit must have told her something. He raised one brow, and she drew a breath.

"Brit said to tell you she's sorry she didn't mention it sooner, Ben," she said, directing her words at him even though her gaze rested on Daniel's phone. "She and Theo have never seen Sweetness. They thought maybe Lolly had embellished the story—turned a regular neighbor into a sweet old woman who lived in the magical forest."

Sounded reasonable. Lolly loved magic and innocence and wonder. Yashi thought it was just her own imagination soaring. Ben agreed but also thought she wanted to give Will some of the magic and wonder that had disappeared from his life when his parents, Yashi's parents and Yashi herself had. Lolly's upbringing had been idyllic, while Will's had been tough.

And Yashi's even tougher.

"So how did she end up living in the woods?" Dusty asked as Booger sat on his haunches and leaned his upper body against her, a thin line of drool running down her pants leg.

"Kenneth," all four cops said in unison. Sam carried on with it. "He used to live in Tulsa, but when his father died, he inherited—"

"More likely stole," Lois muttered.

"—the family property. He and his wife are definitely scary. I bet he muscled in and took over, and the only way for Sweetness to find any peace was to move out of the house."

"Booger is welcome to fart on him any time he likes," Daniel muttered.

"I'd rather see him bite him," Ben added.

Dusty rubbed the hound's long ear. "Booger doesn't bite. He's very gentle. And he came here to work, so unless there's something more we need to know, why doesn't somebody show me this cedar tree?"

Lois added one needless warning. "You guys be gentle, too. Don't hurt Sweetness."

Ben and Daniel both snorted. As if they needed a reminder not to manhandle an eighty-some-year-old mentally fragile woman. After the goodbye, Daniel hefted the backpack Ben had brought, and they headed to the shade of the porch. Ben dropped behind to walk beside Yashi. "You're not going with us."

"I know. I'm not dressed for it."

He didn't mean to let his gaze skim the length of her body. Didn't mean to notice that the orangey-pink color of her top looked particularly good against her golden skin. Didn't intend to appreciate the snug fit of the white pants that ended midcalf or even look at the whimsical flip-flops bearing orangey-pink flowers and sparkles. He didn't mean to let himself notice that she looked as appealing on this hot summer day as a long, tall iced tea and a sweet breeze.

*Damn.*

"Do you think Sweetness Brown has anything to do with what happened?"

It took effort to pull his brain back from its reverent wandering and concentrate. "I doubt it. My great-aunts used to tell us stories about her, how she roamed the woods at night and was always watching little kids who weren't doing what they were told. Great-Aunt Norma said she was a spirit. Great-Aunt Beatrice said she was a fairy. Great-Aunt Opal said she was a leprechaun, and Great-Aunt Weezer said she was a figment of their elderberry wine."

"I thought most of you Little Bears were teetotalers."

"Just Mom, Weezer and me." Yashi knew his father had been a drunk—everyone who'd ever met David Little Bear had known that—and that Ben's younger brother had followed in his footsteps. She also knew neither of those were the reasons Ben didn't drink. He didn't like the taste, and he liked being in control.

Sometimes, in his months with her, he hadn't felt like he had much control. How had he never guessed, in all his life up to that time, that giving up control could actually be a good thing?

His gaze slanted toward her, cool and blonde and beautiful, and he thought of a few specific instances when she'd been totally in control, and heat began spiraling inside him that put the outside temperature to shame.

It had been a very good thing.

They caught up with the others at the back side of the porch. Daniel had delved into the backpack, removing cans of bug spray and bottles of water. Yashi stopped a distance back, having no desire to let the repellant mist drift over her until the bugs had come calling, and watched their preparations.

All three of them wore tactical pants and long-sleeved shirts that were tucked in. While the others sprayed for bugs, Ben unrolled his sleeves and buttoned the cuffs. It was a shame to hide those gorgeous muscles, but likely Sweetness Brown wouldn't be impressed by them, and it would be a bigger shame for him to come back covered with chigger bites or poison ivy.

Apparently bored, Booger wandered down the steps, sniffed his way to the garden, then stopped to watch a hawk soaring overhead. He didn't look like Superdog to the rescue. Truthfully, he seemed to be contemplating sinking down right where he was and taking a nice long nap while those pesky humans tramped through the woods.

But appearances were deceiving. Ben often wore a similar contemplative look, but it was entirely opposite of what was going on inside him.

Finally, after putting on gloves and ball caps, Ben, Daniel and Dusty were ready to go. Ben directed Dusty to what remained of the tomato, then hesitated at the bottom of the steps. "Do you want the keys to my house?"

She shook her head, appreciative of the offer but unwilling to go so far away, and he joined the others with a nod. When they had moved with a rustle past the Christmas tree, she sighed. Sat in an old rocker near the back door. Breathed too deeply of bug spray and coughed. Moved to a chair farther away. Listened to the bees and thought about Lolly's admission that she wanted to get bee hives even though she was sensitive to their stings. *But think of the incredible honey I could give you*, she'd tempted.

*Think of using the epinephrine pen you already carry*, Yashi had responded.

And that was all in the first five minutes after they left. How long would it take them to find Sweetness? Would she be home or off wandering? Would she talk to them, or would the sudden appearance of three strangers and a dog be too disruptive for her to cope with?

It didn't take long for stillness to settle. Not silence, not like the last few times. She was aware of the traffic on the turnpike, and the chimes hanging from various tree branches tinkled with the occasional whisper of a breeze. Someone's dog was barking in the distance, and someone's cow mooed a response. A lazy rooster whose concept of dawn was a little off crowed a time or two.

But the stillness was there, heavier than those distractions, the emptiness of a house that routinely bubbled with life. It was as if the very boards and bricks were aware that their family was gone, that violence had been visited upon them and things might have changed forever.

Will and Lolly, Brit and Theo might never come back.

Yashi's heart stopped beating for a long, painful moment. Her breath wheezed, anguish releasing before she rejected it, denied it. Will and Lolly were strong, and no one would protect Theo more fiercely than them.

They would survive this, and they would come home, and this house would be happy again.

That was the only outcome her wounded soul could accept.

Sweat rolled down Ben's face, and every part of his body was either sweltering, stinging or itching. Daniel and Dusty weren't faring any better, and Booger's tongue was hanging as he picked a path down the steep incline to the creek.

"Why couldn't Miz Brown live in the middle of a nice, cleared pasture?" Daniel muttered, followed by a grunt when he tripped over a rock hidden beneath knee-deep dead leaves.

"Aw, what's the fun of that?" Dusty asked. She gripped a clump of sumac branches in one hand to steady her as she half jumped, half slid down a vertical boulder.

Ahead, Daniel slipped again, and Ben caught him by the strap of the backpack. While he had hold, he pulled out a bottle of water, let him go and took a deep drink. He was pretty sure the sun was reaching inside and leaching out the moisture even as it rolled down his throat. He should have insisted Yashi go to his house to wait. Granted, she would be sitting in the shade on Lolly's porch and not exerting herself, and she would have the advantage of the light winds that they'd lost once they started descending.

But she was alone, and alone at the Mueller house these days was on the far side of creepy. What if the kidnapper got impatient and decided to snatch another family member to let the police know he was serious?

But why would he get impatient? The lack of movement on his proposed trade fell on him. So far, he'd given them two messages, neither including information on where and when he wanted to conduct the trade. He hadn't given them a way to get in touch with him, hadn't contacted them in more than twenty-four hours. Even if they were willing to play along with his outrageous demand, they couldn't play without him.

"Whoo!" Dusty's boots connected with concrete in a solid thunk as she jumped the last few feet to the ground.

The trail had taken them directly to the north end of the two tunnels. The creek flowed through only one, and even with recent rains, it was hardly a trickle. Insects darted about on the surface of the pool at the tunnel's mouth, and Ben thought he saw a mudbug scurrying through the silt.

Boomer went into the tunnel a few yards, sat and regarded his handler with his sweet, sad-looking face. She pulled a contraption from her own backpack, something that turned a bottle of water into a pooch fountain, and he drank heavily before walking the extent of his lead and looking back at her.

"We've had this talk," Dusty said as she opened her own bottle. "I need rest more often than you do."

Booger didn't look happy, but he turned back to studying the other side of the tunnel.

As soaked as the rest of them, Daniel leaned against the wall while guzzling his water. "I don't suppose we could be lucky enough to walk out the other end and see Mrs. Brown sitting on her porch offering iced tea and a fan."

"Stranger things have happened." Like Daniel's fiancée coming back five years after she dumped him. Like Yashi showing up once again in Ben's life and him not running away. He knew his reputation as stoic and strong, but sometimes a man could be too strong for his own good. Dealing with her even in the performance of his duties wasn't a wise move, not given their past. That he'd loved her. Missed her. Still found it far too easy to want her if he let himself.

And he might be tempted to let himself. He spent a lot of time with Daniel, who'd also been loved and betrayed by a woman. Who'd gotten a second chance and was now happily married with a baby due anytime. Exactly where Ben had thought he would be at about this age.

Did he believe in second chances?

Before he had to consider the question, Booger lifted his head, scenting the air, and tugged on his lead. His nose was light-years more sensitive than humans'; was his hearing also that much better? Because the air still smelled the same—moist, stinky of human sweat and decay—and no unusual sounds had reached Ben's ears.

The tunnels opened into more tangled wood, though at least it was level on this side. The stream went quietly on its way, deeper but narrow enough to cross on flat stones that stood a few inches above the surface. Ben expected them to teeter under his weight, but they were surprisingly stable. There went the great-aunts' ideas of

Mrs. Brown's true nature. What need did spirits, fairies or leprechauns have for stepping-stones when they could magically traverse any obstacles?

The sun overhead heated the air but left them mostly in shade, unable to penetrate much of the tree canopy. They were definitely on Brown land now; the railroad right-of-way served as boundary. As far as Ben could guess, they were pretty equidistant from both houses and the Pickerings', though he couldn't see anything but trees to confirm it.

Booger surged forward, dragging Dusty behind, scattering leaves with each touch of his giant paws and floppy ears. His tongue was still hanging out, but it was excitement now rather than thirst. Whatever scents he'd picked up from that chunk of uneaten tomato must be heavier on the air over here.

Their surroundings changed drastically within a few yards. One minute they were stumbling through dead leaves and overgrowth; the next they scuffed into a clearing. In the middle of the clearing stood a shack that didn't appear to have been repaired beyond the urgent in the decades it had stood there, and in an old rocker in front of the door sat Sweetness Brown. No spirit or fairy, just a round gray-haired woman wearing oversize clothes. Her scowl created lines across her forehead, and her hands clenched the chair arms tightly.

Booger closed half the distance between them, sat down, bayed and looked at Dusty. She joined him, rubbing him all over and murmuring compliments before slipping a toy from her pack to him.

Ben and Daniel exchanged looks, then Ben approached her. Though she appeared unarmed, a sufficiently disturbed person didn't need a weapon to be dangerous. Not even a round gray-haired grandmotherly sort. "Mrs. Brown, I'm Ben Little Bear. I'm a detective with the Cedar Creek Police Department."

Her gaze was brown with a haze that made him think of cataracts. It slid across his face, and something there sharpened. As a kid, Ben had heard his elders describe people saying, *The lights are on, but no one's home.* Sweetness Brown might not be home, but she wasn't entirely gone, either. More like standing outside the back door looking in. She studied him for a moment, her head tilted to one side, then she smoothed out her pink cotton shirt and brushed the knees of her green polyester pants.

"Little Bear. I know that name." Her voice was rusty but held soft undertones. "You're one of Weezer's boys, aren't you?"

He crouched so she didn't have to look up so far. "You know Great-Aunt Weezer?"

"Of course. She used to live across the road with her sisters. Where you live now. She used to come visit with me sometimes. Brought me Indian tacos and apricot turnovers. Back when I lived in the other house." Mention of the other house brought fleeting sadness to her face. Longing for the days when she'd lived there with her husband?

Ben rarely needed confirmation that Great-Aunt was a sly old woman, but once again he got it anyway. Telling her sisters Mrs. Brown was an alcohol-fueled hallucination when she knew for a fact who—and what—the woman was. He would like to think it was for Mrs. Brown's protection rather than because of Great-Aunt's pure orneriness.

Mrs. Brown gazed past him. "Who's the pretty boy?"

Ben glanced at his companions, still standing ten feet away. "That's Booger," he replied, and the old woman smiled.

"Gee, thanks," Daniel said drily. "I'm Detective Daniel Harper, and this is Dusty Smith. She owns the dog."

"I've had dogs before. *He* owns *her*. I seen the way she chased after him. I don't blame her. He's beautiful. Smells a little ripe, though."

She must have a nose like a bloodhound herself, Ben thought, if she could separate Booger's distinctive aroma from the sweat-soaked people he'd brought along. None of them were fit to be in polite company.

She rocked a few times, the bare old wood creaking pleasantly. "I guess you've come about the boy."

Ben and Daniel exchanged looks again, and Daniel moved closer as he gently asked, "Do you know what happened to the Muellers, Mrs. Brown?"

"No," she said, shaking her head, then nodding, then shaking it again. Evasion or just confusion?

"But you know the Muellers."

"I know Lolly. Nice girl. Sweet as her name." Her smile this time was vacant. "That's what my Frank used to say about me. Sweet as my name. 'Cause my name is Sweetness. Not made up nor nothing. It's right there on my birth certificate. My mama was happy to have a girl after so many boys. Seven of them. The youngest was twelve when I was borned. She thought she was all done with having babies, and here I came." She laughed with delight, softening the lines of her face, but the emotion faded too soon. "She's gone now. And Daddy and the boys and Frank. I sure miss them."

Ben gave her a moment to grieve, feeling a little of it himself. Outliving everyone she'd loved had certainly never been her goal. It was unfair, God taking her parents, brothers, in-laws and her husband, and leaving her nothing but an obnoxious son who didn't give a damn about her. Life wasn't fair, people always preached, but Ben had spent a long time wondering why not. It was the best model humanity could ask for: a person did good and benefited; a person did bad and suffered. They got what they deserved. After enough suffering, people would stop doing bad, and life would be better all around.

But he wasn't here to solve the problems of the world. Just his own little corner of it. "Miz Brown, when did you last see Lolly?"

Sweetness rocked a few more times before shaking her head. "Lord, I don't ever know what day it is. Two days ago. Maybe. I kind of lose track of time." She waved a hand around them. "No newspaper delivery, no television, none of them computers or phones. I don't have guests or appointments or any need to go anywhere else. I'm a free spirit. Frank used to say that, too."

And that was exactly the way she wanted it. Knowing what he did of Kenneth Brown, Ben couldn't blame her. When he'd moved back home—most likely uninvited—after his father's death, this little cabin deep in the woods, probably built by the first settlers to claim this land, must have been the only place she could find peace and tranquility. Her son was too lazy to tramp through the woods to bother her here. As she'd implied, there were no luxuries, but a spring bubbled nearby. There was a fireplace and enough wood to heat the cabin through several winters, and an outhouse sat at the far edge of the trees.

A hard but simple life for a woman who couldn't cope with change.

"What do you know about the Mueller boy, Mrs. Brown?" Daniel asked.

"Poor kid." She shook her head regretfully. "Oh, he was crying awful. Scared me something fierce. I don't usually run into crying little boys on my midnight rambles. That's what Frank called my little walks in the woods. He'd say, 'Sweetness, you're gonna get hurt out there,' and I'd tell him there's nothing in the woods to hurt me. Hurtin' comes from people, not nature."

"So you saw Theo Mueller when you were out walking?" Now Daniel crouched near Ben. "Do you remember when that was? Do you know why he was crying?"

"Theo. That's a nice name. You don't meet many Theos these days." She focused on him after a moment. "He was crying because he was scared, of course. Let the bogeyman drag you out of your house in your pajamas in the middle of the night and see if you don't cry, too. I cheered to myself, all quiet-like, when Lolly's boy kicked him right square in the shin and ran away. I prayed God to send him to me, and He did, he came running straight at me, and I hid him from the bogeyman. Oh, that man cussed until he finally gave up and got in his van and drove away."

His muscles knotted, Ben straightened and walked to the cabin. Daniel's voice was quiet behind him, kindly with his questions, but Ben's focus was narrowed ahead. The door stood open, a broken screen door laid over the opening in an attempt to keep out the insects. He carefully lifted it to one side and stepped into the doorway. The cabin was one room, the furnishings sparse: another rocker, a battered lawn chair, a wooden table with one short leg fixed by a rock, two wooden chairs, an aluminum camp cot in one corner and another corner making up the kitchen. Open shelves on the wall showed the kind of dried goods he'd expected—beans, rice, flour—along with a supply of canned and boxed foods. Lolly gave the woman fresh vegetables; was she also the one who'd supplied the soup, macaroni and cheese, peaches and tuna and Kool-Aid?

The only other items in the cabin were two cases holding books and magazines, a bureau and an old-fashioned steamer trunk. When Ben spotted two small feet in two small tennis shoes missing their laces sticking out behind the trunk, he swallowed hard, a chill rushing through him. "Theo. It's Officer Bear. You can come out now."

For a long moment, the feet didn't move. Couldn't move? *Please, God, no.* Sweetness was harmless, Lois had said. She wouldn't hurt a little boy. She had no history of violence. She liked Lolly. Surely she couldn't have done a thing to hurt Theo.

Ben felt movement behind him and shifted slightly

to see Sweetness, with Daniel giving her a hand. She eased into the crowded doorway, unaware of the sweat that had broken out on Ben's forehead. Daniel noticed, though. His gaze swept across the room, stopped on the feet, and he blanched.

"It's okay, Lolly's boy," Sweetness said in a cooing, coaxing voice. "You can come out. These police officers are here to take care of you."

Seconds ticked past, and still those little feet didn't move. Then slowly, one disappeared behind the trunk, followed by the other, and just as slowly Theo's head appeared over it. First his hair, standing in a dozen directions, then his pale, tearstained face, then his worse-for-wear ninja pajamas.

"Officer Bear," he whimpered, and he jumped to his feet, ran around the trunk and flung himself into Ben's arms.

Sweat trickled down Yashi's spine as she tried to calculate how long it would take them to find Mrs. Brown's cabin, talk to her and come back again, but she knew enough about scent hounds and searching and woods to know she didn't have a clue. Ben and the others were covering rugged ground, led by a dog who had to separate his particular target from all the other thousands of smells out there. It was miserably hot and humid, putting extra demands on their bodies. The place Mrs. Brown called home might be well hidden, or she might not be there, or she might be too frightened to cooperate. There were snakes, spiders, scorpions and an abundance of biting, stinging insects, to say nothing of rocks to fall off, holes to fall into and scrubby brush to scrape raw any skin it touched.

She'd been rocking but had stopped, tired of mistaking the slight creak of the wood for something important. She'd heard a dog a while ago, like the baying she'd heard on television and movies, but she hadn't been able to pinpoint where it came from. It just seemed to echo off the trees, and it had made her heart race at the same time her stomach knotted.

Now she was pacing the length of the side porch, pivoting at the north end, when a sound caught her attention. It was soft, rustly, not stealthy. A heavy layer of leaves muffling the sound of feet?

She hustled to the back steps, and the noise expanded to include panting, the slap of branches and a distinctly female grunt. Slowly she started down the steps, reaching the bottom just as the branches of the red cedar swayed, pushed out of the way two feet above the ground by a big tan head with ears dragging and jowls swaying. Fifteen feet behind Booger came Dusty, her appearance confirming this had been no walk in the park, and behind her...

Yashi's breath caught. Her heart rate increased so quickly that she got light-headed, and it seemed a balloon was about to burst in her chest. Ben cleared the cedar, lowered his head to speak to the boy he was carrying, then set him on the grass.

"Oh Theo." Tears welled. Yashi had been praying, but she'd lacked faith that God was listening, that her pleas were eloquent enough to get her little cousin back, and *oh, thank You, Jesus*, here he was in his favorite pajamas and his favorite outgrown sneakers that Brit had cut out the toes so he could wear them as house shoes.

A cry catching in her throat, she started toward him, and he began running, too. But when she would have swept him into her arms and swung him around, holding him tightly enough to feel his heart beating safely all the way through her own heart, he skidded to a stop, and his small determined fist made contact with her jaw.

Yashi stood frozen. He was a little boy without much power to put into a punch, so the throb in her jaw was minimal, but the fact that he'd hit her at all… She'd seen it, felt it, but couldn't believe it. Theo didn't hit people, not even Brit when she pestered him out of his mind. He was a sweet, gentle boy.

Who'd been through God knows what kind of trauma. She swallowed back her hurt, her shock, and said, "Theo, sweetie, I've been so worried about you—"

Before she could finish, he drew back and hit her again, this time in the stomach. Her breath caught, and the rushing in her ears dampened the sounds around her—his name called sharply by Ben, and even more sharply by Brit, her steps thundering. The censure in her voice was enough to make Theo burst into tears.

"I hate her, I hate her! This is all her fault! The man took Mama and Daddy, and he hurt them, and he tried to hurt me, too, and it's all her fault! He said so—he said, 'You can blame your cousin Yashi for this.'"

By then, Brit had jumped down the steps and run to join them. She gathered Theo in her arms but turned an anguished look on Yashi. "Are you okay? Did he hurt you?"

Her heart more than anything, but Yashi pretended otherwise, smiled tightly and shook her head. She was in shock. *Her* fault? Was it true? Was the kidnapper putting her family through all this horror because of something *she* had done? Oh God, she couldn't bear that. She'd made enemies, sure. What prosecutor didn't? But a defendant who hated her so much that he would hurt her family?

With Theo sobbing in Brit's arms, they headed for the porch. Dusty busied herself with Booger, and Quint, who must have received a heads-up from Ben to bring Brit to the house, stood quietly near the rocker, his gaze directed toward the road out front. Yashi felt isolated, standing in the bright sun and frozen hard inside. She hugged herself tightly, unable to think of anything to do but breathe, and even that hurt.

The quaking in her muscles was spreading outward, making her nerves tremble, prickling her skin and her eyes. She wouldn't fall apart. Couldn't. Not here. Not now. If she did, how would she ever put herself back together enough to help Will and Lolly?

Ben moved stealthily, as he so often did, and laid his hand on her shoulder from behind. "He didn't mean it."

Theo was terrified for his mom and dad, but he probably did believe she was to blame. After all, the man who'd hurt them had said so, and what eight-year-old boy could overcome his fear to argue with that?

Despite her best efforts, a little sob escaped her. Her whole life, she had treasured Will, all that was left of the innocent part of her childhood, and she loved his wife and children as well. She would have done anything, given up anything, for them, and instead she'd brought danger right inside their home, the one place they should be safest.

Could they forgive her? Could she forgive herself?

"Yashi."

She glanced at Ben's hand, big and strong like the rest of him. He'd removed his gloves, letting her feel skin and calluses and heat where her shoulder was bare. Trembling, she raised her hand to touch his, and his thumb shifted to rub against hers. More heat swept over her as he moved closer, and with it came a sense of security, an offer of hope, reassurance that she desperately needed.

"We don't know much more." His voice was quiet, its cadence calm and even. "That's the first thing Theo's said other than my name since Miz Brown found him by the Christmas tree Friday night. We've called an ambulance, and after he's been checked out, Morwenna's mum is going to talk to him. She's a psychiatrist, and she works with us a lot."

When he paused, the faint wail of a siren drifted on the air, growing steadily louder. Abruptly, it switched off, the silence startling, and an ambulance pulled into the driveway.

"He'll be all right. They all will."

His fingers tightened briefly, then he gently pulled away. Lord, how could she feel so alone after such minimal contact?

She wiped her eyes, stinging from the sweat on her face, and gave herself a mental shake before joining everyone else on the porch. The paramedics began examining Theo while Brit held his hand in both of hers. Poor kid, she looked equal parts relieved and terrified. So thankful to have her brother back and now doubly scared for her parents.

When Theo caught sight of Yashi, his entire little body tensed as if he might launch himself at her again. Brit slid her arm around his shoulders, whispering assurances to him, and he slowly sagged back as if he might collapse without her assistance.

Yashi's heart hurt as she moved away from them. She waited around front instead, thanking Dusty, petting Booger, until the paramedics brought Theo around, strapped to a gurney, his hand still tightly clenching Brit's. Ben and Quint stopped at the steps while they headed on out to the ambulance.

"Dusty, Quint is taking Brit to the hospital," Ben said. "He's offered to give you and Booger a ride home on the way."

"I appreciate it. If you need any help getting Daniel back out of the woods, just give a holler. Yashi, I wish we could have met under better circumstances."

Yashi shook her hand. "You brought Theo home. It can't get much better than that."

Within a few moments, they were gone, leaving Yashi and Ben alone on the porch. She wished he would touch her again—nothing intimate or personal, just her hand. If he held her hand and told her once more that her family would be all right, she would believe him and would feel better at least for a moment.

But when he did finally do something, it wasn't reach out to her. He heaved a weary sigh and said, "Let's get something to drink. Then we need to talk."

# Chapter 7

Ben invited Yashi inside. She hesitated, then lifted the thin, peachy fabric of her shirt away from her body, and it fell back, damp enough to cling to her breasts and middle, and she walked through the door. Immediately, she shivered, goose bumps rising on her skin. His, too, even though it was only seventy-five degrees inside the house.

Granted, his goose bumps might not have anything at all to do with temperature.

He expected her to take a seat in the living room, but her flip-flops slapped across the floor and into the kitchen. Of course she wouldn't choose to sit on the good furniture when she was soaked with sweat and he was a whole lot worse. His clothes were dirty and stained, he smelled of bug spray, and he had a rip in his sleeve from a slide into dewberry brambles and a tear in his pants, dotted with blood, from a run-in with a barbed-wire fence on the shortcut back from Miz Brown's.

She slid into a chair at the dining table next to windows that looked out on his own few acres of woods. Light coming in made her hair look more gold than blond, and highlighted the tension and the guilt in her eyes, the set of her mouth, even the rounding of her shoulders.

He washed his hands before getting two bottles of water from the refrigerator and grabbing the container of leftover cookies. As he set them down on the table, she said, "Thank you for bringing Theo back."

It hadn't been the reunion she'd been hoping for. In her head, she was smart enough to understand trauma, but it must have broken her heart when he reacted the way he did. Ben hadn't expected physical violence, but he hadn't been surprised by it, either. Miz Brown said he hadn't spoken a word the entire time he'd been with her, and he'd done nothing but cling to Ben all the way home—wouldn't even let go so Ben could climb the fence, then lift him over. Ben hadn't seen him speak to Brit, either. He was guessing it might be some time before Theo felt safe enough to talk again.

"Daniel is still with Sweetness Brown, getting a statement," Ben said at last. "She took a liking to him. He's going to stay there until Sam shows up. He wants to talk to her, too."

"He won't make her leave, will he?"

Ben scratched a place where a thorn from a black lo-

cust tree had scraped the back of his neck. "Some people might say it's not an appropriate way for a woman
her age to live."

Yashi met his gaze directly, reminding him for a moment of the ambitious, confident prosecutor he'd seen
in court so many times. "Maybe it's not some people's
business."

"These days everything is someone else's business."
Even things a man said to the woman he loved in confidence could be taken out of context and used against
him in court.

Having neither time nor the desire to let his thoughts go
off in old directions, he took a cookie from the container
and ate half of it in one bite. "Sam's a good guy. He'll do
what's right. But he can't just ignore the situation."

Her mouth, thinned in a line, suggested she wanted
to argue further, but she didn't. She took a napkin from
the holder on the table—a few pieces of wood nailed
together crookedly and slathered with red paint, a gift
from one of his nieces—and chose her own cookie.
"So…we misinterpreted the message spray-painted on
the door. It's not Brit the guy is after. It's me."

She sounded grim and bleak and regretful. It would
be a tough revelation for anyone to handle, but especially Yashi. She wasn't obsessive about her family, but
she valued everything about them—every visit, every
conversation, every laugh. She understood loss too well
and was deeply grateful for what she had. She didn't
take them for granted. It would hurt deeply that she
was in any way responsible for what had happened to

them, even if it was just drawing the bastard's attention to them.

"The pictures the kidnapper stole of Brit…you were also in them. His note and his text didn't reference her. We just assumed because she'd sneaked out of the house that night, it was her he wanted." He finished off the cookie and reached for another. "We'll still talk to the people on our lists that are involved with Lolly and Will, but just to cover the bases. It's your life we're going to look into now."

If he hadn't already felt grim, that statement would have made him so. It was a simple fact, but that didn't stop it from sounding ominous. Odds were, the kidnapper had met Yashi in court when she was with the DA's office. Her practice in the years since then had been civil cases—adoptions, wills, divorces and so forth. And looking at her time in the DA's office would certainly include checking out her personal life. Ben and Yashi had been together a year and kept it hidden from everyone. They'd been broken up for five years, and still kept it hidden. And now, in a day or two or three, it would be common knowledge in his world.

Apparently, her mind had wandered the same direction. Meticulously smoothing the paper napkin in front of her, she remarked, "They'll ask about my sex life now and then. They'll want to know if there's a crazy ex-boyfriend stalking me. I can't lie, Ben. Not with Will and Lolly's lives on the line."

"Good thing I'm not crazy." His attempt at humor falling flat, he met her gaze. "I wouldn't ask you to lie. Even if their lives weren't on the line." Choosing not to let their coworkers and friends know they had been a couple was one thing. Given the nature of their jobs and how often they were thrown together, it had been easier to separate professional from personal. It had given them breathing room to let things go the way fate wanted. But lying in a criminal investigation? Nothing from their shared past was worth withholding information.

She sighed heavily. "What do we do now?"

He took a deep breath, and the rankness of his own odor wrinkled his nose. Standing, he picked up his water. "First, I'm going to shower and change. If Daniel and Ben aren't back by the time I finish, you and I will go into town—" Hearing a grumble from her stomach, he went on. "Get some lunch and go to your office. Since I assume there isn't a crazy ex-boyfriend stalking you, or you would have filed a report already, we'll start looking at the people you sent to prison."

The reference to her cases made a serious mood darker. He didn't need to ask who she would put at the top of her list, just as she didn't need to hear him doubt it. Lloyd Wind wasn't a bad guy, despite being arrested for—and prosecuted for, and wrongfully convicted of—murder. According to the media, he was free, life was good and he held no grudges against the good people of Cedar County.

Though, murderer or not, Ben conceded that four years in prison might make a good, innocent man dream of vengeance. But to actually put a plan like that into play? To hurt other innocent people and terrify a little boy? Not likely.

"I can meet you at my office. I need to clean up, too." Her voice was stiff, her gaze settled somewhere out the window.

He took the steps needed to bring him even with her. His height gave him an advantage in the intimidation game even when the other person was standing straight. Seated in a chair, Yashi couldn't help but think he was looming over her. *You always loom,* she used to tease. "We just figured out that you're the real target here. You don't get to climb into your bright yellow car and take off on country roads alone. Brit has been in protective custody, and she'll stay there. Theo will have a guard at the hospital. As of this moment, your liberties are greatly restricted as well. Don't leave this house without me."

Her brows rose and her eyes widened as if her hair was about to catch fire, but the offense faded as quickly as it flared. One of the things he'd always admired about her was that her independence was tempered with a healthy dose of common sense. Everyone loved to think they could take care of themselves if need be, but truth was, most needed help. Victims weren't generally a threat to an attacker; that was part of what made them victims.

"All right." She picked up another cookie, flashed a weak smile and bit into it. "Make it quick, would you? I feel the sweat drying and cracking on my skin as I speak."

He couldn't help it. His gaze slid down her face, following the curve of her throat to where the rounded neck of the orange top started. It slid across the strip of fabric that crossed her shoulder, to her left arm, golden, not muscular but not slack, either. He still remembered the incredible pleasure of exploring her skin for the first time, of finding it was that same golden shade everywhere, that it was soft and sensitive to his slightest touch, his lightest kisses. If he touched her right now, he was sure his fingers would recognize her very cells, as if their memory was imprinted in his very cells.

A surge of heat rushed through him, literally knocking him a step off balance. He needed that shower more than ever—and colder than he'd intended—but he was hesitant to walk away.

After a moment of his hovering, she shooed him off. "I won't leave. I won't open the door to anyone but Daniel or Sam. I'll sit here and stuff myself with your mother's cookies and wait. Go."

And he went, because he knew she would keep her word. He'd always known that about her, right up to the very second on the witness stand when, in the middle of a major trial, she'd looked him straight in the eye and given him his first clue how wrong he'd been.

*Detective Little Bear, how long have you been friends with Lloyd Wind?*

He'd trusted her, and it had almost killed him. Was he really going to repeat that mistake?

His answer came as he walked out of the kitchen and turned toward his bedroom. He really was, but only professionally. If anyone knew how to keep his personal and professional lives separate, it was him. He would never trust her personally again.

There'd been no sign of Daniel and Sam by the time Ben came out of the bedroom again, dressed in a fresh uniform, his black hair falling in damp strands over his forehead. He smelled of soap and cologne, something earthy and spicy, reminding Yashi on the surface of warm sun, clear skies and new flowers. Underneath those top notes, though, the scent brought feelings rather than images: springtime, life, renewal, hope.

Feeling doubly sweaty and stinky in comparison, she followed him out of the house and across the road to his truck. She avoided looking at the side yard, where her sweet Theo had punched her, and at the porch where he'd clung so helplessly and angrily to Brit. She avoided the house, too, as much as was possible, leaving little besides the woods and her Bug to focus on.

Ben's truck was four-wheel drive, giving her a step up onto the running board. She was about to slide inside when her gaze narrowed on the Bug's hood. Slowly she lowered one foot back to the ground, then the other. She circled the front end of the truck and started toward her car but stopped ten feet away.

"What—" Ben stopped beside her. She felt his gaze connect with her face, then he tracked what she was staring at. "Damn."

He said the word very quietly, with very little emotion, which amped up her tension exponentially. When Ben was quietest, he was angriest or most alarmed. If he wasn't standing right there beside her, she would be running for safety—jumping into her car and locking the doors, taking off like a wild woman down the road, tearing back to his house and hiding in the darkest corner of his bedroom closet.

"Stay here."

She didn't need to be told. She was being a good victim—standing utterly still, saying nothing—not because she *wanted* to but because her body was ignoring her brain's commands to flee. Her emotional side wanted to rush to the car, grab what she could now clearly see was a cell phone, glaringly out of place on the dusty yellow hood, and toss it hard enough into the woods to land in the creek. The only other option her emotions offered was to pretend she hadn't seen it, pretend it didn't look like some deadly black electronic omen, to climb into Ben's truck and demand that he take her home.

Her brain kept her frozen and still.

Ben radioed in, requesting assistance, then took some pictures of the scene with his cell phone. He studied the ground for footprints, tire prints, and walked close to the car to stare at the phone for a moment. She watched him do these things, registered them in her rational mind, but didn't really grasp them. She was too numb.

The kidnapper had been here—after the ambulance had left, after Quint had taken Brit and Dusty and Booger away, after she and Ben had walked right past the vehicles on their way to his house. The man had walked right up to her car, left the phone, and they hadn't seen him, heard him or known he was there.

Oh God.

Her stomach roiled, the cookies threatening to put in a reappearance. She had felt a lot of things while in Ben's house, and chief among them was safe. The cottage was the house version of its owner: strong and sturdy, damn near unassailable. It had stood through drought, ice storms, blizzards and tornadoes and never lost so much as a shingle. One time a wildfire had wiped out every tree and blade of grass on the property, but the house hadn't even blistered.

And while she had been sitting comfortably within the protection of its walls, with the added security of Ben across the table from her, the man who had kidnapped Will and Lolly and so badly traumatized Theo had walked right up to her car across the road and left his little gift. Was he a freaking ghost? Would he ever leave them a clue?

She squared her shoulders. She hated being clueless and helpless, but no way was she going to give in to hopelessness as well. The son of a bitch might get off on tormenting her, or he really might want to trade Will and Lolly for her, which, of course, she would agree to.

Even though the idea terrified her.

A vehicle approaching jerked her gaze to the road an instant before Sam's truck rounded the curve. When it turned into the drive, Daniel was out of the passenger seat before the truck came to a complete stop. "What the hell, Ben?"

Ben looked at both men. "I figured you'd be coming back this way." He nodded toward the woods behind the house.

"There's a trail from Kenneth Brown's place," Sam replied.

"Three bent blades of grass don't make a trail." Daniel's appearance had suffered most from the trek through the woods. His hair stood on end, his cheeks were red with heat, and his normally neat uniform looked as if he'd slept the last three nights on a hard slab of ground while being poked with sticks. "So this guy just drives right up to the scene of the crime in the middle of the day with a detective unit parked in the driveway and drops off a phone?"

At the same time, Yashi and Ben said, "No." She nodded for him to go on.

"There were no cars. We talked in the kitchen, then I cleaned up, and there weren't any cars."

"Maybe you didn't notice?" Sam made it a question, but Yashi knew he understood how very little in life escaped Ben's attention.

"As close to the road as the house sits, I notice every car. Whoever left the phone had to be on foot."

They all turned as one to look at the wood to the east. There was no fence separating it from the road, just an incline that was gentle here beside the driveway, then climbed steeply all the way to the railroad underpass. Not so steeply, though, especially with all the exposed rock face providing handholds, that a person in average shape couldn't manage it. Then it would be a simple matter of hiking through the trees, the growth far less pervasive than behind the house.

Did it make her feel any better that the kidnapper had sneaked through the woods rather than boldly driving up to the house? Logic said it should, but it didn't.

Daniel pulled a pair of gloves and an evidence bag from his pocket and walked to the Bug. After tugging on the gloves, a bit of a job when every part of him was soaked with sweat, he picked up the cell phone and swiped the screen a couple of times. When he held it up to show Ben and Sam, even from a distance, Yashi could see the photograph there.

She'd felt so bad yesterday morning when she'd gotten the text and the picture of Will. She had wanted desperately to see for herself that Lolly and Theo were all right. Now, she'd actually seen Theo, who was far from all right, and here was a picture of Lolly. Her blond hair was limp, huge strands straggling loose of the ponytail she wore. She stared defiantly at the camera, at least, with her one good eye. The other was blackened and swollen practically shut. *The man took Mama and Daddy, and he hurt them...and it's all her fault!*

Yashi's knees wobbled, tears filled her eyes and she was pretty sure she was going to land hard on the ground when strong fingers wrapped around her upper arm. Not Ben, she instinctively knew, and since Daniel was still holding the phone, that left Sam. Through the blur, she saw his concerned face, and despite the rushing in her ears, she heard his somber voice.

"Ben's going to take you home, okay? You're going to get something to eat, drink a lot of water, stay out of the heat, maybe rest a little. You're our key to finding them, Yashi. We need you in fighting form. Daniel and JJ and I will handle things on this end, and Quint and Lois are keeping watch on the kids. Your only focus now is to help us find this guy. Got it?"

She nodded.

He walked her to the passenger side of Ben's truck, where the door stood open, just as she'd left it. He boosted her onto the running board, waited until she was seated and buckled in, then squeezed her hand tightly. "We'll find them, Yashi. Believe that."

She wanted to believe with all her heart. But… "If it comes down to a trade—"

"It won't."

"But if it does—"

"It won't." His gaze locked with hers a long time before he squeezed her hand again, stepped back and closed the door. There were things he wasn't saying, facts he didn't want her thinking about, and she didn't press him. If she gave herself a few moments to think clearly, those facts would come on their own. Somewhere in her brain were statistics on how often kidnap victims were released unharmed. On the odds of a kidnapper letting go victims who could identify him. On the risks of trusting a criminal who'd managed to successfully subdue, control and abduct two adults all on his own without leaving a single clue behind.

A criminal who held such a powerful grudge against Yashi that he was willing to kill her family before he killed her.

He wanted her dead or destroyed.

And by God, she wanted the same for him.

"What do you want for lunch?"

It had been a silent drive back into town. Ben was edgy. Violence made him that way. People getting hurt did, too. Seeing that picture of Lolly, her face distorted by the black eye, had left a hard knot in his gut. Lolly was truly one of the nicest people he knew. She was happy and wanted to share it with everyone. She always expected the best, always believed the best.

And Yashi… In that instant before Sam caught her, Ben had been stricken by her grief. He'd never seen her so lost, so vulnerable. She was capable, independent, standing up for others as well as herself. When the victims of her cases had been too traumatized to be of much help, she used to tell them, *You don't have to be strong. I'll be strong for you.* Seeing her—not weak; he could never call her that—but not strong had shaken his image of her.

Now she sat blankly in the other seat, her gaze unfocused, her shoulders rounded. "I don't care."

"Today's lunch special at the café is chicken and dumplings." She loved chicken and dumplings but had never learned to make them. Why should she, she'd asked, when his mother did them so well?

"All right."

That dull voice grated on his nerves, prompting him to go on. "And Mom won't even mind that you look like you've been rolling in the gutter. Smell like it, too."

Slowly she turned to face him, insult sparking in her eyes. It sent relief gliding through him. "Oh, please. A gutter couldn't possibly smell as bad as you and Theo and Booger did when you came out of the woods."

"Yes, but I—" Abruptly he stopped. *I showered and put on clean clothes*, he'd been about to say. Which very well might lead her to remark that he hadn't offered her the same opportunity. Which would definitely lead him to remember all the times he'd showered after her, the bathroom steamy with all her amazing scents, or the times they'd showered together, or the times they'd done a whole hell of a lot more.

He fiddled with the air-conditioning vent, making sure it was blowing directly on him, wishing he could blame the weather for the sudden rush of heat inside him. "What?" he asked to distract himself. "Dusty didn't stink, too?"

"It's impossible for any female to stink as much as the male of the species." She made a point of sniffing the air. "In fact, your truck is a bit ripe, and it's not coming from me."

"Yeah, Booger kept farting all the way out to the house." He could resist if he tried really hard, but he gave in and grinned. "The dog has forty times the number of scent receptors we do, and his gas was bad enough to make our eyes water, which means it should have been forty times worse for him. He didn't even seem to notice the noxious fumes roiling about him."

"Maybe he has selective scent. His nose magnifies the scents that interest him and blocks out the ones that don't."

"I wish I did." He wrinkled his nose in her direction, and she finally cracked a smile. The tension holding his nerves taut released a little more. She was going to be all right.

If they got Will and Lolly back safe. If they kept Yashi herself safe from this guy. If she got rid of the notion that she would trade herself for her cousins. Ben appreciated that she was willing to make such a sacrifice, but there was no way in this world he was letting her do it. If anything happened to her—

His breath hitched, his grip tightening on the steering wheel, as his brain automatically cut off the thought. He forced himself to let it go, to say the words his subconscious didn't want to admit even to itself: if anything happened to her, it would destroy him. Living without her was bearable, even though she saw other men, even though he saw other women, even though they weren't together, because he knew she was there. Not in his life, but some other *there*, safe and happy and maybe harboring the same regrets he did. Maybe—

"Are you planning to push that car out of the way?" Yashi braced herself with one hand on the dash as he hit the brakes. "Though I imagine a jury would overlook it when you told them, 'My mom was serving chicken and dumplings.'"

He waited for the vehicle ahead of them to turn before easing his foot back onto the gas pedal. "Next time you can just say, 'Slow down.'"

*Next time...*

The lunch rush was over at the café. No one greeted them at the door, though his eldest sister's voice called from the back, "Sit wherever you like."

A lot of Ben's meals at the diner were taken in the kitchen, where he was related to most of the employees—an easy way to catch up on family news and avoid eating alone. The rest of the time, he was with his fellow officers, and they always shared a table in the dining room that faced the creek. With Yashi, they had taken the family dining room, claiming a need for privacy while they worked. Sometimes during those meals, they really had worked. Now he opted for a booth on the creek side. With the hour well past noon, the room was shaded, and the park across the stream offered a few distractions if they needed them.

They were barely settled when a waitress greeted them as cheerfully as if she hadn't already put in a full day on her feet. "How are you folks today? Enjoying this cool weather— Oh, it's you." His sister Emily swatted him on the shoulder. "What are you doing sneaking in the front door? You usually come through the kitchen."

"I don't usually bring other people through the kitchen."

"Not true. Sam comes in the back. Morwenna comes in the back. That cute Detective Harper comes in the back." Emily shifted her gaze to Yashi, looking her up and down. Without hesitation, she stuck out her hand. "Hi, I'm Emily Little Bear, and I'm fairly sure that nothing he's said about me and my sisters could possibly be true, because we are the sweetest, kindest sisters in the world."

"I'm Yashi Baker, and that's exactly what he told me. The sweetest, kindest sisters in the entire world."

"Aw, for saying that, you deserve an extra dessert."

"An extra?" Yashi asked. "I plan on stuffing myself on lunch and skipping dessert."

"Nobody gets out of here without dessert, and because you covered for my annoying big brother, you get two. And I'll put them both on his tab." Emily handed Yashi a menu—she was likely to use the extra one to swat Ben—but Yashi waved it away. "Let me guess— chicken and dumplings."

"Yes, please. With sweet tea."

Emily's smile split her face. "Honey, I like you. Do you know how many people come in here thinking they can give me orders like it's my job?" She made an outraged face and started to walk off, but Ben stopped her.

"Hey, what about me?"

Emily, a younger version of his mother, an older version of Toni and Mercy, rolled her eyes. "Let's see, it's Monday. Chicken-fried steak and mashed potatoes with gravy poured over all, glazed carrots and a dinner roll. You're nothing if not predictable, Benjamin Bear."

He tried to put extra intimidation into his scowl, but she skipped away with a laugh. Across the table, Yashi was smiling just a little. It made her look like a sad, worried angel, and that made him feel bad, sad, angry, sorry, determined.

"Benjamin Bear? Is that your family's name for you?"

"No. It's the name of my teddy bear when I was little. He was a grown-up bear, with glasses and his own books, and I thought Benjamin sounded grown-up. I didn't even know it was my real name until I started school."

"Aw, that's so sweet. Where is he now?"

He'd rather pretend he didn't know, that the ragged bear had gone to toy heaven with all the other worn-out, broken or rejected toys from the Little Bear household, but he told the truth. "He's on a shelf in Mom's bedroom, waiting." For Ben to get married, to have his first child, to give Benjamin Bear a new home. The bear and the giraffe belonging to George had once shared the shelf with loveys—his mother's word, not his—

belonging to his sisters and their other brother, Landon, but now they sat alone at opposite ends.

Aunt Denise's youngest daughter brought their drinks. After draining half of her tea, Yashi gazed out at the park, at kids on the playground, their moms taking cover in the shade or sunbathing on blankets nearby, then turned back. "So…what's been happening since the last time I saw you here?"

Her manner was casual, her tone friendly, but her eyes were still shadowed. He mimicked her with a shrug. "Let's see… Toni had two daughters. Mercy broke up with her boyfriend while she was pregnant with her second son. Great-Aunt Weezer actually went on a date last weekend. That's a scary thought."

That coaxed a hint of a smile. "Has your mother considered it might be time for *her* to start dating again?"

"That's even scarier than Great-Aunt dating." Not that he would stand in her way if she wanted romance in her life. But his father had never been a steady presence—he'd come back only long enough to do his part in creating six kids—and he'd left for good not long after Mercy was born. For Ben's whole life, Mary Grace Little Bear had been a mother, a daughter, a sister, a grandmother and a business owner, but she'd never been part of a couple, an available woman involved with a man.

Yashi unrolled the silverware from the napkin and spread it over her lap. "Has anyone heard from George?"

Ben's features slid back into the familiar blankness. "No." As the fourth of six children, George hadn't liked being in the middle. He'd wanted responsibility but refused to accept it, coddling even when he was too old for it and attention any way he could get it. He'd been the one failing his classes, getting escorted home by police officers, drinking beer with his buddies and smoking dope late at night. After one spectacular argument that had included the entire family, he'd left home two days before his twentieth birthday and had never come back.

"I'm sorry."

He smiled ruefully as Emily approached with their meals. "We're all sorry sometime, aren't we? That's life."

With her stomach full, her body tired and two pieces of chocolate silk pie in a plastic bag, Yashi was grateful to arrive at her house and find it looking exactly the same as when she'd left that morning: no mystery gifts left on the steps or the lawn furniture, no signs of an intruder, just its usual pretty, welcoming, cozy self. She wished she could turn the thermostat down to sixty, crawl into the bed in the loft under a mountain of quilts and sleep until next week, but she could sleep when Lolly and Will came home.

Or, as her college roommate had always said, she could sleep when she was dead.

It had been funnier back then.

She unlocked the front door and crossed the threshold with none of the pleasure she normally found in the action. Leaving Ben to close the door, she headed up the stairs, grabbed clean clothes, then hustled back down to the bathroom. Stepping under the cool water made her breath catch in a good way, the dirt and grime rinsing away in a lather of lavender-scented scrub. For the first time since she'd left the house that morning, she felt revived, with a breath of energy that would get her through the next part of her day.

It couldn't possibly be as bad as the previous hours had been.

Surely it couldn't.

Washed, dried, her skin rubbed with lotion and adorned with clean clothes, with her hair pulled back in a clip to keep the damp strands from her face, she exited the bathroom to find Ben comfortable in a chair, his attention on his cell. He looked bigger than life in her tiny house, which was fair, since he'd always been bigger than life in her estimation. She'd gotten an incredible opportunity with him, but she'd blown it, all for the sake of her career. For proving she was right, he was wrong and Lloyd Wind was guilty.

But she'd been deemed wrong, and the state had paid Wind a fortune to compensate him for the error. She'd lost Ben and given up her career. For nothing.

After sliding her feet into flip-flops and retrieving her laptop and a flash drive from the storage space beneath the landing step, she walked to the door, where Ben joined her. He inhaled deeply. "You smell better."

Such a lovely compliment it was, being told she didn't stink. "I still feel like I've been rolling in the gutter."

"The trick is to not let it show."

She smiled faintly as she led the way outside and to the rear door of her office building. On her first day in court for the district attorney's office, the DA had asked how she felt. *Like I'm going to puke*, she'd replied, and he'd laughed. *We all feel that way sometimes. The trick is not to show it.*

She'd spent most of her life not showing it.

The office was quiet, dimly lit, and felt as if she'd been away far longer than just this morning. She flipped on the hall lights, passed the bathroom and turned into the conference room. The table wasn't antique, just old: oak, battered, scarred by kids with pen knives. She'd bought it at auction when a rural school had closed its doors. The oak chairs had come from the same school, seats worn smooth from decades of accommodating staff's butts. The one she typically used had come from the principal's office.

"How long have you been here?" Ben asked as he walked along, gazing at the frames on the wall: her college and law school degrees, drawings by clients' kids, and photographs she admired.

"A couple years." She sat down and fiddled with her computer while he viewed the last photo. It was the only one from their time together: a peaceful shot of the ancient forest at Keystone. She'd whined so much about going that she was surprised he hadn't left her behind. Wild nature stuff still wasn't her thing, but she'd appreciated the hike once they'd started, and she'd shown him just how much when they got back to his house.

Too bad she didn't have a shot of *that*.

After the computer booted up, she inserted the flash drive, and a list of files came up: one for each case she'd prosecuted. They weren't official records, of course; those were the property of the DA's office. But she'd been allowed to keep her work product when she left—research, notes, things of that sort—and that was enough to jog her memory.

Before she could open a file, though, Ben spoke. "Why did you do it?"

Her hand hovered in the air, trembling like a leaf at the leading edge of a tornadic wind. She watched it a moment before lowering it to her lap, clasping it tightly with her other hand, stilling it while the same quivering spread through her body. Her mouth was suddenly dry, her face hotter than it had been after two hours outside. She wished she'd grabbed a couple of bottled waters from the mini-refrigerator in the file room for her parched throat. Wished she was back in the shower with cool water to put out the fire.

*If wishes were horses*, her mother used to say. Wishing got a person nowhere. It couldn't change the past. It couldn't change the future.

"You know why I did it," she said quietly. "I believed he was guilty. It was your case, and you'd just testified for the defense. You told the jury your doubts. You weakened our chances for a guilty verdict, and I… wanted that verdict." She could have substituted any number of words—*needed, coveted, desired*—but probably the most honest one was deserved. She had argued a good case. She had deserved that win.

He walked around the table and slid into the chair across from her. His dark gaze locked on her face. "No matter that you were wrong. No matter that you were sending an innocent man to prison."

"I didn't believe I was wrong, and I still don't believe Lloyd Wind was innocent. I think he got away with murder."

The only change in his expression was a small one, a shifting of his gaze, but clear enough to express his emotions. He thought she was hardheaded, clinging to her presumption of Wind's guilt out of pride, not conviction. He thought she couldn't admit, after all she had lost—all they had lost—that she'd been wrong.

She had pride in spades. Hardheadedness, too. She'd needed both to make it through life. But she had no problem with admitting she was wrong *when* she was wrong. Her gut instinct that Wind had murdered the man in the alley behind his office had never wavered. Not when she'd presented the case, not when she'd heard the verdict, not when he won his appeal, not even when he won his multimillion-dollar settlement.

"What did you think was going to happen with us, Yashi?" Ben's voice was hard, the words clipped. "You stood in that courtroom and accused me of turning a blind eye to Lloyd because we're both Creek. You questioned my honesty and my integrity and twisted something I'd said as a damn joke to show me as racist. What did you honestly think was going to happen?"

Her brain gave her body the order to stand up, to pace, to walk away, but if she tried, she would probably collapse in tears. Years ago, she had tried to have this conversation, but he'd wanted nothing to do with her then. She'd had reasons and rationale and logical arguments lined up back then, but when she'd finally accepted that the relationship was over, she'd buried them with all the other hurtful memories.

"I thought—" Her voice quavered, and the quick breath she took sounded more like a sob. After a hard swallow, with her fingers tightly clenched for strength, she forced herself to continue calmly and evenly. It was all pretend.

"I thought we would be all right. I thought you loved me enough to understand and to get over it."

His anger exploded, brightening, sharpening his eyes, turning his features stark, flushing his dark skin red, and his voice rose half an octave and doubled in volume. If he'd been writing instead of speaking, every sentence would have ended with multiple exclamation points. "Get over it? You told the jury my doubts about Lloyd's guilt stemmed from the fact that we Creek brothers have to watch each other's back. You told them I was racist, that the white victim wasn't as important to me as the Indian suspect. And you thought I would get over it? That at the end of the day, I'd be waiting at home, that we'd have dinner and go to bed and have sex, and in the morning everything would be all right again? I loved you, Yashi, more than anything in the world, but that's not the kind of thing people get over. You couldn't possibly think it was."

She'd been wrong. Ben wasn't a the-quieter-the-more-dangerous type, as she'd always believed. She'd just never seen him really angry.

His outburst didn't make her eyes burn with tears. It didn't make her jump up and flee the room. It turned her entire being, inside and out, hot with shame and naivete and anger of her own. It gave her a big empty pit in her stomach, a fragile feeling as if one good poke would collapse the shell that she'd become in the last few minutes, and she would—*poof*—disintegrate into nothing.

Had she honestly thought that this afternoon couldn't be worse than this morning?

And in the next instant, it got even worse.

A rap sounded at the opened door. JJ Logan wore an uncomfortable look, and she seemed indecisive about whether to stay or go. Judging by the fact that her gaze darted from Ben to Yashi and back again but didn't actually make eye contact with either of them, Yashi would guess she'd heard at least the last couple exchanges. "I—I can come back—"

Ben's chair made a screech as he shoved it back. "Go ahead and get started. I'll…" He didn't offer an excuse. He just maneuvered past her and out of the building.

JJ came into the room and sat down nearest Yashi. "I'm sorry. I called hello when I came in the back door, and I just assumed you heard. And then I was in the door, and I couldn't think of any way out."

Yashi forced a smile. "Don't blame yourself. As I'm sure you heard, it was *all* my fault. Everything that ever happened and ever will. I was ambitious and stupid and selfish and…" Now it was her turn to run out of words.

JJ laid her hand on Yashi's arm. "Don't be silly. There are people screwing up all over the place. You don't get to take the blame for everything. At times, we're all ambitious and stupid and selfish, and we still mean the world to the lucky people in our lives." She squeezed gently, the diamond in her engagement ring catching a sparkle of light overhead.

"Thank you." Yashi nodded to the ring. "Congratulations."

JJ's smile was satisfied and content. "You knew Quint's fiancée—I guess I should say first fiancée now, shouldn't I?"

"Yes. Belinda was a good person. So is Quint. He deserves to be happy."

"They were together forever. Engaged for years." She studied the ring. "We only met in March, and we're getting married in September. You know all the clichés—life is short. Live for today. Tomorrow isn't promised to anyone." She rolled her eyes. "We're not getting any younger. That's my mom's favorite reminder."

"He needed you. Needs you. You're good for him." Now a hint of moisture stung Yashi's eyes. She tried to live by the clichés, but if that forever kind of love was anywhere in her future, she couldn't see it. She didn't want just a partner, a lover; she also wanted a baby, maybe two, and grandbabies. She wanted the mom experience, the watching-a-piece-of-her-heart-grow-up experience. She wanted to be part of a family of her own—with kids, cousins, in-laws, out-laws. Everyone else had that. Why couldn't she?

Because *that's not the kind of thing people get over.*

And no matter how JJ tried to reassure her, that was most certainly her fault.

## Chapter 8

Ben never shirked work. Because his father had had no work ethic, his mother had overdeveloped hers, and she'd passed it on to him. He never put off until tomorrow what could be done today, but he had spent the last two hours driving around in his truck, air-conditioning blasting, music loud enough to vibrate the air and his cell tossed in the glove compartment. He figured JJ had covered for him, because he hadn't gotten a single call over the radio until ten minutes ago, when the dispatcher told him to meet the team at Creek Café for dinner.

He didn't want to go, but that wouldn't keep him away. Nothing short of an emergency would. JJ had heard all she needed to hear about them—*from* them, mostly him—and she would report it to the others because, private or not, it was pertinent to the investigation. He didn't even care that they knew. He just didn't want to see ornery, pigheaded, impossibly stupid or naive Yashi again, not when it had taken the last two hours for his blood pressure to drop from boiling to merely simmering.

She'd thought he would get over it. Even now, his hands clenched tighter around the steering wheel at the ridiculousness of her statement. The ends had justified the means. She'd won her case and put another bright, shiny star on her résumé, and he was supposed to have realized it was just business. Nothing to affect their personal relationship. She'd embarrassed him in front of a courtroom of people, maligned his character, but hey, that was work. At home, things were supposed to stay the same.

She wasn't stupid. He wouldn't have the patience to fall in love with a stupid woman. Had it been naivete? Or her usual determination to buff up her win record with the added benefit of proving him wrong as well? They'd always been on the same side. He'd done his job; he'd had faith in the cases he'd taken to her. She'd never doubted him, and she'd always argued a good, fair case. Lloyd Wind was the first time they'd disagreed, and even then, he hadn't been convinced of Lloyd's innocence. He hadn't been convinced of his guilt, either.

But Yashi had had no doubts. *Find some proof*, she'd told him. *Show me he's not guilty. Until then, I'll stick with the evidence that says he is.* And Ben had looked. He'd reviewed everything a dozen times; he'd reinterviewed everyone he could remotely connect with the case, with Lloyd or the victim. He hadn't found a thing to point to Lloyd's innocence. Just his undocumented, not-worth-much-in-court gut instinct.

And yet lawyers working on behalf of their incarcerated client had found that evidence: the weapon, the property stolen from the victim and the killer himself. Lawyers, who were generally better at lawyering than investigating, had needed little time to find the proof that had eluded Cedar Creek Police Department's best for months.

It had annoyed Sam, Lois and Quint. Even Daniel, who hadn't worked for CCPD during the investigation, had been ticked off by it. But Ben had thought odds were good Lloyd was innocent and had been more concerned with an innocent man being locked up than the ease with which he'd been set free.

He had also been nursing one hell of a grudge against Yashi, as well as trying to adapt to life without her. He hadn't been in the best frame of mind. Maybe his judgment hadn't been the best, either.

He pulled into the employee lot at the diner. He didn't need to see official vehicles out front to know that Sam, Daniel, JJ and possibly Quint would be waiting inside. So would Yashi. As he'd told her earlier, she couldn't take off alone now that they knew she was the kidnapper's real goal. What were Sam's plans for her tonight? To send her home with Quint and JJ, since they were already watching Brit? Not a good idea to have someone with a target on her back around an innocent kid. That also ruled out Sam and Mila's house, and Daniel and Natasha's, even though little kid Harper hadn't decided to join the world just yet.

Maybe Yashi would volunteer to stay in the holding cell at the police station or downstairs in a regular cell.

Yeah, that was really likely.

He *knew* what was most likely.

He was mumbling when he went in the diner's back door, sidestepped the line cooks and passed Toni. "What's that?" she asked distractedly.

"I wish I'd applied to the Tulsa PD." A bigger city, a bigger budget and broader opportunities for providing protection to a subject.

"Aw, you wouldn't like it at all. You wouldn't know most of the people you arrested."

"I wouldn't be related to some of them, either."

She punched his arm. "You picked me up *one* time when I was seventeen. I didn't even spend the night in jail, though at least there I wouldn't have had to face Mom."

He managed a smile as he headed toward the private dining room. A deeply disappointed mother had forestalled more than a few criminal careers. Toni's sole attempt at playing the wild child with her friends had ended in tearful apologies to everyone involved, especially their mother.

The expected people sat around the table in the middle of the room, Sam and Daniel on one side, Quint, JJ and Yashi on the other. The empty chair next to Daniel was directly opposite Yashi. Ben could suck it up, sit across from her and pretend she wasn't all he could see, all he could think about. That would be the grown-up detective thing to do. Instead, he pulled a chair from another table and put it at the opposite end, where Great-Aunt Weezer sat for family meals.

"Mature," Sam whispered, then said aloud, "We've already ordered. Toni said she'd bring you whatever was handy. To bring you up to speed, Lois and Simpson are at the hospital with Brit and Theo. Theo's still not talking, not even to Brit. Sweetness Brown couldn't give a description of the kidnapper other than 'bogeyman.' He was driving a dark van, no idea what type. No fingerprints on the phone left on the hood of the car. You saw the photo of Lolly. No identifying details in the picture. The message said, 'Maybe I'll give her back, too.' We assume he's implying he let Theo go rather than couldn't manage him."

In the sense that he hadn't wasted time looking for the kid, it was basically true. Even if he had looked, though, Ben would bet Sweetness knew every rock, log and hidey-hole in those woods, and she was accustomed to wandering around there at night. The kidnapper would have risked losing Will and Lolly if he'd tried to recover Theo.

Sam went on. "JJ interviewed Yashi and put together a list of defendants she prosecuted who made threats or seemed particularly resentful, and there's no old boyfriends we need to worry about."

Four gazes swung to Ben's face, stirring a desire to shift uneasily in his chair. Because he wasn't the sort to shift uneasily, he remained motionless, his face blank, his own gaze scanning the length of the table, catching a glimpse of Yashi staring down.

Finally Sam broke his all-business manner. "A

*year*, man? I know you're big on the stern face-hidden emotions-deep mysteries sort of thing, but a whole year, and you never let on?"

Heat warmed Ben's neck. "Don't blame me because you couldn't get a clue." Quickly, he changed the subject. "How many on the list?"

JJ didn't miss a beat. "Six." She handed him a sheet of paper with a half dozen names in Yashi's familiar handwriting. A drug dealer who'd threatened in court to kill her. A woman newly convicted of domestic abuse who'd tried to break a solid wooden chair over Yashi's head. A killer who claimed he'd stabbed his victim seventy-three times in self-defense, another drug dealer who'd asked his buddies in the courtroom to *take care* of her, a homeless man who'd defended his territory with a deadly sharp blade and promised to cut her open the same way he had his victim, and Lloyd Wind.

Ben had been involved in three of the arrests and knew the major details of the others. "Two of these people are still in prison, one is in a psychiatric facility and Lloyd Wind was released a year ago."

"And the other two were released due to prison over-crowding," JJ said. "One disappeared off the radar the minute he got out, and the other one kind of faded from view. These are the ones who made actual threats. Smart criminals don't make threats. They take their revenge without drawing attention to themselves. So there could be other ticked-off people who blame her for the consequences of their actions, or it could be a family member who faults her for sending their loved one to prison."

"Or it could be someone she made the mistake of smiling at at some point in her life," Daniel pointed out grimly. That had pretty much been the case with the stalker who'd followed Natasha to Cedar Creek. It didn't take much for a psychopath to develop an intimate relationship with a stranger.

Toni and their aunt Rebecca's daughter delivered their meals, refilled drinks and greeted Ben before leaving and closing the door behind them. After giving everyone a few moments to make a start on their dinner, Sam spoke again, his gaze shifting from Ben to Yashi and back. "We all know there were hard feelings after the Wind case. We apparently didn't know the extent of them—" that was said with one brow raised at Ben "—but they're not going to be a problem now. Everyone did their jobs on that case, and it's done. The only thing we're concerned with now is whether Lloyd Wind could be behind the Mueller kidnapping. Let's focus on the facts, not the emotion."

Ben never had a problem separating facts from emotion.

Unless Yashi was involved.

Sam went through a quick rundown. "Wind was accused of murder. Yashi prosecuted. Our lead detective's testimony was more helpful to the defense than the state. The jury voted guilty, Wind went to prison, his wife left him and he lost his business. A few years later, another guy confessed to the murder, died soon after and Wind's record was cleared, and he was released."

The line about his testimony stung Ben. His job in court wasn't to help either side; it was to present the evidence in a clear, unbiased manner. He wanted to believe that was what he'd done in this case, but Sam, the fairest person he knew, didn't think so. Ben's doubts had colored his recitation of the facts, which had put Yashi in an adverse position, grasping for whatever means available to recover.

And he had been the means. His relationship with her. His throwaway comment about Creek brothers sticking together.

It *had* been a throwaway, hadn't it? Had he subconsciously been influenced by the fact that he and Lloyd were from the same tribe, that they'd grown up together, that they shared a culture and a history and probably, somewhere along the way, a relative?

He had investigated other Creeks. Had determined their involvement in crimes ranging from petty theft to homicide. Hadn't been swayed by tribal connections. Why would he look at Lloyd any differently? They'd known each other forever, but they'd never been buddies. There was no reason he would give Lloyd preferential treatment.

And yet, what if he had?

"It always strikes me as convenient," Quint said, "when a person makes a deathbed confession that gets another person out of prison. I know it happens, but I also know sometimes easing their conscience is the last thing on their minds."

Something flitted through Ben, leaving him unsettled. Gerry Dillard, the man who'd made that confession, had been in trouble before, but always petty stuff: walking on tickets at restaurants, drunk and disorderly, shoplifting. He'd been a likable guy with a fondness for booze, an aversion to work and a wife who put up with him far too long. They'd never had a spare dime the whole marriage and, thankfully, no kids, either. She'd moved away the day after his funeral without even making arrangements to sell the house where they'd lived the past twenty years. It had eventually been taken for back taxes and razed, and hadn't even provided a decent pile of rubble.

Where had she gone?

And why hadn't she needed the money the house would have brought?

Dinner was over, the meeting breaking up, and Yashi hadn't said more than a handful of words. She knew she'd been included not for her input but because someone had to keep an eye on her, and she'd waited warily for Sam's decision on where she would spend the night. She'd like to go home—alone—and try to pretend that her life hadn't fallen apart. She wanted cozy, familiar things around her, wanted to listen to Bobcat's purrs and the usual sounds of traffic on the highway, wanted to smell the citrusy scent of fabric softener on her sheets. She wanted to pad through the dark to the bathroom or the fridge without a misstep, to not worry about unusual noises. She was even daring to hope that would be the case when Sam stood up, but then he paused.

"About tonight…"

Everybody looked at her, then at Ben, also on his feet. He nodded, resignation etched across his face, and the others joined Sam in getting ready to leave. Daniel checked his cell—anxious about any going-into-labor calls he might get?—and JJ stretched, then stepped easily, naturally, into Quint's arms. The way he smiled down at her…

Sam was going home to his adoring wife and baby. Daniel was going home to *his* adoring wife and soon-to-be baby, and Quint was going home with his adoring partner.

While Yashi got to go with Ben, who hadn't unbent one tiny bit all through dinner. Who radiated stiffness and annoyance and preoccupation with unpleasant things, all surely caused by her.

*Yay, me!*

The others left quickly, probably so they didn't have to feel guilty that they were unfettered by babysitters. She got her purse, and they went out through the kitchen to the back lot. The looks the staff gave them didn't show any particular interest, and there were no Little Bear women to delay them along the way. Yashi was vaguely relieved as she stepped into the muggy evening.

"We'll pick up whatever you need," Ben said, sounding as stiff as he looked, once they were inside his truck.

She opened her mouth to protest, then closed it again. Of course, it was natural he would want to go to his house. His living room alone was bigger than her whole house. There were two bedrooms. A full-size bathroom. It was even more familiar to him than her house was to her. It was logical.

And it was right across the street from Will's house. Where most of her experiences with her family took place. Where they had been kidnapped. Where their kidnapper had left his first and also his latest message for her. Where she felt creeped out by every tree, shrub, shadow and sound.

His sigh sounded long, heavy and defeated as he drove out of the parking lot. "Do you have an extra toothbrush?"

She needed a moment to realize that he was giving in. "Yes. And the chairs make out into beds. Twin size, but comfortable enough. The kids sleep on them when they stay over. Or you can have the bed. Bobcat and I will sleep downstairs." Her rambling stopped with a sudden breath, leaving quiet for his mumble.

"Oh crap, Bobcat."

She stifled the urge to defend her cat. "What about Oliver? Do you need to take care of him?"

"Oliver keeps his own schedule. I leave his food and water on the back porch, and he's got a bed there." He gave her a sidelong glance. "I had to screen it in to keep the possums and raccoons away, then I had to put in a cat door that only opens in response to the chip on his collar."

Yashi turned her head to hide her little smile. Ben would be comfortable with a big dog, something that tipped the scale around 120 pounds. Cats no bigger than his foot weren't manly pets, and Bobcat had done nothing to improve his image of felines.

Some of the stress that had knotted her shoulders all through dinner eased in the silence that followed. Her office came in sight ahead, the large windows dimly illuminated by the lights left on inside. Another ninety seconds, and they would be home—

"What do you know about Gerry Dillard?"

The knots returned with a vengeance. Her glance his way was cautious, but he was deliberately not looking at her. His tone was so even that she knew it was deliberate, too, and his own tension seemed to shimmer around him in the dusk. Did he expect an outburst from her because she didn't believe in Dillard's guilt any more than in Wing's innocence?

"I know he was in jail himself, in Tulsa, when he confessed. His wife said he was lying or crazy, but she always said that about him. He confessed to a pastor, who took the information, per Gerry's request, to Wind's lawyers. Gerry didn't trust the Cedar Creek police or 'that girl DA' not to bury the information where it could never be found again."

"He was never a suspect in the case," Ben picked up as he drove around the end of her building. "Never seen on that night, never interviewed, name never came up. His entire criminal history consisted of grabbing whatever he wanted and running. He never broke a window, threw a brick or kicked in a door. Even his domestic disputes involved a lot of yelling but no touching. And I talked to him at least a dozen times after the murder and before the confession. He wasn't suffering from a guilty conscience. Nothing was pushing him to right his wrongs."

A pole light lit the yard near the table and chairs and shone on Yashi's house, sending quiet pleasure through her. She would have gone to Ben's house and been grateful for the company, but she was so much more grate-

ful to be home. Even if the conversation did leave a lot
to be desired.

"What was Dillard's cause of death?" she asked as
they walked to the porch.

"Alcoholic cirrhosis. He drank himself to death."

"He never held a job longer than it took to quit, did
he? But his wife worked?"

"She worked for a cleaning company. Did office
buildings."

"Not much money in that." Yashi unlocked the door
and spotted Bobcat on the stair landing. He stretched,
his scrawny butt in the air, until Ben came in behind
her, then he leaped onto a shelf and arched his back.
With an impressive hiss, he jumped to the railing above
and landed on her bed with a whoosh.

It wasn't dark yet, but she turned all the lights on,
then closed the blinds on the first-floor windows. Her
predator could sit out there all night—and hopefully
get devoured by a pack of blood-sucking mosquitoes—
but damned if she would let him look in the windows
and watch her. She brought out her computer again and
got bottles of water and the two pieces of pie Emily
had given her at lunch, grabbing a napkin and fork for
each one.

"Let's assume that his death wasn't a sudden shock,
that the disease process took some time to kill him,"
Ben said. "He knew he was dying, leaving his wife
pretty much nothing. He wanted to scrape together
whatever he could for her. All he had to sell was a
story, and all he had to do was hook up with someone's
lawyer who would buy it."

Yashi wished she believed it would be harder than that—that most decent lawyers would balk at being offered an alibi tailored to their client's specific needs. In fact, she knew a lot would. And, in fact, she knew a lot wouldn't, including the type who represented shady businessmen like Wind in their shadier dealings.

"So Gerry confesses to a chaplain at the jail," she remarked as she opened her browser. "The chaplain puts him in touch with the lawyers, so the legal team can say he came to us, we didn't go looking for him. Do you know his wife's name?"

"I'm running her now."

She started her own search on the husband, then opened the cardboard container and beamed. She loved chocolate pie, and Mrs. Little Bear's meringues were legendary, tall golden peaks that reached easily six inches above the custard. She ate the meringue curls first, pulling them off one at a time, closing her eyes and sucking the sticky sweet from her finger. *What happened to my pies?* her mom asked on every day deserving of her special desserts, and then she always zeroed in on Yashi. *One day I'll make an entire pie of nothing but curls just for you.*

They'd had a lot of *one days* planned. Sadly, most of them had never come.

She'd had a lot of *one days* planned with Ben, too. Her mom couldn't have helped what happened to her, but Yashi was mostly—solely?—responsible for what had happened to them. Had she really done it to convict an innocent man?

Lord, she hoped not.

The search engine showed nothing in the first fifty results on Gerry Dillard that Yashi didn't already know, other than identifying his wife as Debbie. His confession had received heavy coverage in the Tulsa media, much lighter in Oklahoma City and only a couple of outlets outside the state. His obituary was painfully short: date of birth, parents' and wife's names, and date of death. He hadn't distinguished himself in school or at work, hadn't had any children or been involved in any churches or civic groups. It seemed a very sad life.

"My pie had better not be pockmarked," Ben said absently as he studied the screen of his laptop.

"Technically, Emily gave both pieces to me."

"And charged me for them."

"Do you ever actually pay?"

He glanced up, his gaze meeting hers. Most of the tension was gone from his eyes, and the hostility. There was still a lot of thoughtfulness and preoccupation, and still some of that unsettledness. If he was willing to consider that Dillard's confession had been bought and paid for, then he would also have to consider that Wind might be even guiltier than ever, letting a dying man take the blame for his crime. That was a lot to wrap his mind around.

"I've tried. She's refused. So I mow the yard, cut the firewood, paint when things need it and do a bit of plumbing. I draw the line at electrical work."

Yashi felt a flash of anguish mixed with pleasure. She'd helped out Will and Lolly with painting, planting and weeding, and they'd done the same for her, just like a real family. If she never saw them again—

She squeezed her fork tightly enough to cause pain. She wouldn't think about that. She couldn't focus on the worst-case scenario and still put all her being into hoping for the best.

"Look up Brightstar Cottages in Arkansas," Ben said as he reached for his pie. "That's where Debbie Dillard's living now."

Brightstar was on a lake in the Ozarks of northwestern Arkansas, a fifty-and-older community for people whose annual retirement income obviously exceeded Yashi's full-time salary. The setting was beautiful, the two golf courses were lush and manicured, the four pools were a rich ocean blue, and the cottages ranged in size from thousand-square-foot condos to ten-thousand-square-foot mansions. It was all very posh.

"Wow." Envy prickled at her edges, and she let herself wonder what life inside those guarded gates must be like, but only for a moment. She was grateful every day for what she had. She didn't covet much, and a fancy rich house surrounded by fancy rich neighbors didn't make the list.

"The cheapest buy-in is $400,000."

He shifted his computer so she could see, and she left hers to go look over his shoulder. A satellite photo filled the screen, centered on a house that would have looked right at home anywhere in the Deep South. The structure was white, with a wide veranda and wicker furniture inviting a view of the blooming crape myrtles and twining vines. The houses on either side were similar, the lawns meticulously groomed, the sidewalks edged—all in all, a picture-perfect scene.

As Ben zoomed out to show more of the street, Yashi bent to rest her elbows on the back of his chair. The position placed her mere inches from his hair. If she turned her head an inch, it would put her practically in kissing range, a temptation that sent tiny thrills racing through her. She was close enough already that the fragrance of his shampoo tickled her nose, and the heat radiating from his skin warmed hers.

*Oh my.* It had been a long and lonely time. Give her a second and she could count it right down to the years, months and days.

But he hardly seemed to notice she was there.

"Seeing that makes my teeth itch."

Startled by the comment, she looked at him, the smooth lines of his face revealing nothing, then at the screen. "Definitely a planned community."

"And a tightly controlled one. The flowers in the beds are all the same, just different colors or arrangements. No variation in the type of grass or the height of it, all watered and fertilized exactly the same. The trees, the flower pots, the blinds, the mailboxes… I'm having a really hard time putting Debbie Dillard in that picture."

So was she, and she'd never met the woman.

Resisting the urge to smooth down the strands of his hair that curled behind his ear, she straightened, took one more breath of his scent and returned to her seat. With regret that not even a crumb was left of her pie, she watched him take a bite of sky-high meringue and gave him a chance to swallow it before quietly asking, "So what do we do now?"

\* \* \*

For a folded-out chair, the sleeper wasn't uncomfortable, but Ben was having a hard time settling in. Maybe it was because he knew the bed upstairs had to be a much better place to stretch out. Maybe because when he straightened his legs, his feet and ankles dangled in the air. Because he wasn't used to the noises here. Because he could see Bobcat's dim shadow on one of the high shelves, watching him, crouched and ready to pounce.

Partly, it was because of the doubts stirring in his brain—that Lloyd was innocent, that Yashi was totally at fault.

Mostly, it was because of her. Because she was in that bed upstairs and having as hard a time finding sleep as he was.

"It's not too late to go to your house." Her voice floated down from above, weary, soft, light as air in the night.

"I doubt I'd sleep any better there." *Doubt.* That damn word again.

A moment passed. "I'm sorry."

"Don't be. I could have told Sam to put you in a cell."

"I would have gone if it wasn't for that whole no-privacy-for-the-bathroom thing."

"And yet your bathroom is smaller than a closet."

"It works for me."

He turned onto his back, gazing up at the ceiling. The night-light plugged into the wall cast Bobcat's shadow large and menacing across the beadboard. "What about the others?"

"What others?"

He should say good-night and shut up, but he didn't. "Others who spend the night here." *No old boyfriends to worry about*, Sam had said. Presumably, he'd meant no boyfriends with a grudge. But there had been men in her life before Ben, and there had surely been men since. Hadn't there?

"Besides the kids, you're the only other person who's spent the night."

*Huh.* "How long have you lived here?"

"A couple years. I've dated. Just not anyone I wanted to see first thing in the morning."

Did that mean no sex, or just no sleeping over when it was done?

Another moment passed, disturbed only by the noise of the central air as it clicked on. He watched Bobcat and felt the animal watching him back as he said, "I've found that few women appreciate my charm first thing in the morning."

That earned him a choked laugh from the loft. She'd always teased that he certainly lived up to the last part of his name in the morning. It was like watching a grizzly dragged unwillingly from hibernation.

The sigh that followed was so quiet that it barely made it down the stairs. "When I said I was sorry, I didn't mean about you having to stay here—though I'm sorry about that, too. I meant…about everything." She hesitated, and when he didn't say anything, she went on. "You were so patient and rational and sensible. You knew how I was about the job—"

"Driven," he supplied. It sounded better than narrowly focused, confident just to the edge of arrogance, morally superior and ambitious.

"I've been called worse." Her voice came from nearer by, as if she'd turned so her head was at the foot of the bed. "Remember what I used to tell you about your cases?"

Ben punched the pillow into shape before turning onto his side to face the stairs. *You always bring me everything I need. We'll never lose, you and I, because we're that good.* That was after he'd noticed how easy she was to look at, to spend time with, and before they'd done a lot more than just spend time with each other. When they'd finally got around to the sex, he'd taken her home with him on a Friday evening, and they hadn't resurfaced until Monday morning.

Somewhere he had a list of all the things so memorable about it. He had another list of the pros and cons of dating a prosecutor, another of the good and bad of marrying a prosecutor. He'd torn the last one up after his day on the witness stand, but something had kept him from throwing away the pieces.

"I trusted your cases, Ben. I trusted that one. And I trusted my own instincts. I believed Wind was guilty, and I believe it even more tonight. I didn't understand your…sorry for the word, but your waffling about it. You'd convinced me that the man was a killer, and I wanted to get justice, whatever it's worth, for his victim."

And when Ben had expressed his doubts in his testimony, he'd become part of the opposition. He tried to never recall that day in any detail, but here in the dark, nothing for her to read but his silences, it was easy enough to summon the highlights. The lowlights.

He'd been through the routine of simply stating the facts on the witness stand dozens of times, but then the defense had changed the gist of their questions. They'd made no effort to disprove him, to suggest biases or tampering or lazy investigating. Instead, they'd drawn out his concerns and expanded on them.

With the clarity of time and distance, Ben could see exactly what Sam had said: his testimony had helped the defense more than the prosecution. He'd gone beyond his usual scope; he hadn't stayed totally professional, *just the facts, sir*. He'd let the defense make it personal.

Then Yashi had made it *real* personal.

His silence lasted so long that when she broke it, she was hesitant and cautious. "Do you not want to talk about this?"

He'd said only one word since the conversation started. She must feel like she was talking to herself, and it was hard, she'd told him once, for an ADA to talk without an audience.

"I'm still considering your choice of the word *waffling*."

Relief warmed her voice. "I could have said *dithering*."

"I think I prefer waffling." He dragged his fingers through his hair, then let a sigh escape him. "I, uh, I think I may have been, uh…wrong about some things. Definitely about some. I just… Hell." He muttered the last part, not meant for her.

It was hard, when he'd been the injured party whose life was totally upended due to someone else's wrongdoing, to give up the martyrdom. He wasn't wrong often.

He had little experience with it. He'd learned right off the bat that it was so easy to put the blame elsewhere, to paint himself as totally in the right. In the beginning, he believed it fiercely, and then he'd pushed it to the back of his mind, where he didn't have to deal with it. Didn't have to examine his own behavior. Didn't have to give up his status of Yashi's victim who'd done nothing but love and trust the wrong person.

"The big mistakes were mine. I was too driven and maybe naive about my expectations. You were the only man I'd ever loved. I guess I thought it meant more. You know, through good and bad, sickness and health, richer or poorer. I thought you would take my questions the way I meant them—as business. Nothing personal."

"We were dating, Yashi, not married," he reminded her. Maybe not as impatiently or bitterly or angrily as he would have done before.

Though the idea of marriage had crossed his mind with increasing frequency in the weeks leading up to the trial. Even if it hadn't, he still understood what she was saying. If they'd been committed enough to consider marriage, they should have been committed enough to work through that one single day. He should have been more professional. She should have gotten less personal.

Neither of them had planned their actions. He'd gotten suckered in by the defense attorneys; she'd reacted. He'd known even then that she hadn't kept track of things he said privately that might be used against him in court. His comment had been recent, and it fit the situation. That was why she'd dragged it up.

The bed squeaked as she resettled, presumably turning to lay her head at the top again, adding six feet of distance between them. "Well, anyway, I just wanted you to know that I really am sorry. For what I did, for any hard feelings I caused in the department. For breaking my heart and hurting yours, too. For…everything."

Hurting his heart. Such an understatement.

The bed creaked again and covers rustled, then she yawned. Half a second later, so did he. He thought he could sleep now, but he had one more question first.

"Does your cat ever go to sleep and fall off one of these shelves?"

"Only on occasion." Her tone lightened. "Don't worry. He always lands on his feet on a chair. Usually right about where your head is." Another choked-back laugh. "Good night, Ben."

"Good night, Yashi."

Words he'd thought he would never say again. He wondered what others might be lurking in the back of his memories that might also find their way out.

# Chapter 9

Tuesday was hot and sunny, humidity and temperature both in the high nineties. Yashi dressed in shorts and a tank top, barely able to stand the idea of clothing wilting against her skin, and sipped her coffee while leaning against the kitchen counter.

Ben, barefooted and wild haired, stood outside the bathroom door. His boxers were black and clung low on his hips, exposing oh, so much beautiful skin and amazing musculature, especially in the long lines of his back. It took her breath away, seeing all that gorgeousness first thing in the morning. He filled the room, sucked all the air out of it to leave her light-headed, but she knew from experience that seeing him almost naked left her light-headed even in the great outdoors. It wasn't too little oxygen. It was so very much him.

He scowled in her direction. "I'm not doing it."

She raised her free hand in self-defense. "All I said was there are towels on the counter if you want to shower. Here. Have some coffee. It'll make you feel better."

It would, too, even if it had nothing in common with the vile sludge he preferred. It also made him grimace when he took the first sip. It always did.

Yashi had loved falling in love with Ben, learning all his quirks. Every day had meant a discovery, and it had been exciting and exhilarating and new. But there was something so very comfortable about already knowing a person. To know habits and routines, to be familiar with his stories and his experiences and his challenges and triumphs. To feel a part of his life.

For however long or short a time it might be.

It had been nice talking to him after they went to bed last night. It was easier to unburden herself in the dark, when only the wobbles or anger or hurt in her voice could betray her emotions. She'd loved after-bed talks with her mom, when she shared her fears and upsets and savored the good things in her life. She had scooched to the side of her bed, and her mother had lain in the space that was left, and they'd talked softly, sang songs and said prayers in the moonlight. They were some of her best memories.

Ben picked up the coffee, grimaced at the flavor and turned to the refrigerator. She'd looked at the pizza still left from Friday night and decided it was past its eat-by date, but he didn't feel such qualms. He took out the box, offered her a slice, then took both when she shook her head. One went into the microwave to heat. The other he ate cold.

"I'm going to drop you off at the hospital before I go home and change," he said. "Dr. Armstrong figures it will do Brit good to spend time with you, but we'll have to see about Theo. Either Quint or Lois will be there all day for protection."

He must have been getting texts already this morning, since she hadn't heard him talking on the phone. Speaking of phones, she hadn't looked at hers in too long. Her business wasn't so steady that she got a lot of calls, so she made do with two numbers on the one phone, but she'd ignored the business ring since Morwenna's call Saturday morning.

Something she could deal with this morning if Theo threw her out of his hospital room.

"You could just take me to your house, and I'll get my car—" When he gave her a sharp look, she fell silent. She wasn't used to not having the freedom to go whenever she wanted. It didn't chafe—she fully understood the reasons—but it took a little getting used to.

Cellophane crinkled when she took a honey bun from the cabinet, then she folded out the dining table and sat down with it and her coffee. "What are you going to do today?"

He gave the second bench a skeptical look, apparently found it lacking and leaned against the cabinets, crossing his ankles. "Looking more into Debbie and Gerry Dillard's backgrounds. See where she got the money for the house. Try to find a connection between them and Lloyd." He paused, then added, "Maybe talk to Lloyd."

"Give him my best," she said sarcastically. She never would have gotten rich in the DA's office, but she'd liked her job. She'd been doing something a lot of lawyers weren't suited for, and she'd traded it, in part because of Wind, for cases that any paralegal could handle if not for the little matter of a law degree. And because she didn't take on criminal cases—there was still way too much of the prosecutor in her for that—she would never get within spitting distance of rich. Maybe, if she continued to work hard and was lucky, she could continue to pay her bills.

Lloyd Wind would be able to do a whole lot more than just pay his bills.

"Now that he's got his millions from the state, he might even be grateful to you."

"I'd still like to punch him in the face." Just on general principles. If he was behind the kidnapping, she'd want to do far worse to him.

"That would be quite a headline. 'Former ADA assaults man wrongfully convicted of murder.'"

She savored the *assault* part but wrinkled her nose at the *wrongfully convicted* part. After scraping a fingertip's worth of frosting from the bun, she paused before putting it in her mouth. "Do you think he's involved in this?"

Ben hesitated. Considering his options? Or thinking about his admission last night that he had been wrong about some things? *Which things?* she'd wanted to ask. Breaking up with her? Siding with Wind? Was he having doubts about the man's guilt or about his own reactions? Regretting that he hadn't given them a chance to recover from her misstep?

All of it, she hoped. She had friends from law school who worked the defense side of the courtroom but married into the prosecution side. She'd wondered how that held up outside the courthouse but assumed it did, since they *were* married. She had no problem with Ben having a differing opinion. It had just been so much easier when they'd agreed on every case.

"I don't know," he finally replied. "But his good fortune in having Gerry Dillard come forward and take the blame so he could be set free… Quint was right. It was awfully convenient that Gerry needed to clear his conscience, especially considering that he never seemed to have much of one."

He *was* having doubts, and that pleased one part of her. Mostly, though, she wanted the truth. Well, *mostly*, she wanted Will and Lolly back safe. After that, she wanted a second chance with Ben. Then she wanted the truth.

He finished his pizza about the same time she took the last bite of her roll. She got shoes, her purse and a jacket, in case the hospital air-conditioning was set on arctic freeze, and he dressed in yesterday's uniform, only mildly perturbed by the cat hair decorating his shirt. He shook it off, glowered at Bobcat, back on a high perch where he could see all and glower back, and they left the house for his truck.

At the hospital, he didn't pull up to the front entrance and let her walk fifteen feet to the door. She hadn't thought he might. He parked to one side, made sure the security guard saw the badge on his belt and went inside with her.

Theo's room was at the end of a short hall on the second floor. The door was open, and voices came from inside—Brit's, Quint's, but no Theo. Was he still trapped in silence in the nightmare of the past few days?

The possibility made her heart hurt. It also made her steps falter before she reached the door. Ben glanced at her, then went ahead. "Hey, Brit. I brought you company."

"Yashi?" Brit's footsteps skittered across the room, and when she looked past Ben, her face lit up. "I'm so glad you're here. I love Officer Quint, but he doesn't know anything about good music, he doesn't have a social media account, he thinks I shouldn't date until I'm twenty-nine, and he doesn't discuss politics. He won't even say whether he likes Grandma Kissed a Gaucho—" she fluttered her left hand with their newly polished nails "—better than You're Such a Budapest." Her right hand joined the fluttering.

From his position leaning on the windowsill, Quint patiently replied, "You and I agreed to disagree about what constitutes good music. You have enough social media accounts for us both, I bet Yashi agrees with the dating, and purple is purple."

Brit made a big show of rolling her eyes as she pulled Yashi in for a hug. "I'm really glad you're here," she whispered. "Theo's still not talking, except when he cries for Mom and Daddy, and I miss them, too. I'm afraid for him, and I'm afraid for them, and— Oh, Yashi."

Yashi wrapped her arms around the girl, stroking her hair and rocking slightly side to side, the way Lolly did. It did her a world of good to hold Brit, and would do a world more to hold Theo, but a glance at him over Brit's head showed him curled on his side, staring at the wall. Poor little guy. She felt helpless and guilty and responsible, and she wanted to make everything right, and she couldn't. That might be the worst part: that she was as helpless as he was.

"Hey, buddy." Ben crouched next to the bed, placing himself where Theo couldn't avoid seeing him. "Are they treating you good here?"

Theo's gaze twitched to look at him, then it twitched back.

"Is there anything I can bring you from home? Clean pajamas? Your pillow?"

Theo didn't respond.

"Maybe that buffalo on your desk? What's his name?"

Again, Theo's hollow gaze shifted back to Ben's face, and he gave the tiniest of nods. "Bernie," he whispered in the tiniest of voices.

"All right, buddy. I'll bring Bernie by later today. I'm leaving Yashi here. You keep an eye on her, okay?"

Theo stole a look at Yashi, then repeated the little nod. Yashi was so grateful to not see rage in those blue eyes that tears tried to seep into her own.

Ben patted him on the shoulder, stood up and came

to the doorway. "Anything you want, Brit, borrow your cousin's phone and text me."

The girl released Yashi and hugged him instead. "Ha. You're not going through *my* stuff, Officer Bear. Who knows what you'll find?"

He grinned as he pulled away. "We've already been through your stuff." He tsked, making her shriek, gave a nod to Quint and walked out of the room.

Brit turned to Quint. "Did you guys really go through my stuff? Did you look in my drawers? Oh God, did you look in my desk?"

Yashi tuned out Quint's laconic responses and watched Ben stride down the corridor. *Stay safe.* When they were together, she'd whispered that every morning when he'd headed for work, every night when he'd gone home instead of sleeping over—pretty much every time he'd left her. Long after their affair had ended, she'd prayed some version of it until finally she'd decided it was hurting her more than it was helping him. She'd had to let him go.

Now she couldn't let him go without falling back into routine.

*Stay safe.*

Lloyd Wind had been in investments before his arrest, working from an office he'd built on First Street on the edge of downtown. He'd razed the original building, replacing it with a modern brick-and-glass cube, about which the best that could be said was *It's small*. It stuck out like a miniature poodle in a pack of bloodhounds.

Ben and Daniel stood in the parking lot behind it,

big enough for four cars and a dumpster. A narrow lane allowed access to the street a block north, and a single door opened into the building. Ben took advantage of the shade from the neighboring building, but Daniel stood in the sun, looking around. When he spoke, his question wasn't what Ben expected, but it didn't surprise him. Daniel was interested in every aspect of a case.

"What kind of money does an investment broker make in a town like Cedar Creek?"

"There were only two in town before Lloyd went to trial. Now there's one." Ben shrugged. "How many people do you know who have money to invest?"

Cedar Creek wasn't a rich town. The residents were farmers, ranchers, teachers and civil servants. They worked in the manufacturing plants or at the grocery stores, they paid mortgages and car payments and sent their kids to school. Their retirement plans, if they had them, were handled by their employers. There were wealthy people in town, but they were a minority.

"But Wind had a Jag and a Mercedes. He lived in a big house up on the hill. His lawyers were high dollar. Where was that money coming from?"

"He had a fair amount of debt. Nothing he couldn't manage, but more than most people I know." Ben rubbed the tight muscles in his neck. Doubting Lloyd's story—doubting himself—was giving him a stress headache, but he couldn't avoid it even if he wanted to. Not with Lolly and Will's lives in the balance. Brit and Theo's future. His own and Yashi's futures. "He could have embezzled a little here and there from clients who didn't notice. He could have had a sideline that paid cash under the table. But from the very first time we talked to him—and I mean before he even finished reporting finding the body—his lawyers were at his side, advising him not to cooperate. We had to get a court order for just about everything, including his books. Moneywise, everything looked legit."

"That's the point, isn't it, when someone's embezzling? That the first set of books looks good enough that the cops don't go looking for a second set." Daniel walked to the dumpster, kicking a beer can against the cinder-block wall behind it. More cans, a few bottles and cigarette butts littered the ground. "People come back here to drink?"

"When the bars close." There were only two in the downtown area, and this spot was halfway between them. "Lloyd's lawyers floated the idea that one of them did it. We checked the regulars, and none of them admitted to being here that night. That was probably the one time there weren't any empties out here for us to fingerprint. Lloyd claimed he didn't know the guy, had never seen him, and that he'd gone home shortly after seven, but his cell phone pinged here at nine forty-five. The victim's cell phone was missing, but carrier records showed that he'd called Lloyd three times before, each call lasting less than ten seconds. Lloyd said he was home before he realized he forgot his phone. His assistant said first time we interviewed her that the man had been in once before—she'd run into him on her way out—but after a second look at his picture, she said she'd been mistaken. The Winds' housekeeper said she heard him and her arguing the morning after the murder about him being out late, but Mrs. Wind said the argument was about another time and that night he'd gotten home a few minutes after seven. By the time he went to trial, the housekeeper had gone back to Oaxaca to care for her elderly father."

Shoving his hands into his pockets, Daniel came to stand in front of him. "Why did you doubt this guy?"

Ben stared a long time at the spot on the blacktop where the victim's body had lain. The knife that had pierced his gut, along with the contents of his pockets, had never been found, though a receipt showing Lloyd had owned a similar knife was. The car held nothing of value but part of a fingerprint that partially matched Lloyd's index finger—ten points, not quite up to the average for positive identification of twelve to twenty points. The car itself had been stolen from one state, the license plate from another. The victim's own fingerprints had come back with five names attached. No one had known which, if any, of them, was his real name, but all of his identities had tied to criminal histories, and none of them had tied directly to Lloyd.

Details that could justify guilt or innocence.

"Gut instinct," he said at last. *Something* hadn't seemed right.

Daniel nodded. He understood gut instinct.

They were in Ben's truck, heading for Chicken Farm Road, when JJ called. Ben put the call on Speaker.

"I called Debbie Dillard. She said I'd confused her with someone else and hung up. But I ran her info, and she's definitely the right Dillard. She moved into the house with a six-month lease two days after her husband died and bought it a week later. The only thing she brought with her was a suitcase. The sales manager said the delivery trucks practically wore out the street to her house for the first month. She said Debbie got a major makeover, upscaled her clothes about a thousand percent and told her neighbors she was an oil widow from Texas who was never blessed with kids. She made herself right at home."

"What about the money?" Ben asked, making a left turn onto a dirt road.

"We're working on it. We're also starting on Debbie's and her husband's work histories. I thought you said Gerry didn't work. In the last ten years, he officially had thirty-one jobs."

"I didn't say he couldn't get hired. He just didn't like the actual work."

"Luckily, Debbie had only two jobs during that time, both with janitorial services. We're getting a list of their clients. Where are you?"

"We just turned onto Rooster Run," Daniel said drily, looking at the GPS. "It runs into Skunk Trail up a ways."

"California boy still doesn't fully appreciate Oklahoma," Ben teased. "The Wind family farm is out here. That's where Lloyd's living now." It was a big step up from his prison cell, a huge plummet down from his house on the hill. But he'd always claimed to honor his heritage and revere his ancestors. Maybe coming to the farm was like coming home. Back to his roots. Though if he really was guilty of murder, his ancestors would have beaten him with those roots.

They talked a few minutes more, until Ben slowed to turn into a narrow drive. Pastures on both sides of the driveway were closed in with pipe fences, leaving a shoulder a foot wide on each side. If they met another vehicle, traditionally the one who'd gone the shorter distance backed up. Realistically, the one who could back up better made the retreat.

The trail led through a stand of trees, not weed thick like on the Mueller place, but deep enough to conceal the farmhouse a half mile off the road. It was grayish brown—everything from the shingles on the roof to the battered shutters and doors to the old board siding and the porch. Any paint that had once been there had long since worn off, except for flakes on the wooden dining chairs lined up along the porch. There were four of them, and Ben remembered, as a kid, him and Lloyd carrying them to the shade of the nearest tree so their mothers and grandmothers could enjoy the breeze while they talked.

"Nice vehicle," Daniel said with a nod. It was a Mercedes SUV, shiny and red, so new it still had its dealer tag.

The front door of the house opened as Ben and Daniel got out of the truck, and Lloyd Wind came onto the porch. Though he was only a few years older than Ben, his hair was streaked with gray that hadn't been there when he went to prison. His smile was the same, though, practiced and phony—things Ben had noticed before—and oily, which he hadn't. There was a look in his eyes, sly and calculating and, when the smile faded, a similar set to his mouth.

Changes in the man? Things always there that Ben had been blind to? Things that weren't there that he was seeing because he'd let his suspicions take control? He hated not knowing. Hated questioning his own impressions and motives.

"Ben Little Bear." Lloyd came down the steps, hand extended. "Long time, no see. I've been wondering when you'd find your way out here to question me. I'd suggest we bring the chairs down into the shade, but there's no breeze, so it doesn't matter."

Ben shook his hand, intently studying the man's face. It was naive, but he thought an act such as murder must be so destructive to a man's spirit that it should leave a mark on a person. It would make Ben's life easier if it did: *See, Judge, he has* killer *branded on his forehead.* Of course, a person who cared so little about another person's life wouldn't be overly affected by the taking of it.

"Question you?"

The sound of Daniel's voice jolted Ben from his stare. He released Lloyd's hand, stepped back and gestured. "This is Detective Harper."

"Detective. About that family disappearing. The prosecutor's family. The one who sent me to prison. If you talk to her—" he addressed the words to Ben "—tell her I'm not holding a grudge. She was just doing her job, like the jury and the judge were doing their jobs. Bad luck I got caught up in it." He smiled again, hands up in a gesture of innocence.

"But your luck did an incredible turnaround," Daniel pointed out, "with that guy coming forward. You should start buying lottery tickets."

"I already won my version of the lottery. Bet you never thought Great-Aunt Weezer and I would be the luckiest people you ever knew, did you?" Lloyd chuckled as he seated himself in the nearest chair.

If it had been luck, good for him. Ben didn't like him calling Weezer *great-aunt*, even though all his friends did it. And if Lloyd smiled that smile one more time, Ben was going to be seriously tempted to punch him in the face. Then the headline could read, Former Detective Assaults Man Wrongfully Convicted of Murder. Sam would be disappointed in him, and Ben would be disappointed in himself, but Yashi would be happy. Making Yashi happy was worth a little risk, wasn't it?

Ben pulled a chair to an angle to face Lloyd. He didn't waste time on small talk. "Where were you last Friday night?"

"Where I am most Friday nights. Right here. By myself. No one who can confirm it, unless the deer family that visits in the evenings learns to talk."

"Do you know Will and Lolly Mueller?"

"Never met her. Him…both businessmen in a small town. We ran into each other from time to time. I heard their little boy was missing, too. That's scary."

"Did you know he was related to Yashi Baker?"

When Lloyd smiled again, it took a conscious effort for Ben to keep a fist from forming. "What I don't know about Yashi Baker would fill a book. I always thought it was a shame, her being so pretty and blonde and *such* a ballbuster. I felt sorry for the poor man— or girl—that got involved with her. No doubt who'd be the alpha in that setup."

"You said you'd get back at her."

Lloyd's features went still. "I'd just been wrongly convicted of murder. I was so overwhelmed I might have said anything."

"So if we ping your cell phone, we'll find it was right here all Friday night," Daniel said, his tone even and easy. "We won't find the GPS in your car gave directions to the Mueller house."

Still holding Ben's gaze, Lloyd shook his head. "I heard there was a lot of blood. I wouldn't haul people who were bleeding in my brand-new Mercedes."

There weren't nearly as many Winds in Cedar County as there were Little Bears. It would be worth checking to see if any of them owned or had access to a dark van. Lloyd knew from his own experience that leaving a phone elsewhere kept it from revealing its owner's location, and no one who'd lived in Cedar Creek his whole life needed directions to Old 66. It was as much a part of the area as First and Main Streets. It was the first half of the quickest route to Wind's place.

"Did you know Gerry Dillard before his confession?" Ben asked.

Lloyd's gaze flickered away, then came back, blander than before. "I'd seen him around, of course. Gave him a few dollars now and then for a bottle when he was broke." His smile didn't reach his eyes or linger. "Guy was always broke."

"So you weren't friends."

"No." Lloyd gave him an assessing look. "I have higher standards for friends."

"And a lowly detective who once arrested him doesn't qualify," Daniel said when they were back in the truck a few minutes later. He watched in the outside mirror as they drove away, then scratched his jaw. "Is it weird to think this guy is more of a threat than the one who picked me up and threw me twelve feet?"

"No," Ben said quietly, his muscles taut, his gut churning. "Not weird at all."

The only thing worse than a long day in the hospital was spending a long day at the hospital. At least as a patient, a person had a chance at getting drugs. Yashi was exhausted by five. She'd talked endlessly with Brit and Quint and, later, Lois. She'd even talked to Theo at Dr. Armstrong's suggestion, but he'd pretended not to hear her. She'd eaten too much sugar and sodium and drunk way too much caffeine and discovered there wasn't a comfortable chair in the entire place.

Lois Gideon stood behind her, giving her a deep-tissue massage that almost made her weep, first with the pain, then the relief. "It's not always such an ordeal," Lois remarked. "Last time I was here was when my youngest grandson was born. Both his daddy and his granddaddy wanted a boy, so it was happy times for the Gideons."

"Last time I was here was when Theo was born. He was amazingly kicked back and easygoing, as if he hadn't just been expelled from his super-dark baby cave into a harsh, cold, loud world. He just looked around and grinned."

"Mom said he must have gotten some of the happy juice they gave her in the delivery room," Brit said from the sofa. "He looks really cool and unconcerned in his birth pictures."

Yashi wished he was still that way. Hell, she wished he had only the usual doubts from a week ago, when the biggest deal was how he would do in the next soccer game. *Not* whether he would ever see his mother and father again.

"The last time before that for me was when Ben got stabbed. He's such a big, strong guy that you never think anything could bring him down, but Lord, it was a scary thing."

Mouth gaping, Yashi turned to stare at Lois. Her chest tight, she breathlessly repeated, "Ben got stabbed?" She was dimly aware of Brit's voice echoing her dismay.

"Oh, sweetie, he wanted it kept out of the paper, and the woman who did it killed herself, so everyone kept it kind of hush-hush. But I figured you surely would have heard about it through the gossip. It happened at Mila Douglas's grandmother's apartment. He lost so much blood—"

"It wasn't so much when you've got as much as I do." Ben stepped into the room, detouring to hand Bernie the buffalo to Theo, who clutched the well-worn snuggly to his chest with both arms. Then Ben scowled at Lois. "It's not worth even gossiping about."

Few women were unintimidated by his scowls, and Lois was one of them. She reached up to cup his face in her palms. "We could have lost you, and we would never have gotten over it."

"I'm never going anywhere."

"A fine promise that you can't keep." Lois gave Ben's cheek a squeeze before letting go. "You two go on, get out of here. Miss Brit is going to do my nails for me. I've decided on blue, to go with my do." She patted her sapphire hair. "Don't worry about the kiddos. We'll be just fine."

Yashi hugged Brit, then paused at the foot of the bed. Theo hadn't hit or screamed at her, but he also hadn't shown any desire to talk to her. "Sleep well, Leo-Theo," she said softly. Being a late-July baby, he'd earned the nickname when Lolly was in her stars-and-moons-and-lullabies phase.

He didn't respond, but Bernie's left front hoof made the tiniest of waves.

The desire to weep swept over Yashi in waves—and for the first time in days, it was with joy. She blinked hard to keep the tears at bay as they walked through the corridors.

She and Ben didn't speak until they were on the nearest main thoroughfare heading toward her house. "I think we should probably stay at your house tonight," she remarked, grateful her voice wasn't shaky. She felt him look at her curiously, but all he did was grunt.

It was the logical choice. They would each have a full-size bed. There was a full-size bathroom. Despite her ambivalent feelings toward Will's place now, she'd always felt safe at Ben's house. She'd always thought one day it would be her home, too.

Maybe…

Before the thought could form, she choked it off. Wonderful possibilities and heartbreaking prospects. She didn't seem able to deal with either one right now.

At her house, she packed clothing and toiletries and was in the process of putting out extra food for Bobcat when Ben finally broke the silence. "You want to take Demon Cat with us?"

Bobcat sat at her feet, his attention firmly locked on the food container she held, every whisker and hair on his body on alert. "I don't know how he'd react to Oliver."

"Oliver's only seen when he wants to be." Ben started to stretch, but the kitchen ceiling, lower to allow for the loft above, stopped him. "Besides, I'd put my money on Oliver in a fair fight. In an unfair one, too. Your cat's ego is much grander than his reality."

She would feel more comfortable having Bobcat with her. If her enemy—Lloyd Wind—the kidnapper broke into her house, he might not hurt the cat, but he could let him out, an experience Bobcat had never had. And it wasn't as if getting him into a carrier was a problem. She'd lucked out there, finding the only stray cat in the state who loved cars.

"Want to go for a ride, Bobcat?"

Before she finished the words, the cat raced to the door, where he sat and meowed impatiently. Yashi stuck his things into shopping bags and slung them over her shoulder before retrieving his carrier from storage in the laundry room. His meow took on a hostile tone, but she scooped him into it anyway. "Just until we get in the car. You know the drill."

The drive to Ben's house didn't take long enough for Bobcat to satisfy his curiosity about the strange vehicle, or for Yashi to settle her nerves. Her stomach was still knotted when she carried the cat inside, making it just past the door before he leaped to the floor, raised his tail high and stalked off to revisit old memories.

She had old memories here, too, every one of them good.

While she put out food and water for the cat, along with placing his litter box in the usual spot, Ben left her stuff at the end of the sofa. Was it interesting that he didn't take it straight to the guest room, or was she reading meaning into the action he didn't intend?

Together, keeping the conversation casual, they fixed dinner. He cooked a steak on a cast-iron grill pan; she tore lettuce and diced vegetables for a salad; he whisked together his favorite dressing; she put bread sticks in the oven. It took them a few minutes to develop the rhythm that had come naturally to them so long ago, to avoid bumps and nudges, but by the time she set the table, it was enough like old times to make her chest ache. Not the same. They were older, wiser, more wounded, but Lord, it was sweet.

They'd made a good start on the meal when Ben finally mentioned the case. "Lloyd said to tell you he's not holding a grudge."

Her smile was tight. "That's okay. I hold enough of one for both of us." Fingers gripping her knife, she sliced the strip of steak on her salad into bite-size pieces, briefly imagining using the same knife until he told her where her family was. "I suppose he has an alibi."

"The most common one. 'I was home. Alone.'"

Oh, if they had a dollar for every time a suspect had told them that…

He updated her on the rest of the case, and she shared the few highlights from her day at the hospital. It wasn't until they were doing dishes that she picked up the conversation with Lois that Ben had interrupted. "Tell me about getting stabbed."

He dried the same plate twice before putting it away, then eased her aside and scrubbed the cast iron with coffee grounds and dried it thoroughly with paper towels before setting it on the stove and finally looking at her. "It was no big deal."

Just the idea was enough to make her legs wobbly, to tighten her chest and send a frisson of alarm through her. Thanks to her job, she'd understood his job long before they'd gotten together. She hadn't overly worried about him. He was well trained, cautious and didn't take unnecessary risks. Putting on the badge every day was like putting on a target, but she'd had faith in his ability, and the ability of the officers he worked with, to stay as safe as possible.

And yet he'd still been assaulted. Stabbed. And she'd never known. She'd thought their connection was more powerful, even after their breakup, that she would somehow *know* if his life was in danger. She'd been wrong. Romantic. Naive.

"What happened?" she asked, proud that her voice was steadier than her emotions and her legs.

He looked around as if to find something to excuse his not answering, didn't see anything and instead leaned against the counter beside the stove. "I was one of the officers protecting Mila Duncan from her mother. You heard about that?"

Yashi's smile was thin. A serial killer in Cedar Creek? And a woman, at that, one who had chosen to kill herself in spectacular fashion when her plans to kill Mila and Sam failed. Everyone had heard about it.

But she hadn't heard that the woman wounded Ben. Just as the effectiveness of small-town gossip never failed to amaze her, neither did the effectiveness of a small town circling its wagons to protect one of its own.

"She got past the officer stationed in the lobby of the building and made it into the apartment. I'd fallen asleep on the sofa, and I woke up the next morning in the hospital." He paused, one hand going to his rib cage to rub. "She liked knives. Knew how to use them, too."

He straightened, seemed to realize he was touching the scar and lowered his hand. "Like I said, no big deal."

A crazy woman had tried to kill him, and it had just been another day on the job. She *should* have worried more. *Would* worry more now.

But he was alive, and he was still well trained, cautious and taking only calculated risks. That balanced out the bad, didn't it? Sort of?

Without waiting for a response, he went on. "I'm going over to check Lolly's garden. You want to come?"

No, she didn't, but she appreciated the optimism in his offer, that Lolly would be back and her garden would be waiting for her in the same shape in which she'd left it. Besides, she didn't want to stay alone, either. She put on a smile a hundred watts brighter than she felt. "Sure, let's go."

# Chapter 10

Ben's mother had had a garden when he was young, one big enough to put all six kids to work in spring, summer and fall. Once, he'd pointed out to her that most home gardens only had six or maybe ten tomato plants, not thirty-five, and she'd swatted him. *Gardens should provide a bounty. And have you ever seen a tomato go to waste in this house?*

Lolly's garden wasn't as big as the Little Bears', but it still provided a bounty. Between weeding, watering, slapping at bugs and watching for copperheads, he and Yashi filled two rubber trugs with everything that was ripe and a few tomatoes that weren't. Yashi used to make a fried green tomato that was even better than his mom's. Maybe he could persuade her to fix them for tomorrow night's dinner.

To be honest, all he'd have to do was ask her. But persuading her sounded like a whole lot more fun.

And Ben Little Bear hadn't had a lot of fun in too many years.

The sun was on the horizon, but dusk was yet to come. The crape myrtle blooms perfumed the still air and buzzed with bees, and small clouds of gnats separated as they flew past, then reformed. He batted a bee away as he waited on the porch steps with his full bucket.

"We won't tell Lolly that I let her okra grow to magnificent heights, will we?" Yashi had two trugs, one with discard okras, some eight inches and longer. "Too bad you can only eat them when they're stubby and short."

Sweat dampened her face and left the hair edging it wet and flat or screwing around at odd angles. Her cheeks were red, but she'd smiled while he told Little Bear gardening stories. She was as close to relaxed as he'd seen her during this whole mess, and somehow she was still clinging to that damn hope. It was in her eyes, in her smile, in the essence of her.

He admired her for it.

She picked up a wicker basket, then sat down on the steps, too. "I thought we could leave some of this for Sweetness over by the cedar tree. Do you think she'll get to stay in her cabin?"

He helped fill the basket from his trug. "She's got Sam and Daniel on her side. Her son sure doesn't want her moving in with him. If there's a problem, I know a good lawyer who would help out, and Sweetness has already met Lolly and Theo, so meeting more family won't stress her."

Her gaze darted to his, away and back again, much like the insects tonight. It took her a long moment to asked, "Do you think I'm good?"

He started to chide her with the fact that she knew she was good. The DA had hired and kept her; the entire police department had respected and worked well with her. But she was scraping by now in an area of law that had never interested her, and there were a fair number of people, like the reporters Saturday, who didn't remember the brighter, more successful cases of her career; they thought of her only as the ADA whose mistake had cost the state millions.

"You're a good lawyer, Yashi," he said quietly. "You're a good person."

She blushed and ducked her head to stare into the basket. He could see that she was smiling, a sweet, delicate sort of smile, the kind she used to smile all the time but that had been rare these past few days. Balancing plum tomatoes on top of cucumbers, squash and bell peppers, she abruptly stood and headed across the grass. At the Christmas tree, she looked around, then hung the basket on a low-hanging branch next to the path.

"Sweetness!" she yelled. "Vegetables!" Then, shrugging sheepishly, she came back and retrieved her own bucket.

When they got home, annoyed meowing came from inside, the curtains swaying as Bobcat paced back and forth on the windowsill. "Oliver doesn't seem at all perturbed, does he?" Ben asked.

The kitten sat on the wicker chair, well within Bobcat's line of sight. He preened for a moment, then strutted to the edge of the cushion to sniff Yashi.

Inside, Bobcat yowled, turning into a prickly orange. Ben snorted, and Yashi elbowed him. "He's not used to having other males around."

Ben appreciated that. Given that they'd parted in serious upset—anger on his part, confusion and guilt on hers—she had been entitled to install a revolving door on her bedroom. She was free to hook up, date, sleep with anyone she wanted, none of his business. She could have fallen in love with one of them. Could have married and had kids with him.

But he was damned glad she hadn't.

Ben gave Oliver a few rubs between his ears—the cat was so tiny that his thumb covered the territory and then some—then followed Yashi inside. On a normal night, he would shower and go to bed within the hour. Sometimes dark didn't come soon enough for him. He was up by four or five, enjoying his coffee, reviewing his notes, planning his day.

But tonight wasn't a normal night, and while he would definitely hit the shower, as far as everything else, all bets were off.

They took turns in the bathroom. He let her go first, knowing she would be quicker and wouldn't use too much hot water. The fact that he would be following her, smelling her fragrances, with clear images in his mind, was just an added bonus.

Per form, she was out within ten minutes, hair damp, wearing a tank top and cotton shorts. The garments showed no more skin than the clothes she'd worn that day, but knowing she intended to sleep in them made them more…interesting.

Per *his* form, Ben spent double the time and also came out wearing a T-shirt and running shorts, both left over from his long-ago academy days. They'd been worn and washed so many times that the lettering was illegible. Even the colors were hard to identify.

"You want dessert?" He'd bought groceries, but his mother had sent a large bowl of banana pudding home with him. It was more than five or six people should be able to eat, but he always managed.

"Of course. Would it be too much to eat outside on the porch?"

"Not as long as you spray that." He nodded toward the bug spray on the table next to the front door. It was a concoction of his sister's, all natural and relatively effective if he ignored those natural smells.

By the time he'd filled two bowls, Yashi was sitting in one of the wicker chairs, her feet propped on the porch railing. Oliver was on the railing, too, studying her with head tilted to one side.

"He looks so serious," she remarked.

"Probably wondering why someone as pretty as you hangs out with Bobcat."

Dim light seeping from the windows barely illuminated her face. She seemed torn between accepting his compliment and defending her mutt of a cat. She decided instead to take a bite of pudding and did an appreciative *hmm-hmm* thing that could make him go weak. That made his hand tremble.

"Oh my. That is—" Her tone was almost reverent, and she skipped words for another bite. When she finally spoke again, she said, "Your mother is a culinary goddess."

"You should tell her that." His mom liked compliments as much as the next person, and given the direction his mind kept wandering, being aware of Yashi's awe for her cooking would certainly predispose Mary Grace to approve of her.

He set his empty dessert dish aside, then stood and turned his chair 180 degrees. When he sat again, he mimicked her position, using the windowsill for a footrest. His legs stretched out a lot farther than hers did, enough to keep him out of the light from inside. They both rested their arms on the chairs' arms, their fingers just inches apart.

He'd missed her fingers. Her touch. Her scents.

Oliver leaped onto the chair back, then strolled down Ben's arm to huddle on his lap, where Bobcat could see him. Ben stroked his back, his mind wandering, as always, back to his problems. An inspirational quote had hung in the restaurant's office since it opened, so long that he'd stopped even seeing it when he was there. *Life is ten percent what happens to you*, according to Charles Swindoll, *and ninety percent how you react to it*.

Following that line of thought, the unhappiness, the losses and the loneliness of the last five years was simply relegated. What Yashi had done: ten percent. How he had reacted: ninety percent.

Once, when asked how he could forgive Natasha for

jilting him just days before their wedding, Daniel's response had been thoughtful. *I had a choice. I could be righteous and unforgiving and alone, or I could have the life and the woman and the family I always wanted.*

It was that simple…though the journey to get to that point hadn't been easy for Daniel. It had taken threats to Natasha's life and his own to reach it.

It was that simple for Yashi, too. When Ben asked her yesterday what she had thought would happen with them, her response had been so basic. *I thought you loved me enough to get over it.* She'd had faith, in him, in them, and she'd made a choice to trust that faith.

Ben had made a choice, too, and like Daniel, he'd been righteously unforgiving and alone.

He didn't want to be alone anymore.

"You're awfully quiet." So was her voice. "Are you contemplating the mysteries of the universe?"

He waved his hand to shoo away the mosquito buzzing around Oliver, then realized the hum came from the kitten, asleep on his lap. Another show of faith, given that he wasn't Oliver's favorite human.

"No," he admitted at last, giving the cat one more gentle stroke before raising his gaze to Yashi's. "Just the mysteries of us."

Yashi didn't look past Ben at the night sky to find the reason for her skin prickling and the hairs on her arms standing on end. She knew there were no storm clouds hiding in the dark, no electrical charges zapping from cloud to ground. All that spark and sparkle was generated by him, by her, and it fed on the nervous energy she'd been living on since Saturday. It was sweetly familiar and strangely new, full of promise and pleasure and danger, and it caught her breath in her chest.

When the knot in her throat loosened, she cautiously said, "I miss us."

"So do I. And… I'm sorry, too."

Something gave way inside her, sweet and warm and overflowing with relief. It had seemed he would never let go of his anger. She hadn't even been certain he should. But now that he'd said those two tiny, huge words, she felt a thousand cares lighter. A thousand times more hopeful.

The chair creaked when he moved, but the kitten didn't twitch a muscle. "I knew you trusted my opinions, my evidence, and I guess I expected that, when I changed my mind, so would you. But you didn't. You pursued the case the way you always did—hell-bent on winning—only this time, instead of persuading the jury to believe my testimony, you discredited it. With words that came straight from my mouth.

"I don't know why I was surprised. Maybe because I was still blown away by the fact that Lloyd's lawyers knew I had questions. I thought that was between you, me, Sam and a few select others."

She remembered the look in his eyes the instant he'd realized the defense's intent. Even as good as his poker face was, he couldn't quite hide the shock. Her brain had banished her own shock and immediately begun searching for a way to sway the jury back to her side. A tad difficult when the lead detective was creating a more-than-reasonable doubt. When Ben's earlier comment had popped into her head, she hadn't thought twice about using it.

*Hell-bent on winning* was in the job description for an assistant district attorney.

It didn't belong in a relationship.

"Anyway…" He exhaled loudly. "When you told me yesterday that you thought we would be all right, that I would get over it, I think you made my brain explode. It was the stupidest thing anyone ever said to me. Except it's not. I never doubted that I loved you, or that you loved me. Our trust got broken, and sometimes that happens, and the options are to fix it or stop loving and move on. I haven't had much luck at the stop loving or moving on—"

Yashi's cell phone rang, tightening the bands around her chest. She wanted desperately to hear Ben's next words, but instinct drove her to pat her pockets before she realized her shorts didn't have pockets. She'd put the phone on the bathroom counter when she showered and left it there when she was done.

Her first rule of phone use was the person in front of her took precedence over the one on the phone, especially when the person in front of her was Ben. But anxiety was entwined with the anticipation inside her, reminding her that these weren't the usual circumstances. Most likely, the call was from a friend or a wrong number. But it could be Brit or the hospital. Something could have happened to Theo.

It could be the kidnapper, finally making another move.

Ben's mouth curved in a rueful smile, and his bare

feet hit the floor without a sound. "Go get it. If it's important, they'll leave a message or call right back."

Gratefully, she squeezed his hand as she bounded from the chair and rushed inside. The phone fell silent as she crossed the living room, then rang again as she turned into the bathroom door. With a glance at the screen—blocked number—she made sure the phone was recording, then lifted it to her ear. "Hello?"

"Hello, Yashi." The voice was male, void of accent and inflection, one she didn't know, and it sent shivers dancing across her skin.

She slowly returned to the living room, her free hand pressed to her stomach to control the queasiness there, but her voice stayed steady. "So you finally called. You know, you could have contacted me directly in the first place and left my family out of this."

"I could have, but what would have been the fun of that? Besides, I wanted you to understand how very serious I am."

Ben came inside, moving as silently as a butterfly, stopping in front of her, brows raised. She nodded. *Yes, it's him.* "I would understand better if I knew who you are."

Ben laid his hand over hers, tilting the phone so he could hear, too. She watched him peripherally, his dark eyes all concentration. "When I'm ready. I like this setup. I can yank your chain whenever I want and control the entire rest of your day. You aren't working, you aren't sleeping, you're focused on me all the time. You're living your life on the edge, and that will never change as long as I have your family. Of course, you've still got the kids. You love them, but Will—he's the big deal, isn't he? He's the only person in the world who remembers your childhood. Who remembers your mother and father. Without him, it's like they didn't exist. Without him, your memories don't exist. They're just the dreams of a kid with nobody in the world who loved her."

Physical pain washed over her, leaving her trembling and nauseated, swaying on her feet. It was true. Will was her only connection to her parents and his, to her life when it was happy and normal. Yes, she loved the kids and Lolly, but Will… Who was she and where did she come from without Will?

At the other end of the call, there was a shout, a thud, then a shriek that broke off midscream. Heartsick, Yashi clutched the phone tighter. The shout had been Will, the shriek Lolly. She found comfort in hearing their voices—thank God, they were *alive*—though that thud was surely Will's punishment for interrupting.

She forced a breath, sharpening the pain. "Okay, I know you're serious. Let's make the trade. I'll come right now. Just tell me where."

The man's voice increased in volume, but there was still no emotion. No anger, no derision. That coldness ramped her anxiety to new levels. "You are such a bitch, always trying to be in control. You have no control here, Yashi. You do what I tell you when I tell you. If you don't, your family will pay the price. Do you understand?"

"I do, I do. I swear. I'm sorry. Whatever you want. Just tell me."

There was a long silence, painful and awkward for her, but she sensed in the emptiness glee and excitement for the kidnapper. Of course he was dragging this out. He was enjoying it.

He finally replied. "I want you to suffer."

Yashi knew he'd disconnected after that, but she couldn't lower the phone, couldn't stop the recording, couldn't do a damn thing but stand there in a fog, hearing echoes of Will's shout, of Lolly's scream, of the man's menace. She was only vaguely aware of Ben taking the phone, pushing her into the nearest chair, crouching in front of her. He rested his hands on her thighs, his palms warm against her chilled skin. She stared at his strong, bronzed fingers a long time before dragging her gaze up to his face. "Was it Lloyd Wind?"

"I don't know. I think... There was something odd about the voice. Like he was using some kind of device to alter it."

Her nod was numb. "They're alive."

"You knew they were." A pause. "You recorded the entire call?"

"Yes."

"I need to hear it."

Hear the man's voice again, and her cousins'. Listen again to the sound that surely caused Will pain. Her stomach heaved, and she shook her head hard enough to whip her hair side to side. "I can't."

"I know. Come on." He pulled her to her feet and stepped back. She just stood there. The guest room was to the left, past the bathroom. She didn't want to go in there, a room she wasn't familiar with, a darkness she didn't intimately know, but she hadn't been invited—

With his hand in the small of her back, Ben nudged her toward his bedroom. "You haven't forgotten the way," he chided softly. "If you want to watch a movie or listen to music, my laptop's on the dresser. If you want to prove the son of a bitch wrong, get some sleep. I'll be in the kitchen. If you need anything…"

She didn't need much. Her life set right. Her soul un-frozen. Her family brought home and her broken heart mended. He could do all that. He was the best detective, the best cop, the best person she'd ever known. He could do anything.

He gave her another nudge, and her feet finally moved, padding down the hall, walking into the dimly lit room. She couldn't guess how long she stood in the doorway. Long enough for Ben to sit down at the kitchen table. Long enough for the hum of voices to let her know he'd started the recording. Long enough for his own voice to drift down the hallway as he talked to someone on his cell.

Bobcat watched her from the bed. She picked up the laptop, settled in bed, with the pillows behind her and Bobcat scooting next to her, and stared at the home screen on the computer. What did she want to do? Sleep, but that wasn't going to come easily. Have wild, crazy sex with Ben?

The possibility warmed her inside and seemed more likely than sleep, but not until he was done dealing with the phone call. She agreed with him that the voice had been altered, but she was certain it was Lloyd Wind. She lacked evidence, but she trusted her gut.

The way Ben had trusted his gut at Wind's trial. One of them had been wrong, but at this very moment, she couldn't consider that it might have been her. She couldn't think of a single person other than Wind who might behind the kidnapping, and without a suspect, how would they ever get Will and Lolly back? It *had* to be him.

The computer screen went dark, and she swiped it awake. Her fingers hovered above the keyboard before she finally began typing. She had loved being a prosecutor, and still would have loved it back in the day when legwork was a large part of the job, but thank the heavens for the internet. With the databases she subscribed to in her practice, she could find out virtually anything without leaving her desk or, in this case, Ben's bed.

She found little she didn't already know, but she was used to that. Sometimes it took looking at the big picture multiple times before the important out-of-place detail showed itself. If Wind was the kidnapper, something would lead to him. Probably something small, insignificant. They just needed to find it before he tired of playing with her and demanded she trade herself for Will and Lolly. She would do it, but was it selfish of her to leave it only as a last resort?

She was looking at satellite images of Wind's current residence when she realized it had gone quiet in the kitchen. No, not quiet. There was a rustle of steps, and the light from down the hall shifted as the lights out there were turned off. Ben's conversation was finished. He was coming to bed. She closed the computer and set it on the night table that had always been hers.

The satellite images could wait until tomorrow.

Ben stopped in the doorway of the bedroom, his gaze automatically going to the bed. The instant he saw Bobcat lying there as if he belonged, he scowled, but instead of growling at the cat, he looked for and found Yashi at the window, one slender hand lifting the curtain so she could see the Mueller house. Worrying? Wishing that suddenly the lights would turn on and Lolly and Will would be standing unharmed on the porch? *It was all just a mistake. We're fine. Come have some iced tea.*

Fine maybe, but not unharmed. Everyone who'd heard the tape—Sam, Daniel and JJ—had agreed that the thud was a punch, and that had been protective rage in Lolly's scream. But there was nothing Ben could do about it tonight. No leads to track down, no interviews to conduct, no reason to go to the Wind house and thump Lloyd however many times it took to find out where Lolly and Will were.

*You get to take a night off*, Sam had said before hanging up. *Put it out of your head. Let your subconscious work on it awhile.*

Ben couldn't think of a better way to relax and take a break than what he was about to do.

Stress lines wrinkled Yashi's forehead, and she hadn't fully lost the pallor that had come over her, but the smile she gave him was faint and thin and held potential. Her blue gaze locked on him as he crossed the threshold and started toward her. It stayed with him when he detoured to the bed, scooped up Bobcat and deposited him in the hall. He closed the door and smiled smugly. The cat had been so off guard that he hadn't even thought to leave a wound or two.

Her smile grew fuller. "You and Bobcat really must learn to get along."

"Not as long as I outweigh him by two hundred pounds."

She gave him a long look, leaving icy heat tingling all over his body. He slowly walked to her. Some of the weariness faded from her eyes, replaced with desire. Promise, and damn, her promise could bring him to his knees.

*I never doubted that I loved you*, he'd told her, every word hard, simple truth. And he'd never doubted that she had loved him. Still loved him. They'd just made a few mistakes. People did that, and they learned from them. Hopefully, he wouldn't need so long to learn from his next one.

Because he could live without her. The past years had proven that. He was strong. Capable. He didn't need a specific person in his life to be happy.

But that life was so much better with this specific person in it.

She turned to face him, her back against the window frame. The first time they'd made love, they'd come from work. He'd been in his usual tac pants and polo shirt. She'd worn her preferred dark suit, this one with a dark blue shirt. She'd taken them off to reveal the tiniest undergarments he'd ever seen, a deep, rich purple, delicate and incredibly sexy. *What's the point?*

he'd asked breathlessly, and she'd wrapped her fingers around his erection.

*That's the point.*

Though her shorts and shirt covered a lot more skin, he wanted her as much now—more now—than that night. Then she'd been all mysteries and secrets. Now he knew her body. Knew her heat. Knew how to touch her, and where, to tease and tempt and arouse and satisfy her.

He knew. Missed. Wanted.

"I threw Bobcat out—"

"He let you put him out."

"For a reason."

Her grin formed quickly and fully and stole his breath. "Because you don't like him sticking his claws in your naked butt, as I recall."

He took hold of her wrists and pulled her away from the window. His hands slid around to her back, finding a strip of bare skin between her shirt and shorts, as soft and warm as anything he'd ever felt. He urged her closer, bent his head and nuzzled her temple before sliding his mouth down to her ear. "Okay, I put him out for two reasons. For the rest of the night, in this room, it's just you and me. Nobody else allowed. Not family, not jobs, not good guys or bad guys, not pets, not anyone. Understand?"

"Hmm." The whispery sound slid over him, raising goose bumps on his arms, straightening the tiny hairs on his neck, twisting hard in his gut. "Sounds perfect."

Her fingers slid beneath his shirt, her palms flattening on his stomach. It was something he'd experienced dozens of times, but it still made him suck in his breath, still made his muscles go taut. When she slid them up his chest, he knew what was coming next. Knew she was going to claim his strength as her own, make him weak and hungry and at her mercy.

And she showed mercy in the best ways.

He took his sweet time moving his mouth to hers, tasting her here and there, leaving a tiny mark on the delicate skin of her neck, finally sliding his tongue between her lips. Kissing, he'd thought as a teenager, was the best thing ever, and he'd been of the same opinion as he got older—at least, until he met Yashi. Kissing *her* was the best thing ever. He couldn't explain it. He didn't believe in soul mates—his mom had believed his dad was her soul mate—but there had been something so right about him and Yashi from the very beginning.

It was still there. The way she touched her tongue to his. The way her hands stroked his body. The way his body responded. Those little mewls of pleasure deep in her throat.

It was like, after a very long time away, he had come home.

It was one hell of a kiss.

The primal part of Yashi that equated sex with survival wanted to strip off their clothes, jump into bed and go at it like horny little bunnies. The part that equated sex with Ben with the best reason ever to survive shared that desire. Some small part of her wanted to take it slow, take their time, enjoy their bliss, but it was outnumbered and definitely outvoiced.

She broke the kiss long enough to sweep his shirt over his head and yank off her own. By the time he claimed her mouth again, she was wriggling and bending like a contortionist, sliding down her shorts and panties. Drawing on past experience, while stroking his tongue with hers, she removed the rest of his clothes with virtually no effort: all she had to do was insinuate her fingers under the waistband of his shorts, wrap them around his erection, and with a great groan of need, he stripped off the clothing himself.

When she tugged him toward the bed, protest came from deep in his throat. She ignored him, twisting out of the way of his wandering hands, making him move with her if he wanted to keep touching her. They fell onto the mattress in a tangle of arms and legs, feverish and restless, moving together as if they always had.

He produced a condom from nowhere—she guessed he'd palmed it before shucking his shorts—and put it on with some effort because of her frantic efforts to pull him closer, inside her, so deep they could get lost together.

And then he was there, cradled in her hips, bracing himself above her, staring at her with more emotion than she'd ever seen in his dark eyes. *I never doubted that I loved you.* The echo of his words made her heart hurt in a good way, the way the razor-sharp need slicing through her body hurt in a good way. She hoped he saw the same in her eyes. Hoped he trusted it. Trusted her.

She hoped she didn't go through this only to break her heart again.

And then he moved, slowly withdrawing, slowly sliding back inside, and he gripped her hands tightly in his and lowered his head to her breast.

And her only hope then was that she survived the pleasure of the night.

When Yashi woke up, the bedroom was dark except for the four watts of light coming from a night-light plugged into an outlet. Ben didn't care about the dark, but she did, and so he had bought the light for her.

And kept it all these years.

The room was quiet, no sound but slow, steady breathing behind her. She lay on her side, so close to the edge that her bent knees extended off the mattress, and Ben's body molded to hers. His arm held her about the waist, and his legs warmed hers.

The big, stoic detective was a bed hog who liked to spoon. How many people knew that about him?

For the first time in days, every bit of tension was drained away. She wasn't sure she could even hold her head up, and she was fairly certain her knees would buckle if she tried to stand. But she didn't want to hold her head up, or stand, or do anything other than what she was doing. She wanted to lie there forever. Or, at least, until they made love a few more times.

Her eyelids were starting to droop, sinking in time with each of his deep breaths, when a sound from elsewhere in the house filtered into the room. A quiet rustle, then a crash followed by a feline yowl.

Instantly awake, Ben let go of her so quickly that she was lucky she didn't slide off the edge of the bed. By the time she sat up, he'd grabbed his gun from the nightstand and was slipping from the room. She dragged his discarded shirt over her head, but damn it, she'd left her pistol in her purse in the living room. That didn't stop her from taking the baseball bat Ben kept behind his bedroom door and easing out the door, heart pounding, and down the hall, hugging the shadows close to the wall.

"Oh, for the love of—"

She rounded the corner to the living room. The bathroom light was on, the door open, and in its faint light, she first saw Ben, shaking his head in dismay, then a spray of pottery shards on the floor. On the shelf the pot had previously occupied, Bobcat watched them with arrogant-cat nonchalance before leaping onto a chair, then to the floor, and trotting off to the bedroom. Ben continued to stare at the floor, his weapon hanging at his side.

"Oh no." Yashi's voice was quavery. "That's one of Louise Pickering's pots, isn't it?"

"It was."

After setting the bat on the nearest chair, she crouched to pick up the bigger pieces. The pot had been beautiful and elegant and way outside Ben's budget. Either he'd saved a good while or, being a friend, Louise had given him a discount. Either way, it was something he would have valued far beyond its price.

"I'm so sorry, Ben. I can replace it. I mean, I can't replace it. I know Louise never does the exact piece twice. But I can get you another one." If she ate nothing but ramen noodles for the next five years. Maybe six or seven.

He pulled her to her feet, took the pieces and set them on the coffee table, then laid his pistol beside them. When he wrapped his arms around her, the tension she'd expected to find wasn't there, and when he spoke, there was actually a hint of humor in his voice.

"I guess Bobcat and I have to learn to get along."

She tilted her head back to see his expression. "Really?"

His grin was rueful. "I may outweigh him, but he can outsmart me. What do you want to bet that right now he's curled up on my pillow, while I'm standing out here getting cold and missing out on sleep."

"I wouldn't take that bet." Rising onto her toes, she kissed his jaw. "You go back to bed. I'll clean this up."

He looked as if he might argue until a yawn split his face. "Thanks."

Wearing nothing but his shirt that hung off one shoulder, she was getting cold, too, so she swept up the pottery shards quickly. She hated dumping them into the trash, but they weren't worth anything anymore.

When she returned to the bedroom, Ben was already asleep. He lay on his side in the middle of the bed, leaving just enough space in front of him for her to snuggle in. With more than ample room behind him, Bobcat was curled against his back. He looked at her, meowed, then did his own snuggling.

"I always suspected you had a soft spot for Ben," she whispered as she circled the bed. "It's okay. I do, too. Just to try not to break any more valuables when you show it."

She slid under the covers, got positioned and, like the boys, fell asleep immediately.

The next time she stirred, it was morning, she was alone in the big bed and Ben's funky coffee was fouling the air. She grimaced, realized the smell was way too close to be in the kitchen and opened her eyes to find him standing beside the bed, watching her with his usual enigmatic look.

Then he smiled, and she felt as if the sun had come out after a very long, hard night.

"Up, up. My presence has been requested by the boss. You've got fifteen minutes to get ready."

She refused to think about what the boss—Sam—wanted to talk to Ben about. If it was last night's phone call, that would place itself immovably before her at the right time, and she wouldn't worry until then.

"I only need half that time," she said as she rose from the bed, shedding the sheet and walking very naked to the bag he'd carried in from the living room. She glanced at him over her shoulder as she pulled garments from the bag. "Shouldn't you be doing something?"

He moved to lean against the dresser, his ankles crossed, and sipped his coffee while he continued to unashamedly watch her. "I am. I'm putting on my gun belt."

A smile quirked her mouth as she donned blue-and-white-striped panties and a matching bra. It soothed her, having Ben look at her with such appreciation. It reminded her of how good they'd been together, and how easily they'd found that goodness again last night. It gave her hope, and today, like every day, she needed it.

Finally he put his coffee down and actually put on his gun belt. She dressed in dark blue capris and a blue chambray shirt, then slid her feet into socks and running shoes. Whatever she did today, she wanted to be comfortable doing it.

After a stop in the bathroom, she went to wait for him at the door. Her teeth were brushed, her hair was in a ponytail and she'd put on minimal makeup. She'd set out fresh food and water for Bobcat but didn't look for anything for herself, though. Once her schedule had been decided for her, there would be plenty of time to eat.

It was a quiet drive into town. Ben was never chatty first thing in the morning, and she wasn't sure it even was morning. The sky was gray and dark, with steady breezes whipping through tree limbs and occasional gusts buffeting the truck sideways and peppering the windows with sand and dirt.

But the clock on the dashboard showed it was 8:53 and—"Oh my word, you're late." Ben was rarely late. A time or two, because he was so incredible and she was so greedy, but never routinely. He had his mother's work ethic and was often at his desk long before anyone else arrived.

"I told Sam you need to sleep awhile longer. He knows you've been having problems."

She reached across to pat his thigh. "That was so sweet of you."

She half expected a sly comment from him: *It was for his protection. I've seen you sleep deprived before.* But nothing like that came. He just gave her a look that focused on her face. She'd thought no one would notice the lines on her forehead, the strain etched everywhere, or the circles under her eyes. Yeah, right. She'd earned every bit of that strain.

At the police station, the gusting wind hurried them across the parking lot. Inside, Ben directed her to the conference room down the hall on the right.

Sam greeted them and indicated a chair at the far end of the room, one scooted up to a battered desk that left her as isolated from the group as the room allowed. He offered coffee and doughnuts, and she took one of each. Ben offered his laptop in case she got bored, and she took that, too.

Soon after the meeting started, she realized once again that the world didn't revolve around her. The detectives and the uniformed officers who came and went were discussing all their cases, not just hers. Everyone was sharing information and offering feedback, and though at any other time, she would have found it interesting, this morning she tuned out their voices and returned to the satellite images she'd been looking at the night before.

She admired technology, bowed at the great computer wizard's feet, but there was something creepy about being able to sit anywhere in the world and call up a photograph of practically any other place in the world. To see the house where Lloyd Wind currently lived in detail, all the way down to the faded colors of the wooden chairs on the front porch. To have never gone within miles of the place and yet know how long and narrow the driveway was, or that another structure had once stood near the house but was gone now except for the foundation. Or that a faint trail started on the house side of the structure, picked up on the other side and disappeared into the trees to the rear.

To imagine that somewhere else, someone else could be doing the same with her house. It raised goose bumps on her arms.

Behind her, the officers were laughing, snatches of words registering in her brain: *tenth time this month... her pet pig...in his bed...* They must be talking about the Greens, she thought with a wistful sigh. They were the only couple she knew of with a penchant for escalating arguments and a pet pig. Not a cute, cuddly thing, either, but a porker that outweighed the two of them together.

Sighing, she refocused. If she'd kidnapped two people, where would she keep them? Not at her house, not where someone could hear their thumping and struggling to escape.

Gazing at the pastures and woods on the screen, she amended her answer: unless the house was in the country and the nearest neighbors were bovine or equine and couldn't care less about the noise. Ben and Daniel had gone to Wind's house, and they hadn't picked up any odd vibes, but they hadn't gone inside. They hadn't looked around. They'd seen what was right there in front of the house, and nothing else.

The homestead seemed good-sized to her—about a quarter section, or 150 acres—with some woods and mostly pasture, but the house itself was small, one story and not much bigger than her own. There was probably a living room, a kitchen/dining room and a bedroom, and that bump-out on the north side was probably the addition of a bathroom decades ago.

Since the pasture hadn't been reclaimed by the wild, she assumed it was in use, if not by the family, then leased to someone else. There was no sign of a barn, sheds or the equipment she associated with livestock in her slight experience. But the Winds had once run cattle themselves. Maybe that foundation marked where a barn had stood. Maybe a tornado had blown it away. Maybe she was grasping at straws. Maybe—

She was following the fence line the best she could through the trees when an indistinct shadow appeared on the screen. When she zoomed in, the pixels blurred, then slowly reformed into a building of some sort, as ancient as the house and far less cared for. Honeysuckle vined over and into it, in bloom when the image was taken, and left little of the actual structure to see: gray boards, empty rectangles where windows or doors had once been, more holes than roof.

Her nerves tingled, her muscles tightening, as she stared at the screen. Where *would* she keep the people she'd kidnapped if she had an old barn on the back forty that no one had remembered in years?

She glanced over her shoulder at Ben and the others. She could show him, and he would tell her to stay put while they got a court order to search the property. That would mean Sam calling the sheriff, bringing him up to speed on the case and persuading him to apply for a search warrant. The sheriff would have to go before a judge, and maybe the judge would grant it right away, maybe not. In a small city like Cedar Creek, it depended on the luck of the draw. And in the meantime…

Filling her lungs, she closed the laptop, stood and walked to Ben, bending to murmur, "I'm going to find the bathroom, then a Coke."

He nodded, giving her hand a pat, right there in front of Sam and everybody.

Aw, why did he have to do something so sweet when she was sneaking out to do something really dumb?

# *Chapter 11*

Ben watched Yashi leave, then continued to gaze out the door, something niggling at him. It wasn't until he caught up with the conversation that it registered: she'd turned left into the hallway. She'd been in the police station enough times to know that the bathroom was to the right.

Maybe she intended to get the pop first.

And take it into the bathroom with her?

She could be stretching her legs. Gone to say hello to any of the employees she'd once known. But the knot forming in his gut wasn't buying those options.

He looked at the laptop, out the door again, then shoved his chair back. When he opened the lid, it took an instant for the website she'd been browsing to pop up, and it took an another instant and zooming out on the image for him to identify it. "Son of a—!"

Interrupted midsentence, Sam looked up. "Do we have a problem, Detective?"

"All this time, cooperating a hundred percent, and she picks today to go off the rails?" Dimly aware of Daniel rising, Ben spun on his heel and strode from the room, leaving his partner to explain. As soon as he turned into the hall, his pace increased to a jog.

The lobby was empty, and there was no sign of Yashi in the squad room. Should he check the ladies' room? If she was truly there, would he feel like a fool for over-reacting?

He'd taken only a few steps behind the counter when Morwenna came out of the dispatchers' shack, a disgruntled look on her face. "I can't believe this," she said, her usual melodramatic flair ramped up. "I know I left my keys right there on my purse. They have a bright green clip on them, and they were hanging from that ring. I always hang them there. Ben, you know that."

She pointed to the leather bag sitting on a table outside the dispatch door. It was as big as a duffel, dark brown with braid and fringe and a large metal ring that he definitely knew usually held her keys.

"Have you seen Yashi?"

"Uh, yeah. A couple minutes ago. She stuck her head in the door, said hello and went…" Morwenna waved one hand to indicate anywhere. "Hey, you don't think— She wouldn't take— Why would she take my—"

Ben didn't hear the last words. He was already half-way to the entrance, his heart thudding, anger rushing like gale-force winds in his ears. He hit the heavy door hard enough to swing it to its outward limit, leaped down the steps and sprinted along the sidewalk to the parking lot most department employees used.

His gaze scanned the lot as he ran, bypassing his own truck, narrowing his gaze against the wind. Morwenna's bright red Mustang stood out the way it should, and standing next to it was Yashi. Relief hit him hard, taking his breath and making his knees go limp, but outrage at the chance she was taking stiffened them right back up again.

He stalked across the lot, feeling the instant her gaze skimmed over him. She went still, prey caught by her predator, and her face drained of color, then flushed guilt red. She held out one hand to stop him, Morwenna's keys dangling by the green hook, but he didn't slow. He walked right up to her, violating any personal space she might ever have, and yanked her against him.

Pressing his cheek against her hair, he blew out a breath and let his eyes close. He didn't know what she was thinking—didn't know *if* she was thinking beyond helping Will and Lolly—but he was seeing all the ways her plan could have gone south.

Truthfully, he was seeing only one thing: her under Lloyd Wind's control. Tied up, beaten, starved and mistreated. Dead, right alongside Will and Lolly.

Because Wind wasn't inviting her over for a chat. His fixation on her wasn't sexual. He wanted revenge. To cause her pain. He had no intention of going back to prison, so he had no choice but to kill her and the others when he was done.

"I'm sorry," she said, sounding strangled from the tightness of his hold.

He moved her arm's length away. "I'd ask if you're stupid, but I know you aren't, so are you freaking *insane*?"

"I'm not sure. Maybe." She hugged herself. "I was looking at the satellite image of Lloyd Wind's property. I started last night when you were on the phone, but then you came to bed, and we…uh, well, anyway. Did you know there's a barn or something at the back edge of the property? It looks about a hundred years old, like only the honeysuckle is holding it up."

Ben stared at her, something vague tickling his memories. The Little Bear/Wind friendship had been between the mothers and the grandmothers, not the kids. But when they went visiting anywhere and there was a kid in the family, the video games stayed home and they played. Their mothers wouldn't have had it any other way. Ben and Emily had spent a lot of afternoons trailing after Lloyd, shooting BB guns, throwing rocks, climbing trees.

There had been some structure—a house, he thought. The first Wind to own that property hadn't wanted neighbors, and he'd claimed the entire section then, so he'd built his house right in the middle of it. Later generations had preferred proximity to the road. They'd also tired of being land rich and cash poor, and they'd sold off most of the original spread.

He leveled his gaze on Yashi. "And you thought that would be a good place to hide any kidnap victims he might have hanging around, so you were going to ignore all of us cops in the room and go see for yourself. And to do that, you were going to steal Morwenna's car." He pulled the keys from her unresisting grip.

While he spoke, Yashi's face got progressively pinker, and she flinched when he said *steal*. "I—I... Yes. You'd have to get the sheriff, get a warrant, make sure no evidence gets thrown out. All I have to worry about is being charged with trespassing, and I know a really cheap lawyer who could get me out of that. If Will and Lolly aren't there, and I don't get caught, even that's not a problem."

Ben massaged the ache pounding in his temple. The man had told her *I want you to suffer* in a menacing enough tone to give four experienced cops the creeps, and she was talking about trespassing. "Whatever else you are, you've never been cheap," he muttered.

Her small smile came and went. "Ben, if Wind finds out the sheriff's asking for a warrant, he could kill Lolly and Will and disappear. He could dump them someplace and leave them to die. And you know he could find out. He's got almost as many ties to this town as you do."

He did know. Too many people couldn't keep a juicy bit of news to themselves even if it did mean risking their jobs. Blood ties ran thick here.

The sound of boots on pavement alerted them both to Daniel's approach, jogging the shortest route to reach them. "Sam's trying to get the sheriff on the phone. This new guy, though..." He shrugged.

That was the go-to reaction of everyone in the police department about the current sheriff. He'd come from out of town with only a few years' law enforcement experience and somehow got himself appointed to complete the remaining term when the previous sheriff died. What he had going for him: good looks and money. What he didn't have besides experience: common sense, logic, management skills or the ability to play well with others.

Ben abruptly reached a decision. He held out the keys. "Give these to Morwenna, would you? In about fifteen minutes, tell Sam we're headed out to search an old barn on Wind's property."

Daniel dropped the keys into his pocket. "I'll call him when we get there."

Yashi blinked a couple times before touching Daniel's arm. "I appreciate that, but you don't need the problems this could cause."

"Do we ever need the problems we get?" Daniel smiled ruefully. "Let's go before Sam comes looking for us himself."

"After telling us we can't do it, he'd probably go with us." Ben clasped Yashi's hand tightly on the walk to his truck. When she started to climb into the back seat, he stopped her, held her close again and murmured something she'd told him hundreds of times.

"Stay safe."

Was she insane?

Quite possibly, Yashi admitted as she crawled through the second barbed-wire fence. Straightening, she looked over her shoulder and saw nothing but trees. Somewhere back there was an old trail on the property just east of Wind's, and parked right in the middle of it was Ben's truck. Ben knew the owner of the land, a relative of an employee at the café, and the elderly man had granted them permission to go anywhere they wanted out there. He'd directed them to the trail, once used to check and repair the fence, now mostly relegated to his great-grandkids' four-wheelers, and he'd sworn to keep quiet, even making an old-fashioned *X* over his heart with a stubby finger.

Though her pistol was holstered on her waistband, her cell was in her right pocket and Ben's folding knife in the left, she was scared. She was shaky and fighting for every breath, waiting for the surge of adrenaline that was supposed to stop her whimpering. "Courage is resistance to fear," she quoted Mark Twain in a whisper, "not the absence of it." Who'd ever guessed she was courageous?

Still, every step that took her farther from Ben required faith and stubbornness in measures beyond what she'd thought she possessed.

It was miserably hot, the wind still sweeping down those plains, battering tiny bits of dirt and spores into her eyes. The only good thing was that it dried her sweat as soon as it formed. Otherwise, between heat and sheer terror, she would be a walking drop of water.

Their plan was simple: she would find the old Wind house and search it. If Will and Lolly were there—*please, God*—she would call Ben, and he and Daniel would ride to the rescue. With regards to being outside their jurisdiction and having no warrant, they would plead exigent circumstances, that they'd been in the area when they received information that two hostages were being held inside the house, requiring entry without delay. Wind's lawyers would surely argue it was subterfuge, the detectives using a civilian not bound by their restraints to trespass onto the property on a fishing expedition.

As an ADA who would have had to counter those arguments, Yashi would have hated this plan. As Will's cousin, she embraced it. And hated it. And prayed for Will and Lolly's sake, as well their kids', that it would work.

The second fence had been the boundary of Wind's land. As soon as she set one foot through the strands of wire, she'd been trespassing. She made her way carefully through a patch of weeds that waved their silky tassels above her head, trying not to think about all the biting things she could run into out here. So of course, she fixated on chiggers, ticks, snakes. Skunks and possums, raccoons, roadrunners, coyotes, feral dogs and cats, mosquitoes, wasps, bees...

*Stop it! You're doing this for Will and Lolly, remember? You'd walk through hell for them, and this is far from hell.*

Clearing the grass, she leaned against the trunk of a scrubby oak, fitting herself into its minimal shade, and tried to get her bearings. Ben had done his best to drop her off due east of the house, but walking in a straight line out here was impossible. She stared back at the fence and the rusty posts she'd crawled between, adjusted her direction to the right and pushed on.

After slipping while climbing over a downed tree, she sat on the trunk and examined the scrape on her shin. It was bloody but fine. The tree had been the victim of a lightning strike; its stump was sprouting new life across a narrow clearing. Life kept trying. No matter what the universe threw at it, those tiny, living cells kept coming back, growing, getting stronger.

Like Yashi and Ben.

Smiling, she drew a deep breath and walked away from the tree. When she reached the clearing, she glanced down at her scraped leg again but noticed something else instead: a depression in the growth. Most of the grass stood straight, but a distinct portion of it was flattened, with a similar section a few feet away. Tire tracks. Someone had driven out here.

Her gut clenched. It could have been the neighbor's great-grandkids on their ATVs, having found a way through the fences. But the wheelbase seemed too broad for a four-wheeler, and surely it required more weight than teenage boys and quad bikes could supply to leave those tracks.

She walked a few steps along the trail before breaking into a run. All she could hear was the pounding of her heart; all she could feel was the short, harsh gasps of her breathing. Sweat ran down, tickling her scalp, dribbling between her breasts, stinging the raw skin on her leg. After fifty feet, she wanted to stop but couldn't. After 150, she needed to stop but didn't until she just couldn't go on. Hurting, burning, throbbing, she stumbled, barely catching herself from pitching forward to her knees. She dragged in a desperate breath, raised her arm to soak up the sweat on her face, and her world jerked to a halt.

There was the house, truly more vegetation than building materials now. It leaned precariously to one side, but the red cedars that had sprung up over the years kept it from falling any farther. Honeysuckle added its own support, the vines covering much of the building.

And off to the side, parked between two trees, making use of their canopy overhead for concealment or shade, was a dark van.

Yashi stood, as noisy as a gaggle of schoolkids, in the middle of the road. Placing her feet carefully, she eased off the trail and behind the nearest tree, a scrawny blackjack that couldn't conceal even the scrawniest of the aforementioned school kids. She carefully worked her way deeper into the trees and toward the cedar side of the house. *That* was a tree to hide behind.

Better yet, inside. She eased apart the branches, prepared herself for the prickliness and stepped in. Inside the Christmas tree had been Brit's favorite place to hide when she'd been young enough to do such things.

Found house. Dark van, she texted Ben. Haven't looked inside yet.

That's enough. Get back here.

I have to know, she responded before returning the phone to her pocket and taking out her pistol. His responding message vibrated against her thigh, but she ignored it as she crept out of the tree's shelter and headed for the back of the house. It was impossible to be quiet with dead leaves everywhere, covering dried twigs and acorns. All she could do was her best as she eased around the corner and to the nearest gaping space that had once held a window.

There were no shadows inside—holes in the roof provided natural light screened through honeysuckle and other leaves—but Yashi thought it might be the most beautiful place she'd ever seen, because sitting against the wall not ten feet away with ropes securing them to an iron rod were Will and Lolly. Battered, beaten and broken, but— Yes! A shuddering groan, a raspy snore. Thank God, they were alive.

Yashi's first impulse was to climb through the hole and rush to them, hug them, cry with them, assure them the kids were safe. She'd even raised one leg to a protruding stone on the foundation before common sense demanded she proceed with caution. She texted Ben: They're here. His response came a moment later. On our way.

The house was only one room, broken boards all that remained of the furniture. The floor was littered with leaves and debris but showed hard-packed earth in places. Rocks from the fireplace were left lying where they fell, dotted like everything else with animal droppings. And there was no place to hide. Not a corner, not a shadow, not a crawl space.

Yashi crept around the far side of the house, nearest the van, to satisfy herself that it was just the three of them, then jogged in the front door, dropping to her knees before them. "Will, Lolly, wake up!" she whispered fiercely, fumbling the knife from her pocket.

Will's eyes slowly fluttered open. Lolly came awake fighting. With her hands tied in front, the best she

managed was a weak kick that barely connected with
Yashi's hip. "Get away from us, you bastard!" she
shrieked before her eyes focused clearly and filled
with tears. "Oh my God, Will, it's Yashi! I told you
she'd find us. I told you!"

Will's startled gaze went to the door. "You're not
here alone, are you? I swear, Yashi, sometimes you have
the sense—"

"Remember how our moms told us don't play with
knives?" She unfolded the blade, locking it into the hilt,
and held it up, wicked sharp, for him to see. Will had
warned her to be careful, but it still took her several
swipes to cut through the ropes binding his wrists. Lolly
eagerly offered hers, not even flinching at the idea of
Yashi sawing away so close to her skin. Her ropes were
tighter—no doubt she'd put up the most resistance—so
Yashi had to maneuver carefully.

When the last strands gave, Lolly threw her arms
around Yashi and began weeping. "Brit," she gasped
out between sobs. "Theo."

"They're fine." Yashi returned the knife to her
pocket, then clenched their hands. "Listen to me. We've
got to get out of here. Can you walk?"

Will's answer was a firm nod. Lolly swiped her
cheeks, her wrists chafed and her arms covered with
bruises, and smiled. "Honey, I can run to the moon
and back."

Life was attitude. Yashi helped Will to his feet, sup-
porting him until his wobbly legs could do the job,
then they both pulled Lolly up. Captivity, abuse, hunger and dehydration had taken their toll, but with a de-

termined breath, she stood straighter and took a few stumbling steps toward the door. Attitude would get her through this.

At the door, though, Lolly immediately spun back. "He's coming. Oh God, hurry, he's coming!"

Yashi heard the distant rumble of an engine, and ice swept through her. Praying it was Ben, she peeked out the front window from the side, and half an instant later, a fancy SUV came into view at the far end of the trail. Not Ben. The disappointment stabbed through her, edged with fear, but she shoved it away. Ben would come. He'd said he would, and he would.

"Come on, this way." She hustled her cousins to the rear window, and Will clambered out. He lifted Lolly down, then gave Yashi a hand.

As soon as her feet touched the ground, she gave the knife to Will and pulled out the pistol and the phone for herself. She punched in Ben's number and braced the phone between her ear and shoulder.

Will looked from his weapon to hers with a weak grin. "Trade you."

"You've never fired a gun," she whispered.

"I've never defended anything with a knife, either."

Daniel answered Ben's phone, road noise loud in the background. "Where are you, Yashi?"

"We're behind the cabin. Wind's coming. He'll be here any second. Where are you?"

"Just turning into his driveway. Can you stay on the phone with me?"

"Lolly will, but once he gets here—"

"Hold on, Yashi. Just hold on."

Lolly's hand was extended for the phone. Yashi gave it to her and listened to the louder engine noise, the vehicle drawing closer. Wind wasn't driving fast, but he wasn't creeping along, either. She hoped those were good signs, that he wasn't expecting trouble.

She intended to give him more trouble than he could handle.

"Hi, Lolly, I'm Detective Daniel Harper. I'm with Ben Little Bear, and we're going to be with you in just a couple of minutes."

Daniel was his usual calm and confident self. The only time Ben had ever seen him lose control was on the rooftop of the Prairie Sun Hotel when Natasha's stalker had tried to drag her off with him. Then, in the building opposite with a sniper rifle, it had been Ben's turn to be calm and confident. He hadn't had a good enough shot to kill the man, and he'd regretted it. A clean shot would have saved them the frantic scramble to free Natasha from the man's death grip.

He'd practiced clean shots since then. Once-in-a-life-time shots, taking advantage of the narrowest target in the narrowest window. He wouldn't settle for less again.

He didn't slow when they reached the house. The Mercedes was gone. He drove between the house and the slab from the old shed and picked up the trail that led into the woods. It didn't look like much, with weeds grown tall and deep ruts from last weekend's rain. The farther he drove, the thicker the trees grew and the harder the ground was. He had to drop his speed ten miles, then another ten. Before long, branches were slapping at the side-view mirrors. He hit the button that folded them against the vehicle. He didn't need to add damage to county property to his deeds today.

Beside him, the mobile on Speaker, Daniel said, "I know you have to whisper, Lolly, and I'm sorry, but I can't understand. So let's do this. You stay quiet as long as you need to, but I'll be here. I'll be listening, and I'll let you know when we get there." He glanced at Ben. "How long?"

"Don't know." Ben's grip tightened on the steering wheel as they hit a rut hard enough to jerk the truck to one side. "Never came back here except on foot, and that was twenty-five years ago."

"He's here." Lolly's voice, feathery and thin, came from the phone, breaking into a squeak at the end.

"Okay. Stay quiet now."

For a moment, there was nothing, then came a distant roar. Lloyd had just walked into the house, Ben presumed, and found his hostages were gone. Shouts followed, the tone threatening, the words indistinct. Then they became very clear.

"Yashi Baker! You've just signed your death warrant! I'm going to kill your precious cousins, and then I'm gonna kill you, you bitch. If it's the last thing I do, I'll kill you!"

Ben imagined the man standing at a window or door, screaming his rage, and worried just how far away Yashi, Will and Lolly's hiding place was for the phone to pick him up so clearly. While he and Daniel had waited, he'd studied the satellite image, and it seemed the only decent place to hide was behind a tree, if they could find one big enough. And all Wind had to do was find one of them to get them all.

"Look." Daniel pointed ahead and to the left. Through the trees was a flash of red—Wind's vehicle. It stood out against the earth tones like a beacon. "Are we going in quiet or loud?"

In response, Ben gunned the engine. The truck fishtailed on a patch of ground before finding traction.

"I guess we're going in loud." Daniel's voice was dry as he turned back to the phone. "Lolly, we're here. You stay where you are, and scream if you need us. I have to get off the phone now."

Daniel had already braced himself by the time Ben stomped on the brakes. He steered hard to the right, and the instant the vehicle stopped, they both bailed. Daniel had their truck for cover; Ben ducked behind the Mercedes. Lloyd hadn't wanted blood in his brand-new SUV. What would he think about bullet holes?

Lloyd came to the door of the house, so enraged that his skin was flushed a violent red and his eyes seemed as if they might pop out of their sockets. He was careful to show only half of his body, which likely meant he had a gun in the hand they couldn't see. Damn it.

"Get the hell off my property, Little Bear!"

"Mr. Wind, it's Detective Harper. You know we can't just go away, not this time. We've got to take you in. We've got to get medical care for the Muellers, and we've got to take Yashi Baker, too."

"Do you frickin' see the Muellers or that bitch?" Lloyd slammed his free hand into the door frame, and Ben was pretty sure the entire structure swayed. "You're trespassing! We're in the county, you idiots. This is Wind land. Creek land. You have no authority here."

Ben crept along the SUV, careful to keep his head below the windows, until he reached the front passenger door. Lloyd had parked at an angle so that, to reach the corner of the house, Ben would be exposed only a moment. He wondered how good a shot Lloyd was, and how willing he was to kill someone he'd known his whole life.

"The sheriff's on his way, Mr. Wind," Daniel continued calmly. "And just to cover our bases, we also called the Lighthorse police. One of their officers will be here soon. It will be safer if you're not holding a gun when they arrive."

"It'll be safer if I'm not here when they arrive."

Lloyd raised the hand he'd punched the door with, examining the damage, and Ben launched away from the Mercedes. A shot cracked behind him, but except for a crazy wild jump in his blood pressure and the pounding of his heart, he was unharmed when he leaned against the north wall of the house. There were no windows on this side, which made him feel less a target...until another bullet tore through the century-old wood, leaving a hole the size of his head.

The next shot fired was Daniel's, forcing Lloyd to forget Ben for the moment and find cover for himself. Expecting him to go out the back and try to disappear into the woods, Ben raced toward the rear of the house, only to skid to a stop when a figure darted around the corner. He brought his pistol up, his finger on the trigger, then just as quickly shifted his aim to the ground.

Yashi pressed her back to the wall, panting hard. When she sensed his presence, her eyes grew big and she slapped her free hand over her mouth, turning her shriek into a squeak. She moved as if to throw herself into his arms, and he wanted to grab her and never let go, but instead he shook his head, then bent to press his mouth to her ear.

"Where are Will and Lolly?"

"In the cedar tree," she whispered back.

"*In* it?" When she nodded vigorously, he raised a brow. It wouldn't make his list of hiding places—hopefully, not Lloyd's, either.

"Mr. Wind," Daniel called, his voice coming from the opposite side of the house. "Let's not do this. You're in enough trouble as it is."

"Trouble?" Lloyd was somewhere behind the house. "I've had nothing but trouble since that bitch came into my life."

Finally, Ben joined the conversation. "You've had nothing but trouble since you killed that man, Lloyd. This isn't Yashi's fault. It's not the system. It's not bigotry against Native Americans. You killed a man, and then you bought a confession from Gerry Dillard to get yourself out of prison. No one's responsible for your bad luck except you."

A moment of silence followed, broken by the crunching of leaves underfoot. "Did you figure that out, Ben? Or did she? I really don't think you're smart enough."

The steps stopped, and something rustled heavily. There was a scuffle, a scream, Will shouting, "Run, Lolly!" Damn it, Ben would give anything for a shelter with a view. Instead, he eased right up to the corner, took a breath and peeked around, ready to retreat in an instant.

He didn't have to. Lloyd was there, twenty feet away, one arm around Will's neck, the other hand holding the gun to his head. There was no sign of Lolly or Daniel. Ben prayed he'd gotten her to safety.

The prayer hadn't even faded when he sensed that Yashi was no longer behind him. A glance confirmed it, along with the knot tightening in his gut. He wanted to think she'd gone to comfort Lolly, but the fear roiling inside him suggested otherwise. He got a confirmation of that, too, almost immediately when her voice came from inside the house, strong and steady.

"Let my cousin go, Wind."

Lloyd dragged Will back a few more yards, his gaze constantly shifting from left to center to right. "He's my ticket out of here. You let me get in my car and drive away, and the rest of you get to live. If you don't, I'll kill every damn one of you."

"Let him go," Yashi repeated. "He hasn't done anything to you. You let him go, and I'll drive you out of here myself."

*Aw, come on, Yashi. Retreat while you can. Go take care of Lolly.*

"You hear those sirens, Mr. Wind?" Daniel asked. "I count at least four. Probably more. Probably at the entrance to your place about now. You only have a couple minutes before they get here. They're going to see you with a hostage and a gun, and they're going to shoot you, no questions asked. Is that what you want?"

For a moment, Lloyd seemed to waver. Then he directed his gaze into the house. "This is because of you, bitch. You're gonna have to live with this the rest of your life."

Terror whitened Will's face. He clawed with his fingers, trying to loosen Lloyd's grip as his captor's finger tightened on the trigger.

Ben settled his weight evenly, took a deep breath and tuned out everything else. Clean shot, narrow target, narrow window. The hum in his ears blocked sound, and his vision blurred except for Wind. Narrow target. Narrow window.

Then he pulled the trigger, and there was no target at all.

Will's second experience as a hostage left far less of a mark on him, Yashi had decided—physically, at least—than the first. By the time she'd vaulted out of the window and reached his side, he was sitting, a bleak, lost look on his face. He'd raised one hand to his cheek, but he hadn't touched the blood splattered there. He'd just grabbed her hand in a bruising grip and held her tightly until Lolly had forced her way past Daniel to join them.

Now her cousins sat in the back of an ambulance, side by side, too stunned and shocked to celebrate that they were alive. At the hospital, they would get to see Brit and Theo, and that would do them more good than anything else. Then they would need time.

Lloyd Wind hadn't gotten the justice he'd hoped for, but he'd been right about one thing: Yashi would live with this the rest of her life. The regret that he'd hated her enough to take it out on her cousins. That they and Theo and Brit had gone through such an ordeal. That Ben had been left with no choice but to kill a man he'd known forever.

But she would live with it. Examine it, deal with it, file it away with other life experiences. It wouldn't destroy her.

She was sitting on the tailgate of Ben's pickup, finishing the second bottle of cold water that the paramedics had provided. They'd arrived after everyone else. JJ and Lois had come first, followed within minutes by Sam and Sheriff Moulton, two deputies and two Lighthorse officers, the Muskogee Creek Tribal Police. Moulton had been in a very pissy mood and simply looking at Yashi seemed to set his hair on fire. Right now, he was around back, supervising officers and crime scene techs who were far more experienced than he was, and probably putting all of them in a very pissy mood.

He couldn't affect Yashi's mood. Her family was safe. Her world was whole.

*Mostly*, she added as Ben approached her.

He sat down beside her but didn't speak for a long time. He was always serious; now he was achingly so. It weighed on him, the taking of a life. He would grieve, and regret, and wonder if he could have done anything differently, and eventually he would acknowledge and accept that the only person responsible for Lloyd Wind's actions was Lloyd Wind himself.

"Moulton's going to want to talk to you soon," he said at last. "Just remember two words—*exigent cir-*

*cumstances*. And when he points out that you were trespassing, don't be flippant and say, 'Then put me in jail,' because he will do it."

"From what I hear, he may do it anyway. That's okay. I could use a few days' rest."

He gave her a sidelong look before turning to face her. She did the same, her knee bumping his. His index finger traced gently over the edge of the bandage the paramedics had put on her leg, and when he glanced up, there was concern in his eyes. "Are you okay?"

"I am."

"Really?"

She nodded, and he abruptly swooped her into his lap and pressed his forehead against hers. "I told you to stay safe. Not confront an armed killer. Not almost get yourself killed." He gave her a small shake before holding her tightly. "Don't ever do it again."

Yashi's mouth started to curve into a smile, but she stopped it. It seemed disrespectful to smile when Wind's body was still behind the house. He may have been a bad person, but there were people who would grieve for him. "I won't."

His snort was doubtful. His breathing was steady, his arms snug around her. The wind had died to a slight breeze, making the afternoon even hotter than before, but she didn't mind. She could sit there in Ben's lap forever.

After another while, he remarked, "We never finished that conversation last night."

Everything inside her tightened, anxiety swelling quicker than when she'd seen Wind's vehicle out the window. All he could have taken was her life, while Ben could take her heart. Her future. Her hope.

With one hand, he maneuvered until her head was resting on his shoulder. He laid his cheek against her hair. "Like I said last night, you let me down. I let you down. We left ourselves with two options—to fix what went wrong or to stop loving each other and move on. I gave up on trying not to love you a long time ago, and I didn't have any luck with moving on, either. I could live without you if I have to, but…"

He looked down at her with such tenderness that her heart hurt. "I don't want to. I love you, Yashi. All of you. Even when you make my head explode. I want that future we'd planned—you, me, kids, cats, forever."

Distantly, she heard sounds—the ambulance driving away, voices approaching. She didn't care about them. Didn't care about anything but Ben and her, this moment, all this promise. She cupped her palms to his face, staring intently into his eyes. "Yes."

A faint glimmer of humor appeared in his expression. "I haven't asked you anything."

"But you will. Sometime. And the answer is yes. Will always be yes. Because I love you, too, Ben, and I still want that future and more. I want to know your friends who stand with you and to be a part of your family. And if I let you down again, well, you'll know how to deal with it, and if you ever let me down, I'll learn how to deal with it. So yes, Ben, you, me, kids, cats, family, friends, forever."

He kissed her, slow and sure and heart-achingly sweet, the kind of kiss that started simply before becoming one of those that ended with fireworks, exhaustion and utter satisfaction. Sadly, he had to stop it too soon, because those voices they'd ignored were only a dozen yards away and the sheriff was bearing down on them.

Ben whispered in her ear, "Exigent circumstances."

She smiled brightly at him. "Like us."

He raised one brow.

"An unusual situation that calls for an extraordinary response. I'm unusual, and you're extraordinary."

"You are definitely unusual," he murmured before the others reached them and he had to let her go.

Sheriff Moulton's disdainful gaze swept over her and found her lacking, then moved on to Ben. When his ice-blue gaze came back to her, there was definite disrespect in it. "Yashi Baker. I understand you're responsible for all this mess."

Yashi slid to the ground, straightened her shoulders and lifted her head. "Then you understand wrong, Sheriff. You see, there were exigent circumstances..."

\* \* \* \* \*

SPECIAL EXCERPT FROM

**H HARLEQUIN**
# ROMANTIC SUSPENSE

*Carrie French is escaping an abusive husband when
she seeks refuge at the Double M Ranch—and forms
a friendship with ranch hand Luke Wright. When they
end up stranded in the Rocky Mountains, Carrie's past
threatens their future—and Luke must ensure they
make it out alive.*

*Read on for a sneak preview of
In the Rancher's Protection,
the next book in The McCall Adventure Ranch series
by Beth Cornelison.*

What could she tell him? Her situation was horrid.
Frightening. Desperate. And that was why she had to
keep Luke out of it. She had to protect him from the
ugliness that her life had become and the danger Joseph
posed.

But he was standing there, all devastatingly handsome,
earnest and worried about her. She had to tell him
something. The lies she'd told friends for years to hide
the truth tasted all the more sour as they formed on her
tongue, so she discarded them for one that was more
palatable.

"A few years back I made some…poor choices," she
began slowly, picking her words carefully. "And I'm

trying to correct those mistakes. Until I get my life back on track, my finances are going to be tight. But I can't make the fresh start I need if I accept money from you or anyone else. I need to do this by myself. To be truly independent and self-sufficient."

"Poor choices, huh?" A hum rumbled from his throat, and he twisted his lips. "We all make those at some point in our lives, don't we?"

With his gaze still locked on her, he inched his palms from her shoulders to her neck, and his thumbs now reached the bottom edge of her chin. His work-roughened hands were paradoxically gentle. The skimming strokes of his calloused fingers against her skin pooled a honeyed lethargy inside her. Reason told her to pull away, but some competing force inside her rooted her to the spot to bask in the tenderness she'd had far too little of in her adult life.

*Luke is the kind of man you should be with, the kind of man you deserve.*

*Don't miss*
In the Rancher's Protection *by Beth Cornelison,*
*available July 2020 wherever*
*Harlequin Romantic Suspense*
*books and ebooks are sold.*

Harlequin.com

HRSEXP0620